FAMILY COMES FIRST

A Novel by
TRACY THOMAS

PUBLISHED BY
PENGAME PUBLISHING, LLC

"STORIES YOU CAN RELATE TO"

This book is a work of fiction. Names, characters, places and incidents are products of the author's imagination and are used fictitiously. Any resemblance to actual events or locals or persons, living or dead, is entirely coincidental and is intended to give the fiction a sense of reality and authenticity.

Published by:
PenGame Publishing LLC
P.O. Box 341361
Jamaica, NY 11434

Library of Congress Control Number: 2006940389
ISBN: 978-0-9771444-0-2
© Copyright 2007 by Deborah Davis-Thomas

FAMILY COMES FIRST CREDITS
Written by Tracy Thomas
Copy edited by Candace K. Cottrell
Cover graphics and design by Candace K. Cottrell
Interior design by Candace K. Cottrell and Daniel Francis

Printed in the USA.

DEDICATION

I dedicate my first novel in loving memory
of my beloved Grandmothers:

Elizabeth Allen (1920-1988)
Doris Weaver (1929-2003)

I know you're looking down at me!

AUTHOR'S ACKNOWLEDGMENTS

First and foremost, I would like to thank God for allowing circumstances to show me a gift I never knew I possessed. I would like to thank every one for believing in me when I decided to step out on Faith to publish this book.

Beginning with my soul mate, best friend, and lover (my wife) Deb... I still remember that January in 1987 when I first laid sight on those chinky eyes of yours. I don't know if it was love at first sight, but I do know it's twenty years later and our love is still strong. Lord knows I've put you through a lot but you've stood firm by my side. You've seen in me what I couldn't see in myself. You've blessed me with a son (who encouraged me in ways he doesn't even know) and are the true definition of a 'Ride Or Die' Chick! *Except you are my queen*!

My mom and dad for reminding me anything I set my mind to I could achieve. To my brother for all his mental and emotional support (can't forget financial) during the endeavor that supported me throughout – *Family truly does come, First*! I love you all!

To the authors who paved the way for the urban fiction genre. (Too much talent to name.)

Special thanks to Mark Anthony of Q-Boro Books. In a time where some people measure manhood by how much 'work you put in' in the hood. You showed me real on a whole 'nother level. You treated the thirteen years that we hadn't seen each other as if it were yesterday! You saved me the headaches of having to learn through trial and error by offering my wife your expertise on the industry, thus helping to secure my future and make my dream a reality.

You have a lot of blessings wished your way, and I just wanted you to know I am one of the people that will be praying for your continued success! **One Love!**

To Candace K. Cottrell for your patience and professionalism. Your expertise is truly appreciated. Much continued success!

To LaQuan Plowden, for the original sketch of the logo.

To those on lockdown, time won't give back time and though they've locked our bodies' they can't trap our mind... cuz our minds still stay on the grind!

To our fallen comrades: (R.I.P) Freaky Tah, Huey P., Black Jus, Bebo, Yammie, T. Burke, Tony Tello, Chris Miller, Rico Sorey, and all the soldiers who passed before their time trying to 'come up' in this madness we call...*The Game*!

To the readers, I humbly thank you for your support... without ya'll there would be no PenGame Publishing!

Peace...

Tracy Thomas

MESSAGE TO THE READER

I was never one to knock the next man's hustle. I was too busy finding my own. It took me three state bids to realize I wasn't going to be one of the chosen few to get rich off crime, I always considered myself a thinker (even thou I'm sitting in a cell with a new bid.) So, I begin asking myself how could I do the time without the time doing me. How could I hustle up my own retirement from 'behind the wall?'

Now I've been a fan of the 'hood' novels for the longest. I did though; feel I could pen a story with more substance, content, and reality. The reality that not every convict was a kingpin, and not every hustler was born with kilo in his hand. That the grass is always greener from the other side of the fence and all that glitter isn't gold! What about that 'nigga' that stays on his grind 'till it's his turn to shine? When you see him in that shiny new Benz, he ain't telling how many cats got crossed fa' him to floss. How many coins got scraped up, or thugs got taped up to get where he's at. Instead, he's fronting as if life is all good.

There are 67,000 plus inmates in New York's prisons alone, who've risked their lives and freedom for far, less than the millions of dollars depicted in some of these urban fiction novels.

These are the stories I write... *Stories You Can Relate To!'*

I hope you enjoy!

P.S. If you look up Shane's case in the law library, you will find there is often a thin line between fiction and non-fiction. (It's *not* a game!)

PROLOGUE
Family Comes First

Right now, I'm sitting in this cell restless because I'm getting out of this cesspool in a week! It's been eight years and 28 days, but who's counting? It's a little late in the game to be getting impatient, but all of a sudden, I've got a NY State of Mind. Damn! Eight years...

All I keep thinking about is how my pops use to say, "Shane, you keep getting yourself in trouble and watch how those years sneak up on you. Now you're 16, next time you'll be 21, then 30 and before you know it, you're 40 years old wondering where the years went and finding yourself trying to make up for lost time." Sure enough, here I am, 32 years old. Ready and itching to make up for lost time.

I have two sons. Chauncey's twelve and Isaiah's eight. I'm not sure where I stand with either of them. I guess it's safe to say I'm a little nervous of what lies ahead. Maybe even scared. But not scared enough to stay in this spot, where all your thinking is done for you.

I swear, this place almost runs itself. C.O.'s got it easy. I'm gonna automatically wake up go to breakfast, program, then chow for lunch and so on. See, my problem was— Shane's gotta have it!—the jewels, the whips, *and* the hoes. My last stunt really took the cake. Armed robbery. What the fuck was I thinking? Forty thousand bucks, that's what! But me not being a stranger to doing time, the judge gave me ten flat to think about what I did. Out of a ten, you gotta do eight years. Eight years for trying to snatch up forty grand. That's five thousand a year when I do the math— *less* than minimum wage!

In the beginning, I blamed my driver. A pimp named Cadillac Slim. His bird ass wasn't in the getaway car when I made my exit. I mean damn, I thought I was that nigga that thought of everything! I picked a nice rainy day for low visibility. I also went over plans A and B with this clown— twice! I even got quarters for the parking meter so a meter maid wouldn't roll up and fuck my shit up on a humble. I didn't anticipate two things, though. One, my driver getting out of the getaway car to tell me he had a change of heart, and two, the jeweler being a retired cop. So here I am. And for a while, all I thought about was how I should've never let that bird be my driver. I knew he wasn't built like that. But I learned a valuable lesson: When doing dirt, anything can happen!

Therefore, for the last eight years I've had to sit in the yard and endure criticism from some of the *self-proclaimed* best in the art of robbery. I guess it's just a coincidence that we all share a cellblock. I swear you can't tell a jail nigga nothing! I've heard it all, from "Shane, you rushed into it" to "Shane, you had the right idea, but it was too much to do by yourself." And my favorite "Nah, he shoulda killed everyone in the damn store!" Yeah, brilliant minds at work. I mean, when I think back, for a dude that got shot during my exit from the spot and despite my coward-ass getaway driver, Caddie, whom I only used 'cause my regular driver wanted too much of a cut, a nigga like me still managed to get enough time to stash the loot. But I haven't told anyone that precious piece of info. Except my dawg, Pryze. But even he missed the point. Had I got away, I would've never stopped, and by now, I'd have life or be dead. I got this time for all the shit I got away with that the District Attorney doesn't know about, because I was doing my thang! But 8 years later, that's no longer me. The kid is officially retired...

it's a wrap!

So what's my plan now? I need the necessities, a place to live, a source of income, and a car to drive. Yes, a car to drive. Now I know a lot of folks would say a car is not a necessity, but more so a luxury. But to me the necessity is that I push a luxury car!

CHAPTER 1
LOST TIME

The C.O. doing his rounds interrupted Shane's thoughts.

"West," the officer called out. "You going to work your last week with us?" he asked with a smirk.

"You call 60 cents a day, work? Nah, my last week here I'm using to get my head right," Shane told him.

"Then you've gotta lock-in till after the count," the officer said as he continued his rounds.

"Simmons, put me down for the phone list, Aight?" Shane called out.

"Twenty-eight, for the phone list and West take that curtain down off your bars!" the officer said as he disappeared down the gallery.

After count, Officer Simmons seemed to take forever to lock A-Block out for the gym. It was the only place Shane could access a phone with the exception of the yard.

"I have a collect call from... Shane West, an inmate at Sing-Sing Correctional Facility. To hear the cost for this call, press 9. If you wish to accept and pay for this call, dial 3," said the automated voice.

"Hey, Shortie," said Shane

"Hey, Boonk," was her reply.

Boonk was their pet name for each other. Although they still used the term, it didn't quite hold the same meaning it once held. When Mia first told Shane about Mark, his reply was, "I wanna make a deal with you, Mia. You won't tell me about your relationship, and I won't ask." And they both kept their word.

But lately, Mia felt as if she was leading him on. Mark had been pressuring her lately about her frequent visits to Sing-Sing. He would often say, "I know you be slobbing all on that nigga, Mia. Don't play me!" It would take her a whole day of pampering to calm him down. It was becoming a ritual she was growing tired of. She justified her actions with the fact that Isaiah had a right to know who his father was. But Mia would occasionally visit Shane alone and leave Mark with the promise to tell Shane that Mark and her relationship had reached the next level.

Whatever that means, Mia thought.

"Mia, are you listening to me?" Shane asked.

"Yeah, I'm here, Boonk," she said.

I can't have him coming home thinking things are going to be the same as they were 8 years ago. Mark doesn't deserve that... Neither of them deserves that, she thought.

"I was just saying, when I get out I'm going to see Mom and Dad first. However, when I hit NY, we need to have a serious talk. I've been putting it off because it never seemed to be the right time. OK?" She could almost hear him smiling through the phone.

"No problem, your parents should be the first people you see."

Damn! She thought. Does he really expect us to start where we left off 8 years ago? Maybe I'm jumping the gun, all he said was we have to talk. She reasoned, then as an after thought. Actually, he said we need to have a serious talk.

"And Boonk?" Mia started.

"Uh-huh?"

"Your right, we do need to talk." She could feel him smiling through the phone again as she said it.

"Ok, little Mama until then love ya," he said then hung up.

Shane took out his little black book and started dialing another number. Again the automated voice sounded, then once again...

"I have a collect call from Shane West. An inmate at Sing-Sing Correctional Facility. To hear the cost for this call press 9. If you wish to except and pay for this call dial 3."

My greasy ass nigga! *What's goood?*" Pryze was high again.

"I'll tell you what's good, one week left. That's what's good!" Shane added, "Did you stop puffing long enough to cop my release clothes?"

"Of course my Versace niggerachi, lemme see... You said tan Timbs. Size nine, right? The dark blue Levi *stiffs* and a tan suede peacoat."

"Good, you did good, Pryze. Rod sent me a Dolce & Gabbana tan scully yesterday."

"What kind of shirt you wearing?"

"Oatmeal colored long john shirt!" They both started laughing.

"I'm picturing that shit, son. You of all people can pull that shit off." Pryze was taking deep drags off the blunt he had just rolled.

"Pryze, I want you to pick me up in the jeep."

"I was gonna take Keisha's car so I can push 160 till the rubber touch rims," Pryze joked. He was *always* joking.

"Naw, P, it's my day, and I wanna get my lean on."

Pryze had just copped the 2004 Caddy Escalade in cocaine white. He and Shane had renamed the pearl white and gave it the nickname of the drug that faithfully fattened their pockets. During the late '90's, they graduated to selling heroin. Shane was the alleged mastermind behind a lot of heists in the early 90's by a clique called *The Family*. All members had a black rose tattoo somewhere on them. Shane's was on his neck.

"Pryze, don't drive that little-ass CLK up here. Besides, we're gonna need the space, trust me."

"Shane, don't do no bum shit like bring all that jail shit home." Pryze laughed.

"Well, it's good to know that if ya business ever falls off, you've got a future in comedy." Now Shane was grinning, "So I'll see you next week?"

"Yeah, see you on the 21st." He smirked.

"The 20th! Pryze, the 20th!"

"I'm just fucking with you, son. Could you honestly think I'd forget?" Pryze polished off the last of the blunt he was smoking.

"In the Caddy?" Shane asked, already knowing the answer.

"Yeah, niggero, in the Caddy."

"No doubt, well yo, kid, I'm out!" Shane said.

"Aight...One!" And then the phone clicked.

They are about to release my Scoobie... New York niggas better hold on to their pockets, thought Pryze as he smiled rolling another chunk of Dro.

Bind up the brokenhearted...Proclaim freedom for the captives and release for the prisoners." Isaiah 61:1.

"That my next tattoo, Rowe. Isaiah 61:1."

Shane was sitting at the chess table with Old Man Rowe. Rowe was a chess fanatic, a jailhouse lawyer and a religious nut but he and Shane got along. The old timer took an immediate liking to Shane. Shane didn't have time for war stories, and after blowing trial he attacked the law library with a vengeance, learning on his own to cite and shephardize cases. Along with the language of law. Had it not been for the Old Timer's intervention, he would still be doing the original 20 years the judge sentenced him to. Rowe had life and had exhausted all avenues of appeal. It was a done deal for him, and not once in their time together had Shane ever heard the Old Man complain.

"Yo, Rowe I'm leaving you my shit. I wouldn't have it any other way. You know you my nig..." Shane caught himself. "You my peeps."

Rowe didn't play the nigger game. He would stress that we've come too far in the struggle to use that word as a term of endearment. To call Rowe a nigger was like talking about his Mom. He was old school; Afro picks with the fist, bell-bottoms, and Black Panthers.

"Youngblood, I appreciate the offer, but I'm cool. You know I don't need for nothing in this camp." And it was true. Rowe was the equivalent in Sing-Sing to Morgan Freeman in *Shawshank Redemption*. If he couldn't get it, it couldn't be got!

"Whatever you say, Rowe... It's my move, right?" Shane asked. "Checkmate!"

"That ain't no...Well I'll be damn! Run it, Youngblood, two more stamps." Rowe was already setting up the pieces.

"Where you going? You gonna run off witcha little one win, Youngblood?" The old man taunted.

"Lock-in is in five minutes and your opening move takes 5 minutes," Shane joked.

"Well, if ya want speed chess, go to the park!" griped the old timer.

"Standing count, lights on fully dressed and no talking on the count!" announced the voice from the cellblock's loudspeaker.

Damn, I haven't seen nor spoke to you in so long thought Shane, while staring at his older son's picture. He had tried his best under the conditions, he reasoned. But letters, pictures and an occasional gift, just couldn't equal up to him not being there.

"I owe you, little man...big time!" he mumbled to himself,

lightly touching the photo. He couldn't call because once he was upstate he only was allowed collect calls. And Chyna's phone didn't accept collect calls. *She wouldn't accept my call if I could get through,* Shane thought.

Chyna was his first love, but their relationship was living proof that there's a thin line between love and hate. She'd done quite well for herself. She kept a new car, a house in Maryland, and was a licensed nail technician. Shane's mother said she also had a fiancée and was due to get married sometime in Spring. She finally got her white picket fence. And he was happy for her, although it reminded him of his many mistakes.

Chyna didn't play any games. She hadn't let up on him his whole eight years. At the age of four, Chauncey broke his leg in daycare. When Shane found out, he asked Mia to place a 3-way call to Chyna. He remembered what she said like it was yesterday because it stung him that much.

"Hello," Chyna answered.

"It's me," Shane said.

"What do you want?" she asked him. The tension in her voice already apparent.

"I heard Chauncey broke his leg. Can I speak to him?" Shane was concerned about his son and didn't feel up to an argument.

"He's asleep right now," she told him, but Shane could hear Chauncey in the background.

"Mommy, I'm thirsty. Can I have some juice?" Chauncey said.

Shane closed his eyes and savored the sound of his son's voice. He never mentioned knowing Chauncey wasn't asleep. He just took what he could get. This was overhearing his son's one request.

"He sounds like he in pain," he stated.

Then came the drama.

Her voice was rising. "Why do you even bother calling? He doesn't even remember you! And when he has questions,

I don't know what to tell him. I suggest when you get out, try and bond with him. Until then, I would appreciate it if you did not call here, 'cause you're confusing him."

"First of all, I don't say anything to confuse him, Chyna. The most I ask is if he knows who he's talking to."

She was yelling now. "Won't you just leave us alone? *I don't want you!!!* I don't want you calling. When Chauncey becomes a man—which is about the next time you'll be out— you can explain your side of the story."

I don't want you. Where'd that come from? she thought.

"Fine, I just needed to hear you say it, to make it official. The way I figure things, if I was Chauncey my first question would be, 'Why did he wait so many years?' But as long as I can tell him you wanted it that way, cool," Shane replied.

He was always logical, too logical. Fuck logical! He's not gonna make me out to be the bad guy thought Chyna.

"Well, when and if he starts asking about you, I'll call your mother or some jails or something. Goodbye!" She hung up.

He and Mia attempted some small talk. She had heard it all on 3-way. At first, Mia thought Shane exaggerated Chyna's anger toward him. Now she knew his stories were pretty close to the truth.

"Boonk." Mia paused… "Happy Father's Day."

"Today's Father's Day?" Shane asked.

"Yeah," she said.

"Wow, I would've never guessed it by that call." Shane tried to make light of the situation.

"Word, I ain't taking sides, but carrying around that much anger can't be healthy."

Mia started laughing unexpectedly."Boonk, I wish you could see this. Isaiah crawled over and snatched two of Boobie's french fries and wolfed them down before she could catch him."

Shane started cracking up. He could hear Mia's sister Boobie in the background beefing.

"Mia?"

"Yeah?" She was still laughing at Boobie loss.

"Thanks...I needed a laugh," Shane said.

Shane lay on his bunk with his hands behind his head. In a few days, there would be no more reminiscing, no more flashbacks, no more standing counts, and no more line-ups for bathhouse.

Thank God for my persistence and Old Man Rowe. Without him, I'd have another 12 years to go. One little loophole, one illegal arrest and here I am. I guess the cops tried too hard thought Shane.

Rowe told Shane he should take them back to trial a second time since his case was severely weakened by the suppression of identification testimony by the appellate courts. But Shane had four years in by then, so when the D.A. offered him ten flat to save the taxpayers the expense of a new trial, he had jumped on it.

"You'll do eight years and some change out of the ten," his attorney informed him.

"Thank you, Mr. Kastin." Shane shook his hand then added, "Do you think you can get me on the first bus back to Rikers?" He went back upstate with a little over four years left. Shane had gotten back a decade of his life.

Shane's day had finally come. He didn't sleep a wink that night, so he killed the time by packing all his belongings. He separated his legal documents and important papers from his property. All he was taking were the documents and his photos. Before he knew it, the officer was doing his morning rounds and Shane was told the words every convict longs to hear.

"West, pack up. Take your mattress and your property to intake."

Shane jumped up dressed and packed. He had his mattress rolled up and ready to go. He dragged out boxes of his personal effects, slid them down to Rowe's cell, and attached a note to the boxes with all the outside information Rowe needed to contact him. Then he grabbed his mattress and state-issued greens and headed for intake.

"OK, gentleman, listen up. If you already have what you're gonna be wearing, now's the time to put it on. Throw your state greens in that corner pile." The C.O. pointed. "If you don't have anything to wear, Pataki is providing you with the standard polyester suit. If you're wearing something someone sent to you and you couldn't have it in population for whatever reason, line it up here."

Shane and two others lined up to get their clothes. The Pataki suits were hardly ever worn. Even the most indigent con would hustle up enough cigarettes to buy a sweat suit before they'd walk out the door in a suit provided by the state.

"Name and number," the officer demanded.

"West, 96A7928," Shane replied.

He was handed a box of clothes. He inspected the contents and smiled. Pryze had done well. *Not too tight and not too baggy* Shane thought as he put the clothes on. Other inmates were giving nods of approval at the quality garments he wore. Shane nodded back.

"Now," the C.O. began. "If anyone has money in their account, line up here."

Mostly everyone lined up. When Shane's turn came up, he signed the receipt and the clerk counted out $490.00. He asked if he could put money in another inmate's account and was told he had to go around front and have it deposited as a visitor would. He was also informed he couldn't deposit it himself since he would soon be a parolee and would need his parole officer's permission to visit a state inmate. One final thumbprint and a signature of receipt for his bus ticket and Shane was headed toward the front gate.

Meanwhile, outside, Officer Kelly was getting pissed. It was his third trip to the front gate to tell the asshole outside to turn the radio down in his truck. He already warned the man that if he had to tell him again, he would be forced to leave.

"Aw, man, here comes bird chest again," Pryze mumbled while pulling on a cigarette.

Kelly used his stick to knock on the SUV's tinted windows.

"Yo, what the fuck is up?!" Pryze asked, rolling down the windows of his Cadillac.

"Don't act like you weren't warned, buddy. The music is too friggin loud." Kelly backed up and stared Pryze down.

Only crackers use words like friggin, Pryze mused.

"The first time I turned down the sounds. The second time I rolled the window up, and now you're out here knocking on my shit with your stick even though I seen yo skinny ass coming! You trying ta crack my window or something? Now get the fuck out my face before I put this stogie out on your forehead, cracker!" Pryze was heated.

Kelly was turning red. He was used to dealing with men who were locked down in a controlled environment, but pride wouldn't let him back down from the confrontation, especially when he saw that Pryze was now smiling.

"Look, pal!" Kelly started.

Pryze was out the door before the C.O. could say another word.

This nigger crazy Kelly thought as his adrenaline was pumping.

But Pryze just walked right past him to give Shane a hug.

Pryze saw Shane standing there as the front gate opened and immediately went to greet his crimee. Officer Kelly was too engrossed in his little altercation with Pryze to notice the front gate opening.

"Pryze, what's up? Let me find out you and toy cop is socializing." Shane knew Pryze was more than likely giving Officer Kelly hell.

"What's up? Nigga, stop playing and come holler at ya boy." Pryze gave him a big hug.

"Now let's be out before I put the beats on Barney Fife over there," He said nodding toward Kelly.

Shane stopped in his tracks. "Whoa! What size are those rims?"

"Twinny Twins," Pryze growled.

"Twenty-twos?"

"Yeah, Twinny Twins...don't worry we gonna set you up for society?" Pryze joked.

"Daddy-O, you must mean set society up for me."

They both laughed. They got in the jeep and went around to the visiting area. Ten minutes later, Pryze came out handing Shane a $300 receipt for the funds he had him put in Rowe's account.

"Where to?" Pryze asked

"We got something to roll them trees in?" Shane asked.

Pryze pulled out four Dutch Master cigars.

"Chesapeake, Virginia, Pryze."

And they were rolling, both figuratively and literally.

CHAPTER 2
CHYNA

"Chauncey," yelled Chyna, while finishing off the last of her morning tea.

"What?" he answered.

"What did you say? I told that boy about answering me like that," she mumbled to herself.

"Yes, Mom?" Chauncey answered.

That's better she thought.

"You better be dressed and ready for school because I can hear you and that PlayStation from down here."

"I am," he said while trying to top his own high score.

"You want tuna or turkey?"

"Aw, Ma, I'm not a kid anymore. Bag lunches are so lame. I'd rather buy lunch at school."

"Excuse me?" Chyna was smiling.

She had to admit that Chauncey was good kid. He did well in school. He watched his manners and he did what he was told. He'd had his moments, but never nothing serious. There were times when Chyna questioned whether she was too hard on him. She never had any men around him. Tim was the only man she felt close enough with to even consider introducing to her son. Though Tim was always respectful to Chauncey, he never attempted any serious bonding. Shane's brother also took him out occasionally to the museum, park, etc.

I wouldn't be surprised if he was waiting for his father to come home and make some miraculous entrance in his life, she thought.

Chyna hated that Shane had left her to deal with so much responsibility on her own. She also had the fear that Shane would get Chauncey's hopes up by making him all types of promises, only to renege on them once he got out. She tried to do the right thing and had allowed him to write directly to Chauncey once he was reading and writing fluently.

After all, he's got 20 years, so how else is Chauncey going to get to know him? she reasoned. But something Chauncey said recently put Chyna on alert.

"If Daddy got an appeal, he could be home sooner," Chauncey had said.

"Yeah, but those things aren't easy to get," She hoped Shane hadn't been getting the boys hopes up.

"I know, but you got 3 chances: state, federal and 440. Sorta like baseball." Chauncey smiled.

Sounding a little too much like a lawyer, Chyna thought.

She long ago stopped monitoring their correspondence, but decided it was time to do a little "investigative parenting" as she called it.

Maybe I'll call Ma West and see if there was any up to date news regarding his situation. It would be just like him not to tell me anything, she thought.

Then she remembered her last words to him. "Don't call here no more. If Chauncey asks about you, I'll call some jails or find you through your moms."

Now that she reflected on it, she knew she had worded her statement in a way to inflict as much emotional damage as she could. She wanted Shane to hurt as much as she did. Despite her opinions of him, he still managed to keep some form of contact with his son.

Well I hope for Chauncey's sake his father has grown up, Chyna thought. She finished clearing the kitchen and made a mental note to call Shane's mother, Ma West.

"Come on, time to go," she called up to Chauncey.

"I'm on the last level. I've never gotten this far. Can I put the game on my memory card...please?" he pleaded.

"You got five minutes; I'll be in the car," she told him.

When she started up the car to warm it up, the radio came on. Dennis Edwards of the Temptations was singing "Poppa was a Rolling Stone."

"Is it true what they say, poppa never worked a day in his life, and momma there's bad talk going 'round the town, Poppa had two children and another wife. And that ain't right."

As the song played, Chyna laughed out loud.

"If that isn't a sign from God to check up on Shane's trifling butt, I don't know what is. I'm calling Ma West today," she said.

Just then, Chauncey came running down the driveway, slamming the car door.

"How many times have I told you about slamming the car door?" she said while fixing his collar.

"Sorry. What's so funny?" he asked grinning.

His father's grin, she thought to herself.

"Nothing important." She smiled back.

Chauncey popped in 50 Cent's "In the Club." Full blast.

"TURN THAT DOWN, BOY. I CAN'T THINK!" Chyna had to shout over the music.

"Ma that's 50 Cent. He doesn't sound right low."

"I know who it is, and he's gonna sound a lot like R.Kelly if you don't turn it down."

Chauncey sucked his teeth, but turned it down just as quick, and started nodding his head so hard Chyna wondered if they were listening to the same song.

I'm getting old, she thought, smiling at her son. She pulled up in front of Chauncey's school and saw his buddy Lamont waiting for him as usual.

"When I get home we need to talk." She kissed him on the cheek.

"What did I do now?" he asked, shoulders slumped as if

he was convicted.

"What makes you think I'm going to accuse you of something? Have you done something I don't know about?" she joked.

"No." He smiled.

"I'll see you later. And no PlayStation until your homework's done."

Lamont and Chauncey were already off somewhere clowning as she pulled off. Chyna had a half hour to get to work, and since the shop was close by, she took her time. She was a nail technician at a salon called Simply Styled. She enjoyed her job. It gave her flexibility. She could check up on Chauncey at home, attend PTA meetings, and go on class trips, or her favorite: just take the day off.

Chyna wasn't just a Nail Technician, she was *the* nail technician of the small town. All the who's who of Bethesda, Maryland agreed that if you got your nails done, you went to her. When she first arrived in Maryland, women immediately took notice of her unique style, dress, and hair. Therefore, when she strutted into Simply Styled looking to set up shop, the owner Sheronda, whom everyone referred to as Sherry, immediately took notice. The first thing that caught her attention was Chyna's eyes. She had what most men called bedroom eyes. They appeared slanted, as if she was mixed with Asian. She had a high yellow complexion of unblemished skin which seemed to shine whenever she entered a room. Her full lips glowed as if she kept a never-ending supply of lips gloss applied to them. She stood 5'8" with long, muscular legs that stopped at her small waist. Her 36C breasts strained against the sheer fabric of her top.

She looks like that actress LisaRaye who played Diamond in that movie Player's Club, thought Sherry.

Sherry was originally from Brooklyn, but had moved to Maryland for a change of pace. However, she visited her hometown enough to know Chyna was dripping with New

York style, from her Coach bag to her Manolo Blahnik
Timbs to the black and pink Vanson leather she wore.
Sherry intended to hear her out. *She'd be great for business,*
Sherry thought. Chyna had brought her portfolio, more for
potential customers to see than for the owner.

"What is this called?" one customer asked

"How much do you charge?" another asked

"I saw a girl at the club with a pattern like that one, but
your colors blend better," another customer added.

Chyna was hired immediately and quickly earned a
reputation as someone who'd work with you on those days
when a special event fell before payday. She was also
responsible, and Sherry soon enlisted her for extra duties
around the shop she liked to call 'favors.' Some of these
favors included closing up shop or picking up Dana on her
way to work.

Dana worked the front desk at Simply Styled and was a
straight-up gossip queen. She was short, light-skinned and
on the verge of being fat. Her hips and breasts were bigger
than her stomach, and many men still found her attractive.
Even if she gained another twenty pounds, she'd still have
plenty of fans.

"Men like 'em thick," she would often tease Chyna.

"Not too thick, girlfriend," Chyna would shoot back,
emphasizing the word *thick*.

"You think I'm fat?" Dana would ask and start pinching
her sides.

Chyna and Dana had become close. Occasionally, Chyna
would slip up and share something personal with Dana. The
girl couldn't help but gossip, though. It was to the point she
even told her *own* business. Nonetheless, they were friends.
Chyna picked up Dana every morning and every morning,
Dana ran late. However, Dana opened up the shop, so it
came down to picking her up or waiting in front of the shop
for her. Dana lived three blocks from Chauncey's school, so
it worked out well for both of them.

Dana was 25, but acted ten years younger. And even though Chyna only had her by six years, they didn't seem to have much in common. Chyna was responsible where Dana wasn't. Chyna was punctual when Dana was always late. Chyna pulled up in Dana's driveway and checked her front door. It was open as usual, so Chyna let herself in.

"Dana, ya chunky ass better be dressed!" Chyna always called her Chunky. Short for Chunky Butt. She gave her that nickname since all of Tim's friends referred to Dana as her girlfriend with the fat ass. Dana must have thought so too, because with each passing year, her skirts got shorter and her jeans tighter.

"Make some coffee. I'll be right down." Dana told her.

"I had tea already. You know I don't mess with no coffee," Chyna yelled up.

"Well make me some then!" she hollered back.

"We don't have time. If you hurry, we can stop at Dunkin Donuts." Chyna sat down in front of the TV. The news was on.

Meanwhile, Dana was upstairs squeezing into some tight blue jeans. She looked good in the tight brown sweater. It showed just enough cleavage and her nipples showed through the sweater. *My nigga magnets*, she thought, as she stretched the fabric.

"It's about time, what takes you so long every morning?"

"Damn, do you gotta start the day off bitching? It's still morning. I see I'm gonna have to have a little talk with Tim." Dana picked up her coat.

"Talk to Tim about what?"

"About hitting that thang right, or giving up some lip service. 'Cause I swear, nobody could be as bitchy and uptight as you if they were getting it like they wanted, Angryman!"

Angryman was Dana's nickname for Chyna when she got in her moods, which was often. Sometimes she called her Angry for short. Their own private joke, Chunky and Angry.

Once after hearing them joke, a customer mistakenly called Chyna 'Angie.' They continued their debate on the way to the shop.

"You don't know what you talking about because Tim does his thang," Chyna replied, taking up for her man.

Dana loved to talk about men and would say anything to keep the conversation going.

"That's exactly my point. Tim does *his* thing. When is he gonna start doing, *your* thang?"

"You talk like you're up in our bedroom getting play by play info. As a matter of fact, I wouldn't be surprised if ya nosy ass was. Are you a Peeping Tom, Dana?" Chyna was laughing.

"Whatever! I'm just saying, Tim is responsible, reliable, and a hard worker. But he's so... *bland!* So I can understand the coochie got you cranky." Dana started cracking up.

"Dana!" Chyna squealed.

"Yes, Sweetie?" she answered, still laughing.

"Fuck you." Chyna smiled, giving her the finger.

"My point exactly, you wanna fuck me because he's not fucking you." Dana always gave her opinion whether it was asked for or not.

Chyna stopped at an intersection while Dana kept on.

"I don't think Tim makes you happy. I think you just feel secure with him. And you have a right to. He'll probably never fuck up, and if he did, it wouldn't break your heart because you settling. Ain't I right?" Dana thought she had everyone figured out.

"No, you're not right, and if you spent half the time you spend analyzing other people's relationship on yourself, you might have a man!" Chyna told her.

"Hold up, girlfriend. Half of the girls in the shop is where I get my info from, and to keep it real, everyone's exchanging dirt. So there's always something to talk about. I'll even go so far as to make you a bet. I'm going to go the rest of the month without spreading any gossip, and I bet you all the girls will go crazy, get mad, or think of shit I can use just to keep the ghetto soaps going."

"No bet," Chyna said, then finished the sentence with her. "'Cause you know you'd lose."

They hi-fived each other.

"So, Dana, what do you think people say about your string of one-night stands?" Chyna knew Dana's real reason for not sticking with one man was that she couldn't get one to commit.

"I don't be having no 'string' of one-nighters. I'm just making sure I find Mr.Right. There's a reason they don't have one flavor at Baskin Robbins." She started the same speech Chyna had heard plenty of times at the shop. "How do you know butter pecan is your favorite if you haven't tried any other flavor? Now I'm not saying try them all. I'm just saying if any other flavors looked more appealing, then why cheat your taste buds?" Dana had a look on her face as if she'd won some sort of debate.

"Dana." Chyna kept her eyes on the road.

"What?"

"When they say 'waiting to exhale,' they don't mean between blow jobs."

They both started laughing.

"Fuck you, Chyna."

Dana was laughing so hard her eyes were tearing. And Chyna almost passed Dunkin Donuts. She backed up her Honda and Dana got out.

"You want something Angry?" Dana asked, eyes still watery.

"Yeah for you to hurry up." Chyna was getting impatient.

"First appointment of the day isn't until ten," Dana informed her. "We got time."

"I need to make a call before Sherry comes in," Chyna explained.

They arrived at the shop by 9:15AM, and Dana started

her daily routine of getting the shop ready for business. It was Friday, the shop's busiest day. The shop would stay open until 1AM. All the working women came in around six in the evening and everyone would be done around eleven. They'd pass around cups of red Alize and catch up on the weekly gossip. It was the weekly ritual at Simply Styled. Sherry had all types of promotional gimmicks that kept her place the hottest spot in Maryland to get your 'do did.' Even Chyna ran specials for manicures and pedicures. Simply styled was also just that... simply styled. Sherry had her stylists' booths along the four walls, with Chyna's section in the far corner. The waiting area was a sunken floor with a rust-colored sectional leather sofa. The floors were cherry wood and the walls were classic red brick. Every tool the stylists owned were chrome, from the blowdryers to curling irons, and they all sat in neat chrome cages.

Usually Chyna helped Dana get the shop ready, which didn't entail much more than getting the coffee pot brewing and turning on the shop's big screen TV. They usually showed the latest movies and occasionally daytime soaps or talk shows. Anything that would catch customers' interest while they waited.

Chyna went into Sherry's office to call Shane's mother. Chyna could have made the call from her station, but she wanted some privacy from Dana.

"Hello?" Ma West answered.

"Hello, Ma West," Chyna said, "How've you been?"

"Oh, I'm fine. How's my little man?"

"He's fine. He thinks he's grown sometimes, but he doesn't give me any problems.The reason I called is because I was talking to Chauncey and he started mentioning his father. The next thing I know, he's speaking about appeals and tainted evidence and misidentification and a few other things only Shane could have put in his head. I don't really want Shane getting Chauncey's hopes up." She paused. "Anyway, I was thinking of visiting him and maybe even taking Chauncey to see him."

"You haven't spoken to Shane?" Ma West asked her.

"Not in years, Ma West. Nor have I written."

"He still should have told you... I don't know about that boy sometimes." Mama West sighed.

Chyna was confused. "Tell me what Ma West?" Chyna braced herself.

"Well his friend Bernard—the one who calls himself Pryze or something like that—called last week explaining that he was going to pick Shane up from the jail and that he wanted to know if he could pick up his jewelry. But I told him Shane would have to call me and tell me to give it to him because I don't want to be in the middle of any misunderstandings about that boy's stuff. I remember once..."

Chyna was no longer listening, she couldn't believe Shane had the nerve to tell Chauncey he was getting released and get him to keep it from her. He knew the address and could have had the decency to write her and tell her something. She had the right to know.

"Ma West, when he calls or shows up could you tell him to call me please?" Chyna was hoping Shane's mother could not detect the anger in her voice.

"Well I'm sure you are going to be one of the first people he contacts." Ma West wasn't sure she believed it herself.

"I wish I was as sure as you are Ma West."

Just then, Sherry walked into her office.

"Well I'll speak to you later Ma West." Chyna hung up.

"You didn't have to rush off the phone because of me," Sherry told Chyna.

"No, it wasn't that. Besides, I've heard all I needed to hear." She sounded a little tense to Sherry.

"Good news I hope?" Sherry asked.

Dana was bringing Sherry her morning coffee just as Chyna spoke

"I just spoke to Shane's mother and she said he's getting out."

"When?" Dana blurted out.

Chyna and Sherry both looked up; they hadn't even realized Dana was standing there.

"This week," Chyna answered.

"Well today's Friday, what day this week? Dana said, stating the obvious.

"She didn't say." She wished Dana hadn't heard the news.

Sherry, seeming to read Chyna's mind, told Dana, "And please don't go putting the girl's business out there like you've been known to do."

"Who?" Dana asked playing dumb.

"You, that's who."

"I wouldn't even care, Sherry. I'm so tight right now," Chyna said.

"Why? What's wrong? Aren't you at least happy for Chauncey's sake?" Sherry asked.

"I think Shane told Chauncey not to tell me he was coming home." Chyna was trying to figure out the best way to discuss all of this newly absorbed information with her son.

"Where'd you get a crazy idea like that?" Sherry asked.

"Come on, Sherry; it's obvious." Dana had to add her two cents as usual.

"Shut up, Dana! It's not obvious! Chyna, sweetie, don't jump to conclusions. But if you find out you're right, you take it from there. Keep in mind, you told that man not to call you. You didn't tell him to call you when he's about to get released," Sherry added. "But if you're right, that's foul. I can understand not telling you, but if he's got Chauncey keeping secrets from you, he's dead wrong."

"Sherry, I think I'm right because the reason I called in the first place was that Chauncey's been talking about things he couldn't possibly know about. You know, appeals and suppressing evidence and stuff. I had just called to get his info and talk to him about not getting Chauncey's hopes up and found out he's getting out."

Dana jumped in the conversation. "Aren't you glad he's home?" she asked

"It makes me no difference. That's besides the point," Chyna replied.

Dana went to open the shop, leaving Chyna and Sherry alone.

"Humph, I don't believe you just told that bold-faced lie." Sherry was never one to bite her tongue."We've talked too many nights in this shop about how you want Chauncey to know his father for you to be fronting now."

Sherry looked Chyna dead in the eyes, embracing her friend at arm's length.

"Girlfriend, whatever issues you may *think* you still have with him, let it go. For your son's sake, let it go!" She repeated.

Sherry left Chyna in her office, thinking that a few minutes alone might do her some good. Chyna sat there for a moment, thinking that she liked Sherry because she kept it real and was blunt about it.

And she's right; I gotta let it go before it eats me up.

She took a deep breath and got ready for her day to begin.

CHAPTER 3
LIL' MAMA MIA

"Can anyone give me the definition of psychology?" Professor Harris asked. "Anyone...how about you Mia?"

Mia was busying herself jotting down reminders of things to do after class. She looked up.

"Psychology is the science of the mind, its nature, and functions," she answered.

"And what would be our purpose in studying the mind?" her professor pushed on.

"Well, in order to analyze something we must first understand how it works...or in this case, functions." Mia wanted to counsel troubled youth, making Psychology 101 one of her favorite classes.

"Very good." Before Professor Harris could finish, the bell rang signifying the end of her Psychology class. Her last class for the day.

Mia was the first one out the door, she had no time for her usual good-byes. She had just enough time to pick up the groceries she had written down. The week had been hectic and she was trying to get a head start on the weekend. By the time she got home, the whole clan was watching a DVD and eating popcorn. Isaiah had two handfuls.

"Guess who called?" her sister Boobie said in a teasing voice.

"Who?" Mia asked while Isaiah helped his mom with the

groceries.

"Shane...and it wasn't collect! He was with that fool Pryze." Boobie continued. "He said they were going to his mom's then back here to New York."

"Yep, today's his day. What else did he say?" Mia inspected the groceries and turned toward Boobie.

"I told him you wasn't home yet. He asked for Khalid's number at work." Boobie turned the TV down.

"I think he wants Khalid to find him a place to live," Mia said. She was thinking that if Shane was looking for a place then maybe he wasn't assuming they would resume their relationship where they left off. "Khalid's coming through later, so we can get the 411 from him. You know that nigga gonna give up all the details. Did Isaiah speak to him?" she added.

"Yeah, those two did most of the talking," Boobie told her.

"What were you and daddy talking about?" Mia asked her son.

"He said he was going to Grandma's to pick up his stuff and that he would see me soon," Isaiah explained, while his eyes never left the TV. "I told him you would be home early because your day to cook was today." Isaiah grinned showing the same dimples as his mother.

Mia turned around hands on her hips.

"Well go ahead and say it, because I know he said something slick." She started grinning along with Isaiah.

"He said he knows the whole house is trying to get full off junk food before you get here," Boobie jumped in.

"You know that's right!" She and Isaiah started laughing.

"Ha, ha, ha," Mia said sarcastically. "Y'all just crack yourselves up don't yall? Just for that, we're having Hamburger Helper."

Boobie leaned toward Isaiah and whispered.

"We were probably having Hamburger Helper anyway.

Too bad it doesn't help her hamburger." Isaiah was trying not to laugh.

Mia was smiling and thinking how Shane too had those jokes that were so stupid you had to laugh. *If you didn't know him it was a totally different ball game. Non-talkative, observant, yet at times moody best describes him.*

Mia thought of how different Shane was from other guys she'd met. He had taught her the do's and don't's of his world. *"If a nigga claims to know your peoples, do a background check. See if they'll vouch for his loyalty, character, affiliation...whatever. Just like a job checks references, Lil Mama, 'cause the streets is watching."*

He stayed schooling her. He taught her how to read body language, tension in a person's movements, telltale signs of fidgeting that may mean a person's lying, and how to discipline oneself from showing those same signs. *"The game is 90% mental,"* he'd often say. Just then, Boobie interrupted her thoughts.

"Oh yeah...I almost forgot, Mark called." Boobie wasn't too fond of Mark and purposely let Mia hear the dislike in her tone of voice when his name came up. However, Mia ignored it.

"What did he say?" she asked.

"The usual...call him." Boobie started flipping channels with the remote.

Mia went to run her bathwater, a Friday afternoon ritual. She soaked in the water while her feet played with the bubbles. The steam was forming bangs near her temples once she started to sweat. Nevertheless, it felt relaxing after dealing with the cold October wind. Mia laid back and closed her eyes.

School work and this night gig are kicking my ass.

Mia worked as a bartender at a club called Foxy's Den near Third Avenue in Brooklyn. The rules of the club were strictly enforced, and if the girls got caught breaking any they were fined. The VIP room had no rules whatsoever and cost thirty dollars to enter. A customer had to have a 'date' to enter, and whatever the two had worked out was between them.

Mia was debating whether to call in sick to Foxy's tonight. She was listening to "Jimmy," a song off *Truth Hurts* album. Truthfully speaking, the song took her back to when she was two months pregnant with Isaiah. Shane was robbing everything. If he didn't do it, he was behind it! Drug spots, jewelry stores, check cashing spots, and pharmacy payrolls; it was even rumored he was behind a few bank jobs. Shane had definitely changed over the years. Mia sent him books on everything from real estate, investing, entrepreneurism, federal and state loans, and business management. All he asked for were books.

She knew he definitely had big plans upon his release. She wished him luck, but Mark on the other hand still hustled. At first, she figured being with Mark was hardly as stressful as being with Shane. So why not see where the relationship went? Shane's occupation had been so violent you could feel the tension weeks before a *job* was done. Even afterwards, the whole neighborhood would be hot. Snitches were put under pressure, newspaper articles, TV coverage, the works. Just the mention of a name and that person would be put under surveillance or worse, picked up. Even when they got away, it wasn't over with when it came to *The Family*. At least if Mark got away with a sale, that was it. Mia's philosophy was to let her man "Do Him," as she put it. The way she looked at it, she would rather know what was going on than be kept in the dark. That way it was her choice to deal with the situation or not.

A nagging bitch is always the last to know what's going on.

Most dudes wound up telling on themselves anyway. Mia had a way of making you feel you were with one of the fellas until all of your bad habits and trifling ways were out in the

open. She knew how to work a nigga...she knew the *street*...
a little too well! Lately she started feeling as if she wasn't
sure what she wanted.

"I'm getting too old to be fucking with these dudes and
their dead-end lifestyles. I'm not doing any more bids
with niggas. Shane was it! I'll make that my New Year's
resolution," she promised herself.

She got out of the tub and dried off, then stood in front
of the mirror inspecting herself. She was 5'7, 115 pounds
and although slim, her 115 was in all the *right* places. She
was a smooth, chocolate complexion with lips that seemed
to be pouting even though she never did. She had dimples
and long, black, shiny hair with a tiny waist. Shane used
to tease her about her round 'tight little apple bottom.' He
used to call her Little Mama Mia. However, he stated to her
that she wasn't so little anymore, so he started calling her
Mama Mia instead.

She put on a dark DKNY that was cut low to show her
stomach and matching gray sweatpants. She braided her
hair in two long ponytails. Just then, Boobie knocked on her
bedroom door.

"Mia?"

"Yeah, what's up?" she answered.

"Khalid is here."

"Tell him I'll be right out."

Mia came out her bedroom eating a can of Pringles.
Khalid was on his knees slap boxing Isaiah.

Pooh got a little skills.

Khalid was trying to back Isaiah up with a flurry of jabs,
but Isaiah stood firm, letting his forearm catch the flurries.
Soon as Khalid turned to greet Mia, Isaiah shot a left jab to
Khalid's jaw.

"POW!"

"Oh Shit!"

"Khalid ...you all right?" Mia asked laughing, and then
added. "Pooh Bear, apologize to Khalid."

Before Isaiah could apologize, Khalid handed him three dollars. "A deal's a deal, shorty!" He turned to explain to Mia. "I told him I would give him three dollars if he could connect once." Khalid was rubbing his jaw and grinning. "Your boy's a beast, Mia, just like his pops!"

Mia instructed Isaiah to put one of the dollars in his piggy bank.

"That's gonna be a tough little nigga there." Khalid took some of Mia's Pringles.

"So what's up, Khalid? Boobie said Shane called here for your job number." Mia had to snatch back her Pringles.

"My bad, Mia. You know you can't eat just one," Khalid joked. "Anyway, check it. That nigga Shane must have called me right after Boobie gave him the number. He said he needed a realtor who understood his credit and reference situation. I told him I can dig where he coming from, but my company only deals with houses, not apartments."

Khalid was still eyeing the Pringles, so Mia handed him the can.

"Thanks! So you know what this nigga tells me?" Khalid continued drawing out the story.

"No, fool, what did he tell you?" Boobie asked, trying to rush him to the point.

"He told me he knows that, and to find him a three bedroom ranch house complete with basement and backyard. And check his last statement out, he says to start looking now!" Khalid was looking for some sort of reaction or comment from Mia or Boobie, but saw none. "I told him that type of set-up would run him $350,000 to $480,000 depending on the neighborhood. Then he starts naming areas like Elmont, Valley Stream, Rosedale, any Long Island hood close to the Queens borderline."

Mia called for Isaiah to bring her the other can of Pringles.

"I was telling him since it was only a ranch house he could probably get away with spending $380,000 if he was willing to stay close to the border. I also asked him what kind of down payment he was talking." Khalid was obviously excited. "This nigga tells me he can do up to ten percent down, *plus* closing costs! He also insisted on a big backyard. I'm impressed, Mia. Shane making big moves for a nigga fresh out the joint. I've got a few houses lined up for him to check out." He began eyeing Mia's fresh can of Pringles.

"Forget about it. You polished off the last can!" She then asked, "Are you excited for yourself or for Shane?"

"Both!" Khalid answered, continuing.

"The way I see it, this is probably the beginning of major moves. I was just complaining about how slow this real estate money is and how I missed that paper I was touching in the days of The Family. And who of all people pop up and pretty much guarantees me a commission right out the pen? Shane!" Khalid was hyped. "Mia, you think he got that kind of dough, or something lined up for The FAM?"

The way Khalid was talking had Mia worried.

"Damn. Khalid, you got him heading back Up North off of one phone call. Slow down, nigga!"

"Mommy, what does uncle Kha mean by The FAM?" Isaiah asked.

Mia gave Khalid a dirty look and handed Isaiah the Pringles. "Nothing, Pooh. Go to your room for Mommy. Were talking grown folks business, OK?"

"Khalid, you have to watch what you say around Isaiah. I'm just as guilty sometimes," Mia added to take the sting out of her words.

"Yeah, I know you're right. Sorry about that...you know Shane sounded like he already has that money. What do you think? I sure could use that commission money. Fats been tight with the profits lately."

Fat Pockets, a.k.a Fats, was the leader of The Family. He was ruthless and all muscle.

"Well think about it, Kha. You know Shane. If he said start looking now that pretty much says it all. What you need to do is invest that commission and get your head right because nobody gonna make it happen for you but you." She smiled and asked Khalid, "Are you staying for dinner?"

"What are yall having?" he asked.

"Lasagna...and I'm cooking."

"Hell yeah. That's the shit!" Khalid started helping Mia set the table.

CHAPTER 4
HOME SWEET HOME

Pryze was making good time. He reached the Chesapeake Bay Bridge ahead of schedule. The Cadillac drove more like a car as he gunned the V8 engine forward, exceeding the speed limit by 15 mph the whole time. Shane wanted to hear music, but Pryze wanted to watch a movie on the DVD player. As a compromise, they watched music videos.

"You ain't saying much, homie," Pryze noted. "Everything alright?"

"Couldn't be better." Shane was mixing E&J Cask & Cream in his coffee. "I was just thinking of how I'm gonna go about getting myself situated. I called Khalid about setting up the crib, now I'm plotting on the whip."

"How much you trying ta spend?" Pryze asked him.

"I figured $2,000 down and $2,000 for insurance, plates and all that other shit. I don't want no bullshit whip, but I gotta stretch this bit of paper I'm sitting on, so I'm gonna try to finance it." Shane was sipping his coffee concoction and rolling another dutch.

"Well peep it, if you can find a co-signer, I can put you on to the cat I fuck with. With $8,000 down, you can hit New York in a $50,000 whip, fucking with him. But Shane, don't miss a payment! He'll put you in something quick, but he'll repo ya shit even faster." Pryze handed Shane a business card.

D'Amico Auto Consultant? He examined the card closely. "And this dude don't care about me not having a job?" Shane was skeptical.

"Shane, I gave this dude 'Whitebread' $9,000 down on this Escalade. He likes to keep shit under ten thou anyway. You know how that goes with the cash transactions. And trust me, this cat is one of us. His lot has only top shelf shit! Do you know I was this close to copping the new drop top Volvo C-70? Believe me when I tell you Whitebread will have something you like."

"I think my brother will co-sign." Shane was already plotting on a way to make things happen. "I've put aside twenty grand for this house." Shane took a long pull from the blunt he had rolled and passed it to Pryze.

"And how do you plan on doing all this shit with no job, nigga?" Pryze was starting to think Shane was trying to do too much at once, but kept his feelings to himself. *Shit, the Man had 8 years to think about it, who am I to question his actions? I'd be speeding too!*

"I'm going to rent the basement and start an at-home business," he answered, never letting his eyes leave the video. He was feeling mellow from the weed and E&J coffee mix and felt Pryze picked a bad time for Q&A, but he answered him nonetheless.

"What kind of business? Because I'm looking to invest in something legit." Pryze passed the blunt back to him.

"I'll let you know how things turn out, but the initial investment's gonna be my risk alone. I'm only taking a chance because I want to be doing something I like for a living. But I wouldn't feel right risking the next man's money, you feel me?"

"Oh hell yea, I feel you. And I appreciate ya honesty too. Lemme tell you, the economy's fucked up, son. It ain't like when you was running with The Family. Speaking of which, ya man and them is off the fucking chain! Kidnapping, extortion, all types of shit. Who the fuck does kidnapping and extortion in 2004? That's some real 80's shit right there. Fats has got them niggas starving! Word on the street is that niggas await your homecoming like you the fucking Messiah or something." Pryze finished the rest of the weed since Shane turned it down.

"Well, I hate to disappoint niggas but The Family and me is a wrap! The only family I'm running with is Chauncey and Isaiah. Fats ain't got no business letting his soldiers starve, 'cause word that came through the pen was he's that nigga right now." Shane was looking through Pryze's CD changer.

"Pryze put on that *TP-2.com* joint by R. Kelly. I wanna hear that greatest sex song...Shit, I wanna hear the whole album!"

"Speaking of the greatest sex, you gotta hit the VA strip clubs before you go." Every stripper in VA knew Pryze or 'knew of' Pryze. The strip clubs were his second home. It surprised Shane that Keisha never got wind of his extracurricular activities.

"Yeah, I'm wit that!" Shane reclined back in the SUV and dozed off to R. Kelly.

Pryze started to think of the conversation they had when they first left Ossining. It was then that he realized it was Shane's way of thinking that made him an asset to anyone who had dealings with him.

My nigga turned around a bad situation and made it work for him as best he could. Pryze knew Shane would be calculating his stash, so he let him know that the outfit he was wearing was on him, that way he had his whole forty grand. Shane had just got off the phone with Khalid and from what little Pryze was able to pick up, it sounded like half of Shane's bankroll was accounted for in business with Khalid.

"I appreciate it, Pryze. I never spent the money anyone sent me. And I only spent ten percent of the prison industry pay. So I got about sixty grand all together." Shane noticed

that Pryze seemed shocked at the amount he had amassed.
"Twenty grand? How'd you swing that?"

"When I came through Downstate C.F. I had a 20 year
sentence, so I told my counselor there wasn't much he could
do for me except transfer me to a prison where I could
work industry to learn a trade. Now you know me, Pryze, I
couldn't give a fuck about learning a trade. Yet, it was the
highest paying job in prison. If you double your production
they double your pay. So if I'm making $25 every two weeks
off of 42 cents and hour, and I got an 80% bonus, that gets
me a total of $45. That's $90 a month, which I looked at as
$1,080 a year. So I'd spend the $80 and live off the packages
you and my family sent. I saved *all* ya'll money orders. I
figured if I gotta come home in my late forties I'd better
stack every dime," Shane explained.

"That's deep, son. More dudes should think like that."
Pryze told him. "Niggas spending mad dough on Timbs and
sweats like they still in the hood while you was stacking ya
loot. You always been the thinker of the clique."

Shane went on. "The way I see it, trying to get money is
what got me locked down in the first place so I placed my
concentration on removing that aspect from the equation."

Pryze cut him off... "By the way, what's the big words
about? 'Aspect from the equation', you starting to sound
like that Muslim from *In Living Color,* the one in jail using
intellectual words in the wrong context." Pryze began to
mimic the character from the comedy skit waving his arms
around, teasing Shane.

"You see, my brother....the ramifications of my
incarceration resulted from the solemization of the white
man and my melanin-ful sistah." They both started
laughing.

Pryze snapped out of his brief flashback just in time to
notice he was coming upon his exit. As he swerved to the
right lane, he noticed that Shane was still sleeping.

Prison has definitely changed my dawg. His whole vibe

has matured. Seeing the change in Shane reminded him just how much he needed to get his own act together.

Mama West was thawing out the turkey and washing collard greens to prepare a homecoming meal for her son. The phone had been ringing off the hook since noon, but Mama West could talk and cook at the same time. As a matter of fact, she was quite used to it. she was in the process of giving her youngest son directions on the quickest route to Virginia from New York.

"Ron, make sure your writing this down," Ma West told him.

"I am, Ma. I should be there by tonight. Or should I say tomorrow since it'll be after midnight. And if things get too confusing, I'll be calling you back," Ron told her.

"You do that. I'll be waiting for you...talk to you later. Bye." Ma West hung up the phone.

Her husband John was cleaning the house, not that it needed much cleaning. John had just finished mowing the lawn. At 63, he had an abundance of energy and liked to keep busy. The Wests had moved to Virginia six years earlier. They were both retired and decided that New York was getting a little rowdy for their age. They decided to move somewhere quiet where they could enjoy their retired years together. They had gotten a smaller house since their children had moved out long ago and they didn't need the space. The house was a brick ranch with a sunken basement. It had three bedrooms and a kitchen with a breakfast nook. The stairs leading down to the basement revealed a second mini kitchen. A pool table for John and his friends sat in the middle of the entertainment area. It seemed most of their time was spent in the basement. After John finished cleaning, he took Shane's belongings out of the storage closet. He started the laundry since he knew Mama West had her hands full and finished just in time to watch the ball game.

When Shane woke up, him and Pryze were 20 minutes from his parents' home. He didn't call because they knew he was coming.

"Pryze, before we get to my parents' house, stop at a bakery for me." Shane wanted to bring something knowing Ma West would cook something special for the occasion.

"I gotcha." Pryze answered and drove toward the town. The town had an old fashioned feel to it. The main strip consisted of businesses lined up on both sides of the street. Even the barber shop kept a vintage look, including the classic red, blue, and white striped barber pole. Minutes later Shane came out the bakery with a Sweet Potato Pie and a Cheesecake. "What are you eating? I hope you didn't dip into the pie, foolio?" Pryze knew Shane probably had the munchies after smoking so much weed.

"Naw, its codfish cakes...want one?" Shane offered.

Pryze wrinkled his nose and shook his head.

"Suit yourself. These are the shits. They just greasy as hell." Shane commented.

Pryze grabbed the desserts from Shane and put them under the passenger seat. "And watch them greasy ass hands on my interior, nigga!" Pryze passed Shane some napkins so he could wipe his hands before getting inside the truck.

"Listen, don't forget to get everything ready wit yo man Whitebread, cuz I can't take ya skinny ass barking orders at me much longer. And I know as long as I'm riding shotgun in yo shit, I'm subject to the abuse," Shane told him, smiling.

"Done deal! When you trying to go?" Pryze answered.

"As soon as you pass my cash, fool."

"I can set it up tomorrow and bring ya dough with me in the morning."

"Cool," Shane answered, tearing into the codfish again, and with a mouthful of fish added, "I'm pressed for time."

"Consider it done, Daddy-O," Pryze said, as he pulled off toward Shane's parents' house.

He parked and before they got out, Shane gave him a pound reminding him again about Whitebread. He grabbed his coat and legal papers but was struggling with the desserts.

"Lemme get that for ya," Pryze said and headed down the Wests' driveway. Before they could ring the bell, Ma West opened the door. "I saw ya'll struggling and was about to come help.Ya'll got here quick." Ma West called downstairs, "John, look who just pulled up."

As John came up the stairs he saw Shane hugging his mother.

"You look like you've lost weight." She said, "Isn't it supposed to be the other way around?" Shane smiled.

"I stopped eating red meat." He told her.

"Hey Shane, let me see ya". John said, grabbing his son by the shoulders then hugging him. "You look healthy."

"You too Dad. That's a good look for you." Shane was referring to his father's graying temples.

Pryze stood there smiling and taking it all in.

"Come in before ya'll catch cold," Ma West said.

Pryze handed her the desserts.

"What's this?" she asked.

Pryze pointed to Shane. "He bought 'em. It's a Sweet Potato Pie and a Cheesecake."

"That's perfect! Saves me the trouble of making the pie. But I'm afraid I can't eat any more cheesecake. The doctor said I have to watch my cholesterol," Ma West said to no one in particular.

"Are you staying for dinner, Bernard?" Mr. West always called Pryze by his real name, teasing that his mother did not name him Pryze *and* spell it wrong.

"Nah, Mr. West, I appreciate the offer but I will be stopping by tomorrow ta see my boy here." Pryze looked at his watch, it was nearing six and he had to pick up his daughter Kiah from dance class.

"Well, I have to be going. Kiah's expecting me to pick her up on time for a change." Pryze said his goodbyes to Shane's parents and kissed Ma West on the cheek.

"I'm going to walk Pryze to his truck." Shane told them.

"What kind of truck is that Bernard?" Mr. West asked.

"A Cadillac," Pryze answered proudly.

"So they're making those big trucks now, huh? You've gotta take me for a spin one day." Mr. West liked cars, especially Cadillacs. He was known to keep a nice set of wheels himself.

"You got it, Mr. West."

Pryze and Shane walked down the driveway.

"Pryze, I'm only here today and Saturday cuz Monday morning I've gotta see my P.O., so I've gotta move fast."

"I *gotcha!* And your dough will touch down in the morning, my nigga. I'll have everything set up with Whitebread. I'll even stress to him that you're my peoples." Pryze gave Shane a pound, slipping him the weed that was left.

"That's for when Ron gets here and ya'll start building... Stay up, nigga!"

As Shane walked away, Pryze told him, "Oh, by the way, I hope your chess game has stepped up, because mine has."

Pryze pulled off, checking the clock on the dash; five-fifty. *Looks like I'm gonna have to hear Kiah's mouth after all.*

Ron got to his parents' house around ten o'clock that night. His father was about to go to sleep when he noticed a car going up and down the street.

"Hon, do you see that car outside? That's the third time it's drove past." John was interrupted by the phone ringing as Ma West went to answer it.

"Hello?" she answered. "Is that you out there? Well you're very close, back up one more house," she instructed her son and hung up.

"John, that's Ron outside." Ma West tied her robe and followed her husband to the door. Ron was walking up the driveway with his bag thrown over his shoulder. At times it was hard to remember he was ten years younger than his brother. When Ron got to the door he hugged both his parents. He looked tired.

"You're early," Ma West told him.

"I didn't think I'd wake up until tomorrow if I went to sleep so I decided to push myself and make the trip right after work." Ron dropped on the couch feeling exhausted.

"Well, this is a nice surprise. Your brother is here already," John told him.

"Word. He's early too, huh?"

"Well he told us he has to see his parole officer on Monday so he came straight here for the weekend. He's probably not even supposed to leave the state, but I guess as long as he makes it back by Monday, everything will be OK."

Ron pretty much knew what his father was getting at but chose not to feed into his statement.

"So where is he?" he asked, smiling at his father.

"He's out back," John answered. "Ron, you know where the bedroom is. I've got to get me some sleep. I'll talk to you in the morning." John went to get himself some shut-eye.

Ma West sat down and motioned for her youngest son to sit with her.

"It's good to see you... So how's everything?"

Ron knew when his mother started a conversation that way, it meant she had something on her mind. So he did what he usually did, which was let her steer the conversation at her own pace.

"Everything's good," he answered.

"What's that?" Ma West asked, pointing to the small box Ron was holding.

"Something for Shane."

"I sure hope that boy has learned his lesson this time."

She sighed.

"Yeah, Mom, I know. You try and get you some sleep and we'll talk in the morning." He kissed his mother and headed out toward the backyard.

"Ron, he hasn't said too much since he's been here. Maybe you can talk to him."

"Has he said anything?" Ron asked, trying to clarify his mother's statement.

"Yeah, he talks. Just not that much. He seems a little distant."

"I've got just the thing for him Mom. Now you get some sleep and let me go holla at him." When Ron went outside he saw Shane sitting by the back porch sipping on a drink.

CHAPTER 5
AM I MY BROTHER'S KEEPER?

"So what's up, bro?" Ron asked smiling at Shane, then added, "You look smaller."

Shane jumped up and hugged his brother. "Nigga, what the fuck? You putting steroids in ya Captain Crunch or something?"

Shane was referring to Ron's size and muscles.

Ron joked with Shane, "Yeah, there'll be no more snatching the chicken off of my dinner plate."

Shane laughed at the fact Ron remembered all of their childhood antics. "Ah-ight, Schwarzenigga, sit down and put me on to the goings on. We've got mad ground to cover and a lotta catching up to do. I snatched up a bottle of Dad's liquor too! I didn't expect you so early though... Talk to me, nigga!"

Ron pulled out a black velvet box. "First things first - remember our last visit and what we talked about?"

"Yeah, why what's up?"

"Nothing, I'm just reminding you to stick to ya plans," Ron told him, handing over the box.

When Shane opened the box, he let out a long whistle. "Now this shit here is special, Ron. Fa Real!"

"Yeah, bro, in more ways than one. It represents your past and future."

Inside the box was an 18K rose gold set of dog tags with baguette diamonds encircling each tag and inscribed on each one was. "People v. West-752 N.Y.S 2d 070." The inscription was the case site to the New York Supplement's second division. The first number represented the volume's book number. The second number represented what page you could find his particular case on. Shane put them on immediately.

Ron told his brother, "The inscription on the dog tags is so you'll never forget. These crackers will lose you if you ever get caught slipping again! And the dog tags represent what you said you wanted to do. But imma leave that one in the air."

"I see these tags came with a speech too."

Ron twisted up his face.

"Fix ya face son, I'm fucking witcha!" Shane replied.

The brothers drank the night away, smoking blunt after blunt and catching up on old times and new events. Shane decided to crack on Ron about co-signing a vehicle. Ron knew Shane had the money but not the credit or job history to secure a loan, so he agreed. Ron hipped him to who was doing what in the hood. He also touched on his two nephews, and Shane got emotional.

"Chauncey and Isaiah are the only ones I feel I owe. Out of this whole ordeal, I've made my sons the biggest victims. Chyna hates me and I've gotta hope that shit ain't rubbed off on Chauncey. Mia's a sweetheart, Ron. She'd bring Isaiah up every other month my last year, so I don't think I'll have a problem bonding with him."

"So are you gonna start fucking with Mia again?"

"Ron, like I said she's a sweetheart, but she's too naïve when it comes to men, and besides..."

"Spit it out, bro." Ron smirked.

"She's moved on."

Ron nodded his understanding. "Long as you know, bro. Long as you know." Ron started pouring another two fingers of Hennessey. Shane started rolling another blunt.

"Yo Ron, Chyna may act like a real bitch when it comes

to me, but dawg I swear not once during my bid did I ever worry about Chauncey being OK, cuz she has her priorities straight. But Mia? She's not as independent, she's the *I need a man* type. Thank God she lives with Boobie now. She's been unstable for a minute now."

"Yeah but fuck that, bro, 'cause the broads are gonna be broads. But I need to hip you to some serious shit." Ron took on a serious tone. "Fats and them niggas is talking!"

"Yeah, no doubt, put me on, nigga." Shane kept admiring the dog tags.

"First of all, The Family ain't been the same since you left. Those niggas like fifty deep now, but Fats is the only one truly eating. He's running shit like they the mob or something. Niggas gotta kick back ten percent off anything they catch to Fats on *independent* work and fifteen off anything *bought* to the table. Niggas ain't happy! But even worse, he telling these cats things will be better financially once you come home. How he knows you're getting out is beyond me."

Ron gulped down some of his drink. Shane could see he was getting hype.

"That ain't hard to find out between the internet and his connections." Shane passed Ron the weed, waiting for him to continue. "Anyway like I said, shit ain't the same! They even tried to kidnap Fat Shawn and failed. They also got a serious beef with the Bloods. Some shit that started over that clown Caddy. Fats figured you'd want him hit up. The Family's got money and artillery, so basically they've been untouchable."

"Nobody's untouchable, Ron. So how does this shit affect me?" Shane asked

"Niggas want you back, that's how. The talk is they miss the *big* jobs. The payroll heist, the inside jobs, and Fats ego is so outta control he might not take no for an answer... Then what?"

Ron offered the blunt to Shane, but he passed.

"I ain't doing shit! First of all, in these days and times any nigga caking like you say Fats is has either one foot in the grave or the penitentiary. Feds probably watching them. Besides I paid my dues—"

"That's what kills me, even a solidified gang like the Bloods would let a nigga drop his flag. Especially after doing the kind of bid you did. Even Fats doesn't know how many times the DA came at you talking deals. You stood firm, bro!"

"I wouldn't assume that Fats didn't know, Ron. But what kills me is what you said about dropping my flag. Ain't no flag to drop! The *original* Family crew was Jerry, Rashaun, Jef, and all them cats from Linden and Hollis. But us, we started as a bunch of lil-ass niggas robbing, partying, and crashing at Pryze crib. Niggas don't know that when Fats refers to Family...*he means Family!*"

Shane subconsciously rubbed his black rose tattoo, the mark of every true member of The Family.

"Yo Ron, get some sleep. I got a car to buy tomorrow."

Both brothers cleaned up the mess they made and called it a night, figuring tomorrow was going to be a busy day. Ron went straight to bed from being worn out since making his trip right after work. Shane was too amped to sleep, so he spent the night going through old belongings his father had dug out of storage and placed in the guest room. His clothes appeared to be cleaned and pressed. Shane smiled to himself. *I've got some good parents,* he thought.

He placed everything on the bed and took inventory. Most of the clothing consisted of jackets and coats. There was also about thirty hats, two dozen pairs of shoes and boots, and an 18K rose gold presidential Rolex with a baguette diamond bezel and matching pinky ring. He took another look at the dog tags his brother purchased, thinking Ron really did his homework in choosing this particular gift. He layed out his clothes for the morning which consisted of a tan suede nubuck jacket, tan nubuck Timbs and light blue Sean John jeans he'd purchased out of a catalog once he got his release date. He threw the tan scully to the side, along with an outfit and dug out a tan mock-necked sweater. He had a thing for basic black clothing and earth tones ever since Chyna told him it brought out his honey-colored complexion.

That was the good old days, thought Shane. Chyna was his soft spot, but just as quick as the stress entered his head, he shook it off. *Tomorrow's the day you've dreamed about.* The thought brought a smile to his lips. He turned on the television and whether by coincidence or fate, R. Kelly's "Ignition" remix was playing. Minutes later, the Hennessey started to take effect and he finally dozed off. He dreamed of luxury cars and chrome rims.

"Another successful Friday night at Simply Styled," Dana slurred, she was so drunk her movements were reduced to a two-step off of Jahiem's "Put That Woman First" and was singing all off key at the top of her lungs. Her regular.

"That nigga better put thisss wumen fist!" she yelled, stomping off beat as she tripped over her words.

"You taking her home?" Sherry asked Chyna. It was 2 AM.

"Do you know anyone else who gonna deal with that singing?" she smiled.

"I know that's right!" Sherry laughed, high fiving Chyna.

Dana kept on singing.

"So many times...acking like a bitch ain't veally nuffin... whoo!"

"Dana, please. You will walk home if you keep that up." Chyna sipped on a Malibu with cranberry juice.

"So when you plan on calling Chauncey's father?" Sherry started cleaning up the remains of the shop's weekly ritual. Chyna helped her just to get a break from Dana's antics.

"I don't know. I figured the end of the weekend. I'm not

sure I'm looking forward to making the call." Sherry stopped
what she was doing and took a long look at Chyna.

"Girl, sit with me for a minute." She held Chyna's hands
in hers. "Talk to me."

"I know where you're going with this, Sherry, and I don't
even know where to start,. I don't even like talking about
Shane. I don't even know if he's the same person I remember.
Shit, prison could've made him worse."

"Or better," Sherry told her.

"Well, I'll call him Sunday after he gets his partying out
of the way."

Dana sat down and both women fell silent. "No ya'll
didn't!"

"Yes we did," Sherry answered. "Dana, I'll be the first
to admit sometimes you give good advice, but most people
clam up for fear of having their business repeated."

"All right already, but I got something to say then I'm
ready to go home." Dana took another swig of liquor and
started up. "Chyna, do you agree most women have that
one man that just causes them to act like they stupid? That
nigga that cause you to go against ya better judgment in
the name of love and all that other shit." Dana waited for
the women to give some form of a response, a head nod or
something. She got none, but continued anyway. "OK, ya'll
be like that. But when it comes to Chyna, Shane is that
man! And from what I've noticed about you, it's probably
not that he's super fine or anything. I think it's 'cause you're
old fashioned and want what your parents had or didn't
have. The white picket fence, the dog, well maybe not the
dog," Dana laughed.

"And what's your point, Dana?" Sherry jumped to Chyna's
defense.

"Maybe she ain't want to be nobody's baby mama. Maybe
she wanted the whole package deal and felt betrayed. But
girl, if he wants to be in Chauncey's life, most women would
be happy a nigga's willing to do the right thing. But if prison

hasn't matured him and he's still a fuck-up, then at least it won't be on your conscience. Anything else is irrelevant, so make that call! Oooh that's my song – gotta go." Dana went back to her two-step.

"You know what's scary?" Sherry asked looking at Chyna.

"Yeah, sometimes she almost makes senses."

They both laughed.

"Actually, I'm scared Shane will expose Chauncey to some bullshit from his past or let him down in some way. But you know me, Sherry. I'm gonna do the right thing. Let me take Dana home while I'm still below the legal drinking limit."

Sherry smiled.

"Let me know how everything turns out, OK"?

The two women said their goodbyes.

Meanwhile on Third Avenue in Brooklyn, patrons at Foxy's Den watched a fleet of luxury cars pull up to the popular strip club.

"Whoa, some money just pulled up in this motherfucker," cried a slim youngster with a cigarette dangling from his mouth.

The six cars parked right in front of the club, ignoring the no parking sign. The bouncers knew to let these gentlemen have their way. The rules changed anytime *money* came to Foxy's, and these cats definitely smelled of money.

The first car was a triple black BMW 745, the second was a white CLK 430 Benz with white interior, next was a black Hummer H2, then a Lexus SC430 convertible in platinum gray, and the fifth was an S-600 in a champagne color. But the last car was what caught everyone's attention. The triple black Bentley GT coupe was definitely the head turner of the night. Fats got out the Bentley, his full length Chinchilla swinging. He wore black Timbs, black jeans, and a black waffle-knit Henley with a forty-inch Cuban link platinum chain supporting an iced out cross. All eyes were on him, and he intended to play his part as usual. Skatman, the driver of the white CLK, got out and walked up to Fats, whispering.

"How long is this gonna take? I've got shit ta take care of."

Fats looked at Skatman with attitude. He knew the kid didn't particularly like him, but Skatz served a purpose, so Fats let him get away with an occasional slick comment, but there was no love between the two.

"It'll take long as it takes, nigga... When you gotta go, just go! Fa now I figure all of us should show a gesture of good faith by showing up. Shane's a stickler for details, so I know he's gonna ask this broad everything under the sun once she gives him my message."

Skatz started to place a call on his cell.

"While you sap rapping go see if these mothafuckas can get us a table!" And to add insult to injury, Fats clapped his hands and added, "Pronto!"

Skatz was left steaming.

Gunnz, the driver of the 600 Benz, was Fats's right-hand man. Seeing the exchange between the two, Gunnz intervened, mainly because he saw that Skatz wasn't about to play errand boy for Fats and kept right on engaging in conversation on his cell phone. Gunnz liked the young kid, so he stepped in before Fats could overreact as usual.

"Fats, you see the nigga's on the phone. How you gonna try ta play my Scoobie, huh?" Gunnz turned to the young teen with the cigarette, asking him, "Youngblood, ask the man in charge if he's got a table for six open. If so, ya next drink on me, lil homie."

The teen ran inside the club, happy to be of service to the group of ballers.

A group of Foxy's dancers just coming to work took inventory of the small group of bandits. Black Cherry took an immediate liking to Skatman.

"Check out baby boy in the Sixers warm-up suit. He's looking real chocolatey, ain't he?" Cherry asked her homegirl Poison.

"Since when did the Sixers color become red? Lemme find out his shit is bootleg," Poison cracked.

"Bitch, that's they *vintage* shit, red with the white stripe. See the round Sixers logo? That's they uniform from the 70's or something. Now don't say no dumb shit like that in the club,' cause I'll act like I don't know ya ass if you embarrass yo'self tonight."

"Whatever, you can throw the pussy at lil man if you want, but I'm going for Mr. Chinchilla. He's *obviously* leading the caravan." Poison smoothed out her Coogi dress, trying to get Fats's attention to no avail.

"Girl, if you tryin ta get that nigga's attention you better off taking ya funky ass inside and squeezing in them work clothes," Peaches laughed.

"You know that's right!" squealed Cherry, laughing at the truth in Peaches statement.

"So Peaches, did you see the dread that stepped out that 600 Benz?" asked Cherry, picking Peaches' brain. Peaches was by far the prettiest and thickest of the three, so Cherry figured if she set her sights on one of the young hustlers, a bitch better be willing to settle on a consolation prize.

"Girl please, that dread is cute but he looks like he ain't trying to make no friends. Uh-uh, boyfriend look like he done sent a nigga or two to hell."

"True dat, let's go get this money, ya'll."

Just then, the young teen bolted through the door. "Yo dread!" the teen shouted to Gunnz. "I asked the owner about that table and some cat in a black Armani suit said he's got ya'll covered. Said something about Family always welcome."

Skatz flipped his cell phone shut and walked over to where Gunnz and Fats were standing. "That's Khalid, we just got off the phone."

"Well why you ain't say nothing?" Fats started bitching as usual. "Why am I the last to know everything around here? Did you know Khalid was gonna be here?"

"Khalid is always here, and you told him to show up tonight. He wanted to know if we were still coming, that's why he called." Skatz signaled to the rest of the team that they were going inside. The passenger side window of Gunnz' Benz came down. It was his cousin Fatal.

"I'll stay out here and baby-sit the whips. Ya'll know how I feel about clubs." Fatal rolled the window back up not waiting for a response.

Most of the Family members were relieved he opted to stay outside, because Fatal was the loose cannon of the group. When him and Gunnz were sent on various 'errands' by Fats, it was rumored Fatal wouldn't just kill a man but take pleasure in torturing him with a slow death. Instead of a handgun, Fatal kept a Heckler & Koch MP5 on him at all times, so they knew their whips were more than safe.

"Yo Gunnz, when we leave remind me to check my trunk ta make sure Fatal ain't stuff a body in it while we in here partying," Pretty Boy, the driver of the Lexus joked.

The Deejay at Foxy's was playing Dr. Dre's "The Next Episode." The crowd parted as Fats and the Family made their way through the packed club. Khalid was in the far corner next to the VIP room at a round table feeling up on two dancers. He pried one hand away long enough to wave his peeps over.

"This is Cocoa and this is Ebony. Girls, this here is—"

Skatman stepped forward cutting Khalid off.

"Evening, ladies. Can you excuse us for a minute?"

The strippers sucked their teeth, but made a hasty retreat.

Khalid straightened his clothes out. "That was some rude shit, Skatz. If you wanted a bitch—"

Again, Skatz cut him off. "Nigga, do I look thirsty? These

hoes handling johnson after johnson and you letting 'em stroke yo face like a real trick. You ain't got no wifey, so do your thing. But I ain't coming home to my bitch smelling like ass." Skatz didn't mean to come at his homie so hard, but what was bugging him was Fats' theatrics of the whole fiasco.

Fats didn't need six crewmembers to deliver a message to Shane's baby mom. The way Fats seen it, he had a better chance of getting Shane back in if Mia relayed the message that *every* member seemed to be eating lovely. The way Skatz saw it, either Shane was in or out. Shane didn't strike him as the type whose decision could be swayed because the Family was making a little money.

Truthfully, Khalid's car dealership connects were the reason everyone was driving. The Family seemed a lot more prosperous from the outside than things really were inside. Everyone sat down. Khalid spoke first.

"She's at the bar," he said, referring to Mia. "I didn't mention you wanted to speak to her."

"Good, Good. Gentlemen, I know this is a bit much, but the truth of the matter is, I want Shane back with us, and my gut instinct is he won't even holler at us if we don't come correct. I feel by all of the lieutenants showing up we'll give the impression I'm trying to make. We're gonna cater to his ego." Fats smiled.

Like we cater to yours, thought Skatz.

"Throw him a surprise party...A welcome home party! That way he can't turn down an invitation he's not aware of." Fats grabbed the hand of a brown-skinned dancer walking by. Handling her five dollars he said, "Miss Lady, you take that there just for lighting up the room with your presence and do me a favor? Tell the bartender we're ready to order." Then he added, "The pretty petite one."

"I'll tell her, but don't let the outfit fool you baby. She don't give no lap dances," the dancer told him.

Fats laughed at her remark. "Nah shorty, I just want

some drinks for me and my constituents." And with that, the foxy brown dancer slid off.

"Ya'll niggas kill me...Get around some hoes and all of a sudden we *constituents*," Pretty Boy, the driver of the Lexus joked. Even Fats had to laugh at that one.

Pretty Boy was the comedian of the group. He had wavy hair, green eyes, and a very light complexion. He was in charge of the Family's prostitution, whorehouses, escort services and even had a few $25–a-fuck hole in the walls he started for those working class men who wanted a quickie before returning home to the wife and surrendering their paychecks. Those spots were basements where the front rooms had hoes lined up wall to wall. A trick would pick a chick and go to the back where some selectively placed sheetrock made it possible to transform the back of the basement into eight cramped rooms. Your $25 got you fifteen minutes. If the business dealt with pussy, Pretty Boy a.k.a P.B. was the go-to man.

Also at the table sat Emanuel Smith a.k.a Manny, the driver of the BMW 745. Manny's job was to cop, bag, and distribute the Family's product to the various dealers affiliated with their peeps. Manny dealt with crack, coke, weed, dope, and ecstasy.

Skatman and Khalid's jobs were to give the Family more legal outlets to wash their dirty money. Skatz was that nigga in his hood of Laurelton Queens a.k.a L.A. His dream was to finish what Mikey D started and be the biggest artist to come out of Queens. Fats thought Skatz had potential and backed him with a fully furnished 24 track soundproofed studio. Between the mix tapes, studio time he charged other artists, and the *'smoke only my weed in my studio'* rule, Skatz made Fats his money back in less than six months. It wasn't until Skatz started spitting on Jadell & Rello tapes and formed Skatzman records, which was mostly just a label on paper, did Fats start acting funny.

Khalid, on the other hand, was simply a real estate agent

with connects. He wasn't from the streets. Shane knew him as being Mia's childhood friend and suggested Fats use his knowledge as a real estate agent to counsel him on the proper way to get away with those large purchases. In time, Khalid's duties grew from real estate to car purchases, insurance scams, as well as inside information on bank drops and payrolls. So Fats kept him around but never learned to appreciate his contribution to their floss game.

Gunnz, the driver of the S600, his cousin Fatal, and a kid named Skillz, the driver of the H2, were the backbone of the Family. They kept everyone in check. Their duties included robbing overzealous dealers who overstepped their boundaries, extortion, kidnapping, heists, hits, and anything that dealt with violence. These three were the only members who weren't obligated to kick back a percentage of their earning to Fats.

Mia came over ready to take their orders when she realized it was Fats and his crew. "Oh so now ya'll wanna come visit a bitch, huh? Ya'll must be the ballers these hoes were talking about with the spinning rims and shit." Mia sat down. "So what brings ya'll slumming?"

Fats spoke for the group as usual. "We thought it would be nice to throw Shane a surprise welcome home party. And we can't pull it off without you, lady."

"OK, just name the date, place, and time," Mia told him.

"That's just it." Fats smiled. "We want you to do it all. Rent the spot, bring some of these hoes too. They'll make plenty of dough. Just must sure it's a surprise."

Mia nodded her head. "Well look, before I start jaw jacking, what are ya'll drinking?"

The group placed their order and a few minutes later Mia came and handed the gentlemen their drinks. Each man placed a hundred on the table. Fats told Mia to keep the change. Mia had to make sure she heard him right. "Keep the change? Five hundred dollars for bringing ya'll drinks, what ya'll up to?" Mia put her hand on her hip, eyeing the table suspiciously.

"Nothing, use the money to throw the party," Pretty Boy joked.

"Please." Mia sucked her teeth smiling. "Ya'll crazy!"

Fats wanted to end the conversation and get to more pressing matters amongst his peers.

"So Mia set it up and I'll have someone drop off the dough." He told her.

"And we want receipts," Pretty Boy interrupted.

"Pretty, shut up." Mia picked up the money and started to leave.

Pretty shouted after her, "And don't forget to invite those hoes. I'm trying to expand the stable."

Mia waved him off, laughing.

"All right, Skatz, you're on your own time so I wont hold you up."

Skatz got up and gave everyone a pound. "If I hurry I can still make this studio session." And with that said, he broke out.

Khalid belted down his drink and grabbed the drink Skatz ordered. "Well now that that's done, I'm gonna go get my dick rubbed." He went to find Cocoa and Ebony to finish what they started earlier.

Pretty Boy got up too. "I know ya'll got shit ta discuss, so imma see if any of these hoes looking fo' a pimp." This time Pretty wasn't joking.

Once the other crewmembers broke out, Fats, Gunnz, Skillz, and Manny were left at the table. Fats voice took on a serious tone, as he leaned forward whispering. "Listen up, we got a problem with The Cab Stand."

CHAPTER 6
WHITEBREAD

A light tap on the door caused Shane to stir in his sleep. By the second tap his senses were together. As his eyes adjusted to the room, he realized he was still in the guest room of his parents' house. He smiled to himself. He almost expected the view to be the cold steel bars of his old cell. But he could feel the bed he slept in was a far cry from the metal prison cot he'd been forced to become accustomed to.

"I'm up," he said, wiping the cold from his eyes.

"Shane, pick up the phone, it's Bernard," his father said through the door.

Shane checked the clock, it was 8 AM.

"Damn, nigga, you know what time it is?" Shane bitched, barely able to get his thoughts together.

"Aww nigga, shut the fuck up," Pryze joked. "You trying ta take the bus home or check fa this deal on wheels? Ain't you get enough sleep in jail, son?" Shane smiled at Pryze's enthusiasm.

"You know, a nigga would think you're the one buying the whip wit all that energy you got."

"Ya'll got an hour ta get ready. Breakfast is on me." Pryze hung up before Shane could respond.

Shane went to inform Ron that they were on the clock. He showered and got dressed, then noticed his parents were in the kitchen talking.

"Up so early?" Ma West asked.

"Yeah," he answered. "I've got business to take care of."

His father added, "Just keep ya nose clean."

Just then the doorbell rang. Pryze stood at the door grinning from ear to ear. "It's that time, dawg. I told Whitebread have his ass there by ten."

Pryze was ready to leave when Shane's father called out. "Bernard! You wasn't thinking about leaving without saying hello, were you? I'm sure ya'll business can stand a minute or two." Mr. West gave Pryze a knowing look.

"Hey Mr. West, Mama West. Pardon my manners."

"Um-hmm, I'll let you fellas go and do what you have to do. We know not to wait up." Mr. West smiled.

As the three men left, Ron started up his 2004 white Navigator. Shane told Pryze, "I'm riding in that!"

Pryze laughed and handed Shane a roll of big faces.

"Forty thousand, partner."

Shane peeped that Pryze was driving the black Benz coupe he'd given Keisha.

"Ya'll ready to roll?" Ron asked, leaning out the window.

The trio's breakfast consisted of steak and eggs, cheese grits, silver dollar pancakes, and hot chocolate.

"Yo Ron, you still own that record shop?" Pryze asked still chewing.

"Yeah, but we don't sell CDs, strictly wax. Real DJs want that wax!"

"Good so you co-signing won't be no problem then," Pryze stated, then added. "Give Whitebread nine gees and another gee for insurance, etc. The whip will need a V.A. address. Is your parents' house cool? Can you use their address?"

Shane thought of Fats connects and how one phone call off his plates could give up his parents' address. "I'd rather leave them out of this."

"No problem," Pryze answered. "I've got an address for you. Just send ya payments straight to Whitebread and no one's the wiser. Shit is real lax down here."

Pryze paid for the meal and the group made their way to D'Amico's Auto Consultants.

The name should've been D'Amico's Exotic Car Showroom. He had everything: Benzes, Cadillacs, BMWs, Lexus, Hummers, the works. They pulled right up to the lot's trailer. Once Whitebread saw Pryze he knew his peeps weren't just window shopping. These gentlemen were there to buy. Immediately...according to Pryze. Before Prize could introduce Shane to Whitebread, him and Ron were already checking out the array of exotic imports. Shane had his eye on a black Jaguar S-type.

"You feeling that?" Ron asked.

"The interior looks cramped," Shane commented. "I want something small yet classy. The type of whip that makes a statement without really trying." He walked over to a white S500.

"You don't want that, bro...everybody and their momma pushing those in N.Y."

"A Benz is a Benz though. I did want something I could look good in a suit *or* my Timbs in." Shane winked.

To Whitebread, Shane looked like the average daydreamer, but Pryze was never known to waste his time, so he decided to indulge him even though he wasn't impressed with either of the two men. Whitebread saw none of the big flashy jewels that Pryze was known for wearing.

"My friend, a Benz is a Benz but the rumor is they're changing the shape of the S-class in a year or two," Whitebread commented.

Shane looked Whitebread in the eye telling him. "I have more of a problem with the color than the shape."

Shane rubbed his chin and Whitebread thought he noticed a bluish shimmer of light trying to escape his sleeve. In his most humble accent, the car dealer asked him for the time. "My timepiece seems to be off lately, my friend," said Whitebread as he stepped closer to get a good glimpse of his watch.

Shane was wise to the car dealer's shenanigans but

thought to himself, *'whatever floats his boat.* If that's what it took to be taken seriously, then Shane planned to flash the time for the old timer. He never was flashy unless the occasion called for it. Being a stick up kid himself, he vowed to never succumb to the same flashiness he used in picking his former victims. Keep it simple! He lived by those words. Instead of telling Whitebread the time, he let him see it for himself. Whitebread was so busy appraising the diamond-encrusted Rolex, Shane doubted he even peeped the time. Whatever the case, he took him to the back of the lot to show him the S-class Benzes in three other colors.

Pryze was busy laying his mack down on a big breasted salesgirl standing near the lot's trailer. Ron walked in the rear so Whitebread could spit his spiel at Shane. While Whitebread talked horsepower, Ron pointed to a blue BMW X-5. Shane shook his head no, then noticed a vehicle in the rear covered by a nylon tarp. The 180 spoke spinners caused Shane's curiosity to rise.

"What's that over there?"

As Shane pointed, Whitebread couldn't help but notice the pinky ring. Immediately thinking to himself - *'What the hell he can afford it.'* Whitebread called out, "Sergio, remove the tarp!"

As soon as the tarp was removed, Shane walked toward the vehicle slowly and told Whitebread, "That's the one! How long will the paperwork take?"

Underneath the tarp was a triple black 2004 Range Rover with black interior. Pryze immediately left Big Breast to see the vehicle.

"Aw hell nah!! Bread you been holding out on me? Motherfucker that shit is fire!" Pryze yelled.

"No...that shit is mine," Shane smirked.

"That's definitely you son," Ron elbowed his brother.

"You leave the deposit, yes? Give me $9,000 now, $1,500 a month, and we have a deal, yes?" Whitebread asked.

"Yes!"

The two brothers signed their paperwork. Shane paid Whitebread and threw in a little extra. He needed a few hours to make it happen so the trio hit the mall. Shane wanted to shop. Ron wanted to eat and Pryze wanted to smoke. The three of them chose to ride in Ron's navigator while Pryze rolled.

At the mall Shane bought a cell phone, Timberland boots, and a navy blue peacoat. Like a true don of the streets, Shane bought classics not fads, so a lot of his clothing before his bid were still fashionable as far as coats and suits went. So he shopped conservatively. He planned to stick to his word and not blow his dough. *This money ain't a lot if I'm stupid with it. But it's more than enough if I stick to the plan.* he thought.

Pryze on the other hand, seemed to have money to burn. Ron had to help carry his bags. Shane bought a few CDs then they went to the mall's food court to eat. Shane was programming numbers into his cell between bites of his grilled chicken salad. Pryze hollered at every female that passed and had scored more times than not. By the time they'd returned, Whitebread had Shane's truck out front. Sergio had waxed and polished the Range. He showed Shane how to work all of the truck's features, which included a DVD player and Playstation 2. Shane noticed the truck had temporary plates. Pryze promised to send the plates express mail as soon as they arrived.

"Well Pryze, ya man's the truth. He came through like you said. I'm outta here in the morning, gotta go see my P.O. Monday." Shane gave him a pound and they went their separate ways.

He and Ron made their way back to their parents' house. Their father was returning with the afternoon newspaper just in time to see his sons pull up to the curb. He waved at his boys and left the front door open for them. As they got out the SUVs, Ron walked over to Shane.

"Well you know Dad's gonna hit you with the speech,

right?" Ron laughed at him.

"I know, he's supposed to say something, right?" Shane shrugged his shoulders.

He knew the purchase of the luxury vehicle would raise questions. As soon as the brothers stepped inside the house, their father was sitting in the living room waiting for them.

"I'm glad you're here. Sit down and let me talk to you." His father motioned for Shane to sit. Ron tried to slide off to no avail. "Ron, you might wanna hear this too." Ron shot his brother a look that said, *Thanks to you now I gotta hear the speech too.*

"I'm gonna make this brief cause I know ya'll don't really wanna hear it. Ya know me and your mother is not getting any younger. All we ask before we pass on is to know you two are all right. And I don't mean financially; I mean morally."

"Dad, I have no more bids left in me. The crimes are a wrap for me. I'm gonna start up a business."

Shane knew his words would not ease his father's doubts. He also knew no amount of words would make a difference, his father had heard it all. In fact, Shane figured his pops only gave him the speech because he felt it was his duty as a parent. He never expected him to listen, because he had never listened to anything his father told him. Shane didn't know how much it had broken his father's heart.

"So whose vehicle is that outside?"

Just then, Mama West walked in and sat down sipping a freshly brewed cup of coffee.

"It's mine. I bought it today." Shane wanted to get the mini-interrogation over with, so he dove into the conversation headfirst. "Dad, Mom, I know what ya'll thinking. I also know there's nothing I can say to convince you I've changed. So I won't even try. All I can do is hopefully show you."

His parents looked at each other skeptically. Shane could see the worry on their face. His father looked out the window as if he expected the police to surround their house at any given time.

"So I've gotta ask Shane, how'd you buy that vehicle?"

Shane simply told his father the truth. "I bought it with the money they never recovered from the robbery. I did the time for it, so I feel the money's mine!" Shane could see on his mother's face his words disturbed her, but he went on. "And while I'm confessing past sins, I want ya'll to know the rest of the money, the twenty thousand, is money that I saved during my prison bid. I need every dime to start over."

His father raised his hand cutting Shane off. "You don't have to explain anything to us. Just make this time count, because this is your last chance as far as the man's concerned. You're a grown man now, so the days of talking to you till I'm blue in the face are gone. I've told you more than enough times, we didn't raise you this way. And quite frankly, we're getting way too old too worry like we used to." His father chuckled. "I mean...you're gonna do what you wanna do anyway, right?" Before Shane could respond, his father cut him off smoothly telling him, "Look, time will show us whether you've changed. I just want to enjoy tonight's dinner and hear what your plans are."

Shane was surprised that his father was able to handle the truth with such ease.

After hearing his parents' request to see the newly acquired truck and answering their questions on how much it cost him, Shane retired to his room to prepare for the trip back to New York. He packed his belongings, showered, and got ready for dinner. In the dining room, the Wests were enjoying a hearty meal of baked macaroni and cheese, candied yams, fried chicken, baked chicken, potato salad, and a three different desserts. They discussed various subjects and by midnight, everyone was full of good food and a touch of liquor. Shane went straight into a deep sleep as soon as he hit the bed.

CHAPTER 7
DADDY'S HOME

Shane was finally heading back to N.Y. enjoying the smooth ride of the Range Rover's suspension. *One down, two to go,* he thought, referring to his eight years of planning. *The car's out the way, next the house, then a business.*

He constantly thought about what type of business he wanted to own. He knew he wanted to enjoy doing whatever he chose to do. That way it wouldn't feel so much like work. As he kicked around several possibilities, his cell phone rang. He looked at the screen and didn't recognize the number.

"What's up?"

"That's how you answer the phone?"

Here we go

"What's up, Chyna?"

"Nothing. Your mother gave me your number, in case you're wondering."

"I know, I told her to."

"Well, I'll make this brief since I know you're a busy man." Shane sensed a bit of sarcasm in her statement, but decided to let it slide.

"I'm listening."

"That would be a first!"

"Chyna, I know you ain't wait 8 years to start an argument. So say what you called to say."

"If it weren't for Chauncey, I wouldn't have called at all!"

She started to raise her voice. *Tell me something I don't know,* he thought.

"Anyway, what's your intentions as far as Chauncey goes?"

'This chick ain't changed a bit!'

"To be a father to my child!" Shane started getting defensive when Chyna went in for the kill.

"Well, I won't stop you, but as a parent I've got to lay down some ground rules. First, I need to inspect your residence for guns, drugs or any other bullshit you may put Chauncey at risk of finding. Second, I don't want him around none of those hoes you know. Third, keep ya lowlife friends away from him. I don't want him coming home cussing and carrying on. And fourth, don't leave him with anybody! You are to spend time with him only, no one else. Now if you can meet my conditions I might be able to work with you!"

"Not a problem. Is Chauncey there? Can I speak to him?"

"No."

"No, he's not there, or no I can't speak to him?" Shane was getting frustrated. He never anticipated Chyna giving him problems about seeing his son.

"No, he's not here." Chyna's voice softened a bit.

"Well, until I meet your....*conditions.* Is it OK if I call?"

"Do what you want."

"When's the best time to...." Click! The phone went dead. Unbelievable, thought Shane. She's still got issues.

"What the hell is wrong with me?" Chyna stared at the phone in her hand, questioning herself. Shane seemed to bring out the worst in her and it bothered her. She contemplated calling him back and just as quick dismissed the thought from her mind. Chauncey walked inside the kitchen.

"Mom, can I watch Spiderman on the big screen?"

"Go ahead...and don't forget to put the movie back in the case when you're done."

She replayed the phone call in her mind and realized Shane hadn't said anything to deserve the attitude she'd given him.

I want him in Chauncey's life, yet every time he makes an attempt I go out my way to sabotage it.

She began to rub her temples as if she felt a headache coming on.

"Lord, give me the strength to not let my personal feelings get in the way of doing what's best for my child." She knew there were no guarantees she would not get an attitude with him in the future, but she promised herself she'd give him a chance to do right by their son. She spent the next half hour thinking about Shane. She wondered if he looked any different from what she remembered. She questioned herself regarding her decision to not visit him nor allow Chauncey to see him for eight years. She asked herself why she broke off her engagement to Tim not long after she'd discovered Shane was released from prison. An event she'd done less than six hours ago. An event she still hadn't summoned up enough courage to tell Sherry or Dana. She knew her girlfriends; Dana would immediately connect the breakup to Shane's release. What Chyna found troubling was the fact that she subconsciously questioned the coincidence herself.

That's ridiculous! Tim wants kids and I don't, besides we haven't been on the same page in awhile and I refuse to just 'settle' for a man, let alone a husband.

Chyna justified her decision in her head.

And Shane left me to run the damn streets and impregnated that chick Mia, so I'd be a fool to beat myself up over letting him do the 8 year's he got himself! She shook off her moment of self-doubt and called out to her son.

"Chauncey! Rewind the movie, I'm gonna pop some popcorn and watch it with you."

"Rewind it is!" Chauncey shouted.

Chyna laughed. "That's my little man!"

By the time she finished popping the corn, she convinced herself she'd tell Chauncey that his father was home and even decided they would pay him a visit. When she walked into the living room, he was wearing his Halloween outfit, a Spiderman suit equipped with the web shooter. "I see somebody's ready to do some crime fighting." She smiled at her son admiring his enthusiasm. Chauncey hit the remote and Chyna noticed he had skipped the previews so the movie started exactly at the beginning. She and Chauncey sat through half the movie making small talk before Chyna brought up Shane.

"Chauncey, did your father tell you he was being released when he wrote you?"

"No" Chauncey told her, just then his mother's question sunk in.

"Dad is coming home?" He asked.

"Your father *is* home!" She told him, searching for some sort of reaction. He smiled, pressing for more information.

"Did you speak to him yet?"

"Yes! He was leaving Nana's house."

"Did he ask about me?" Chyna felt a stab of guilt for lying to Shane earlier.

"Yes, he did. I'm thinking of taking you to see him real soon...would you like that?" She already knew the answer by the way her son eyes lit up at the news of his father's release.

"Yes!" he answered, quite animated.

After a few minutes of watching Spiderman fight crime, Chauncey broke the silence. "What was Dad like?"

Chyna told stories of when Chauncey was born and how Shane was scared to pick him up. They both laughed at that. She reminisced about little stuffed animals Shane would buy baby Chauncey that he never paid any attention to. He would throw the stuffed animals and Shane would say, "Chyna, I think we've got a quarterback on our hands!" She turned toward Chauncey and asked him in a sad tone, "Do you remember your Father at all Chauncey?"

He thought about the question for a moment.

"No Mom, I've tried, but I don't."

"Well, hopefully I can get you down to New York to see him soon....real soon. I'm going upstairs, you got everything covered?"

"Yep!" Chauncey rewound the movie for a second time.

Chyna went to retire to her bedroom. Her eyes watered as she thought of the last eight years Shane had cheated their child out of. She went to sleep after rummaging through old photo albums of the two of them in happier times.

CHAPTER 8
THE CAB STAND

The Cab Stand was a front for a door–to-door drug delivery service. In the last week their drivers had been robbed twice. Manny was instructed by Fats to keep the business flowing, while Gunnz, Skillz, and Fatal investigated the matter. The robberies had the makings of an inside job, so the trio agreed to lay low in hopes of flushing out "the fungus among us"—Skillz's favorite saying.

It was a brisk Sunday morning, and the streets were bare with the exception of a few early morning churchgoers. The trio of bandits laid in the cut, slumped back in the seats of a smoke gray Chrysler 300M. Sundays were good days for The Cab Stand. It was the beginning of their week, when the drivers would drop off their weekly take to Manny and re-up their product. Gunnz figured today would be an ideal opportunity for the stick-up kid to strike. Instead of Manny keeping a tight lip on business, the Family decided to set the bait and freely spread the word that they'd double-up this Sunday to make up for the robberies from last week.

You really think this fool gonna push his luck and expose his hand?" Skillz asked from the back seat.

"I don't know," Gunnz answered "But if the dude was smart he would've hit us on a Sunday from the jump. So I'm hoping he can't help but go for a missed opportunity."

As usual, Fatal sat silent in the passenger seat of the vehicle waiting patiently. Just then one of the stand's drivers pulled up. Manny came out of the stash house with a bookbag and looked up and down both sides of the street before getting in.

"The show's about to start fellas," said Fatal. He cocked back the slide on the Heckler & Koch MP5 tucked in his trench coat and patted the two sixty-shot clips that hung opposite the swing-arm holster.

The Chrysler pulled off at a safe distance, so as not to be detected. Losing the vehicle wasn't a concern since the trio knew their destination anyway. As they reached Farmers's Boulevard, they noticed a black sedan smoothly pull up behind the car Manny was in.

"You peep that, Gunnz?" Fatal pointed, putting his brethren on point.

"Yeah, I hope these fools don't try no shit until Manny gets to the house, though."

Skillz sat in the back seat fingering the .40 caliber glock in his waistband. As Manny's vehicle made a right turn, the trio set their plan in motion. They turned down the block and doubled back around, parking at the corner. From their angle the gunmen could see both the front and side entrance to the house. Everyone was in place; they just had to wait and see if the robber took the bait. Manny and his driver Cal were also packing heat. Earlier that week, they'd even taken the time to cover the floors and walls with plastic. This was done in preparation of their plan. The only thing they knew about the robber was that thus far, he worked alone. Gunnz saw the vehicle creeping toward the house and spoke into his cell phone's two-way radio.

"Heads up, ya'll. He's making his move."

"We ready," was the reply.

Inside the Chrysler, the trio sat impatient.

"For this dude to come to our spot alone he's gotta be getting inside info When I'm done with him we'll have the name of our 'fungus' and any other info I can dig up." Fatal was smiling, something he rarely did. He had his 'special

utensils' with him and intended to put them to use. The
lone gunman crept toward the back window of the house,
unaware that his every move was being reported to his
prey.

Meanwhile, Manny and Cal appeared to be unaware of
the presence lurking outside. They pretended to be busy
bagging up. The zip-lock bags on the table were filled with
baking soda; they'd bagged up the actual cocaine the night
before. Manny listened to Gunnz through an ear-piece.

"He's testing the doorknob. Be on point!"

The gunman was surprised to find the door unlocked.
*This must be my lucky day.After this I'm done. I can't keep
pressing my luck.* He smiled, took two deep breaths, then
charged through the door.

"Nobody move!" he shouted, raising his gun hand.
Confusion kicked in as he stared down the barrels of two
semi-automatic handguns.

"We've been expecting you," Manny taunted as he cocked
back the hammer on the Sig Sauer handgun. Face kept his
gun level, slowly backing out of the doorway when he felt
the nozzle of Fatal's MP5 touch the base of his skull.

"Your exits been x'd out, little man! Drop your weapon
and maybe you'll make it out of here alive," Gunnz lied.
They had no intention of letting him leave, let alone live.

As Face began to weigh his options, Manny bashed him
in the temple with the butt of his pistol. Face crumbled to
the floor moaning. As he made a feeble attempt to get up,
he noticed the plastic coverings and thought back on Manny
words. *We've been expecting you.*

He started to panic and began to struggle, which earned
him another smack upside the head with the pistol. This
time he blacked out. When he woke up he couldn't move. He
was tied to a chair with some sort of wire. The wire cut into
his flesh as he struggled. It took Face a minute to get his
faculties together. As his vision came into focus, he gazed at
the dread seated in front of him.

"Damn, ole boy. Thought you'd never come to," Gunnz commented with a sly grin. "Let me break it down for you, shorty. I'm gonna put you through a little Q&A. Now some questions we already know the answers to, some we don't. If you feel the need to man-up, I let my boy take over, you understand?"

Face nodded, looking at the man Gunnz pointed to. Fatal paid the young robber no mind as he went about the business of setting out his tools of trade. His tools consisted of a mini ball peen hammer, pruning shears, a hunting knife, a lighter, a spoon, and syringe needle. The teenager's eyes grew wide with fear as Gunnz continued.

"Just so we understand each other, youngblood, when I use the phrase 'man-up', I'm referring to you trying to get thugged out on us, thinking you can plead the fifth and stay quiet. Ya feel me?"

Face nodded, sweating profusely. *I'm not built for this torture shit.* He planned on telling these men exactly what they wanted to know. He tried to put up a brave front even though he was scared to death. He just wanted to get the interrogation over with.

"What ya'll wanna know?" he asked as his voice cracked.

This is gonna be too easy, thought Gunnz. He decided to turn up the pressure a bit. "I ask the questions, lil nigga, so shut the fuck up!"

Fatal sat back and observed the show, all the while pointing his submachine gun at Face.

Manny and Cal started packing up to leave. As they headed toward the door Manny spoke. "I left the baking soda so they'll think shorty got murdered trying ta pull a fast one." Manny winked at the hog-tied teen and left. Cal followed suit, laughing as he closed the door. Gunnz began throwing questions at the youth.

"How'd you know when and where to hit our drivers?"

"I, um...just watched ya'll," Face lied.

Gunnz raised an eyebrow, signaling he knew better. Fatal

put his gun on the table and began pointing out his tools. "That's your first and last lie nigga! See this hammer? That's for your toes!" He picked up the pruning shears. "I'll use these for each one of your fingers, and if you last that long, I'll heat these spoons until they're red hot and rest them on your fucking eye lids!" Fatal grabbed the hammer, walked over and took off one of Face's Timberland boots.

"Ask'm again!" Fatal snarled, gripping the hammer, ready to strike.

"Hold up! OK, OK! I know this crackhead broad named Lonnie, who was copping from ya'll. I did my homework from there and...." Fatal brought the hammer down on the youngster's toes. Face let out a piercing scream, toppling his chair in the process. "Aaaaagh!" and passed out. When he revived he told Gunnz everything.

The most important piece of information was the identity of the person setting up The Cab Stand. The news angered and saddened Gunnz at the same time. But there was no doubt in his mind the youth was telling the truth. Face left out no details. He wanted to keep the nine toes he had left. He told Gunnz how he met Ray-Ray, how easy the first robbery had been, and how Ray-Ray supplied the times and places of various drops.

Ray-Ray was The Cab Stand's dispatcher. She was a 22-year-old single mother attending LaGuardia Community College. The Cab Stand was just something she did to make ends meet. The pay was good and the hours were virtually non-existent since she worked from home. Gunnz now wished he never knew because he was the one who recommended Ray-Ray for the job. Knowing Fats, that'd be more of a reason for Gunnz to be personally responsible for dishing out her punishment. Gunnz thought about her two-year-old daughter and the father of her daughter, Jason who was doing ten years. Jason was the reason Gunnz fought with Fats to give Ray-Ray the job. Jason was doing the ten years for a robbery he and Gunnz committed. Had he implicated

Gunnz, he could've received a lighter sentence. Gunnz felt indebted to him. He looked at Face.

"Give me one good reason why I shouldn't let my man here kill you, shorty." Gunnz started packing up to leave.

Face started to sweat. "Homie, I was just a pawn. The bitch coulda got anybody ta do the robberies. Give a nigga a headstart outta town. Please!"

What bothered Gunnz most was how quick Face was willing to sell out Ray-Ray to save his own ass. His lack of courage sickened Gunnz.

"Act like a man and die wit yo head held high nigga!" Gunnz started to chuckle.

Face started to realize his chances of coming out of this alive were slim to none. As Gunnz headed toward the door, the thought of being alone with the madman and his 'tools' caused Face to blurt out, "I still have the money, I can tell you where it's at!"

Gunnz paused, walked toward Face, and sat back down. "How much?"

Face saw a chance to live and jumped on it. "I've got $38,000 in a shoebox at the crib! We didn't spend a dime, bro. We was gonna head outta town and cut our losses... start fresh! She said she was getting bad vibes lately."

Gunnz silently wished Ray-Ray had listened to her gut. He eyed the coward in front of him and said with disgust. "Oh, now it's 'we.' You was trying like hell to sell the girl out a minute ago. Next time your bitch say she's got a bad vibe, yo ass need ta listen. Yo greedy ass probably begged her for this last one...The two jinxes leading to the joint every convict'll tell ya. 'This was suppose to be my last one,' or 'my broad told me not to go.' Dumb ass!" Gunnz paused, stroking his goatee. "Thirty-eight grand, huh? Tell me more and ya might make it outta here, gangster."

Face explained that the money was at home, but that he lived with his sister and mother. He told Gunnz that they could take him to his house, retrieve the money, and leave him there and he'd be on the next bus headed out of New York. Gunnz rejected the plan, he had a better one. As he sat pondering the ins and outs of his plan, Fatal stared at Face with a sinister look, snapping the latex gloves he wore.

Finally Gunnz spoke. "OK, shortstop, I give you my word that *I* won't do shit to you if I get that dough. But this is how it's going down. I've got a driver outside. He's going to go to your crib. Once he's there I'm gonna let you speak to your people and you're gonna convince them to give my driver what he came for, and remember your life's on the line, so get creative!"

Face took a deep breath. He had chance, he just had to convince his family not to ask any questions, which wasn't going to be easy. His mother was strict and his sister was a square who didn't run the streets. But the odds at home looked better than him trying to bust out of his restraints and disarming the crazy looking dude with the submachine gun. *Word ta blood, if I get outta this one I'm through with the streets! Me and Ray-Ray can still start over.* He watched as Gunnz got on his cell phone and explained everything to Skillz.

"OK, what's your address?" Gunnz asked, repeating the address to Skillz.

The Chrysler pulled off toward the Conduit. Skillz was heading toward Rosedale, Queens. When he got to the mouth of Snake Road, he made a left. When he found the house he was looking for, he called Gunnz as instructed. Gunnz was busy relaying the information Face gave him to Fats, when his cell phone indicated he had another caller trying to get through.

"Yo Fats, that's Skillz trying ta get through. Lemme see what's up and I'll holla back at you in a few." Gunnz clicked over to Skillz.

"Talk ta me."

"I'm in front of the house. White with blue trimming like you said. What now?" Skillz asked.

"Hold on." Gunnz walked over to Face and smacked the shit out of him. "Now listen up, li'l nigga, it's showtime! You got one chance ta make this shit go smooth. Any fuck up and yo ass is a wrap, ya feel me? I'm gonna put you on the jack now. This is what I want you to say..."

As Gunnz briefed Face on what to say, Skillz took the semi-auto glock out and tucked it in his waistband as he started walking toward the front door. Face had already guaranteed Gunnz he would make it his business to insure his own safety by getting the bandits what they wanted.

"Yo Skillz, I'm putting shorty on the phone now, so ring the doorbell."

Skillz rang the bell and a teenage girl around the age of 16 answered the door. "Whas up?" the young girl asked, chewing on her gum as if it were the last piece on earth.

Skillz handed her the cell phone with a bored look on his face. "For you," he mumbled. He knew Gunnz would make sure their prisoner said nothing to alert the young girl of her sibling's predicament. As she listened, he noticed her little adolescent curves starting to fill in and smiled to himself.

She's gonna be proper in a few years. At least she won't have to worry about her brother cockblocking these hot-ass little niggas, Skillz thought, referring to the fate he knew awaited her brother.

"Yo Glen," referring to Face's government name. "Mommy told you 'bout bringing ya bullshit to our doorstep." She rolled her eyes and popped her gum into the mouthpiece of the cell phone.

"Listen Dee-Dee," Face pleaded. "I really don't have time to argue with you right now. Go to my closet and give the dude standing in front of you the Timberland shoebox with the Jay-Z sticker on it...please! I'll explain later."

Something about the urgency in her brother's voice and the silence of the man at her doorstep gave the young girl the impression her brother had gotten involved in something serious. "Ok Glen, I'll get it. Hold on." She turned to go upstairs and retrieve the box.

Skillz grabbed his cell phone and kept the line open until she returned with what they wanted. He opened the box, checked the contents, and spoke into his phone.

"Touchdown!" he told Gunnz. "Cool, Fats said it's ours so hurry ya ass back so we can split that!"

"I'm on my way, dawg." Skillz jumped in the Chrysler heading back to the Blvd.

Gunnz looked to Face telling him, "You did good homie, so Imma keep my word."

"You talk like you blood. You blood, homie?" Face asked, hoping he could find some sort of common bond between himself and his abductors.

"Hell no! I detest you dudes, ya'll got the hood hot for nothing! I just like the ring of that word....*homie!*"

"So we straight now?" Face stuttered, hoping he'd now be released.

"I don't know about 'we', but I'm straight! And I'm gonna keep my word too. Like I said, I ain't gonna do shit to ya shorty."

Face breathed a sigh of relief until Gunnz pointed to Fatal and said... "He is!"

CHAPTER 9
MAKING MOVES

Mia spent Monday morning calling various clubs, caterers, and DJs in preparation for Shane's party. She was finishing up the process of sealing the invitations when the phone rang.

"Hello?"

"Someone called me?"

"Yeah Fats, it's Mia. Shane's party is scheduled for Friday. That's the nearest date I could get considering the notice you gave me. Is Friday cool?"

"Yeah Babygirl, that's cool. The invite's a formality 'cause I've already spread the word. Where's that nigga Shane anyway? You speak to him?"

"I've spoken to him, but I haven't seen him. He's been laying low. Handling his business, I assume."

Fats' voice got deep in what he assumed was a sexy tone. "So Mia, what are you wearing?"

Here we go again, thought Mia.

"See, Fats, that the shit that pisses me off about you. When you say things like that you not only disrespect me, you disrespect ya man Shane!" Mia was getting fed up with Fats' flirting and inappropriate comments. She knew he meant every word because he never made a pass at her around members of his clique.

"Damn, girl, why you so sensitive? I'm just playing! You act like Shane's ya man or sum' thin'. Ain't you still fucking

with lame-ass Mark? He still working for my boy Harry-
O?"

"We aren't discussing Mark." Mia sighed, deciding to cut
the conversation short. "I'll see you at the party, Fats." She
hung up.

"You need to tell your little friends ta keep my fucking
name out they mouth!"

Mia jumped. She didn't realize Mark was in the room.
He had his arms folded and had an attitude. It was obvious
he'd overheard her conversation with Fats.

"Mark, you scared the shit out of me. I thought you were
still sleep, boo." Mia eased over to hug her man, hoping he
wasn't going to start an argument. Mark backed up, "What
the fuck is Fats asking 'bout me for?"

"Mark, don't start. And stop cursing. You're acting up
over nothing."

"Nothing huh? And what's this shit I'm hearing 'bout a
party for Shane?"

"Baby, the man asked me to throw Shane a welcome
home party. Why are you tripping? He's footing the bill so I
felt it's only right to update him on where his money's being
spent!"

Mark saw Mia was starting to get angry and decided to
switch tactics, putting her on the defensive.

"I don't like all this sneaky, secret squirrel shit, Mia. If it
aint't about nothing, why didn't you just tell me about it?"

Mia took a deep breath. Mark knew he had her.

"I was going to tell you about the party. I was just waiting
until I confirmed the date, place, and time so I could fill you
in on the details, boo."

Mark had been trying for months to get close enough to
Fats to convince him to front him some drugs on consignment.
Harry-O was good to him, yet he found himself more drawn
toward what The Family represented. Their unity, strength
in numbers, and reputation appealed to him. He looked at
the party as an opportunity to reach out to Fats.

"Are you going to this party?" Mark asked

"I have to go. Someone has to bring Shane without him knowing it's a surprise."

"Am I going?"

Mia paused, she'd asked herself the same question a dozen times. She wanted him to attend the party, she just wanted to explain to Shane that her and Mark were involved. She had lied to Mark months earlier stating she told Shane about them, leaving out the fact that Shane had cut her off before she'd gotten in depth about the relationship.

I'm going to have to talk to him before the party.

"I asked you a question!"

"Yes, Mark, I heard you. You can come. But you're gonna have to meet me there. Is that OK?"

"I can live with that." Mark grinned. "Wouldn't wanna spoil the surprise."

Mark sat on the couch in his blue velour RocaWear sweats and lit a Newport. "So, you gonna re-do these conrows or what?" he asked, taking a drag off the cigarette.

"I can't do your hair right now, I've got things to do. When I get back, I'll braid it."

She pecked Mark on the lips and headed out the door.

Shane was surprised to find Khalid outside waiting when he pulled up to his office at 10AM. Khalid didn't seem to notice him, so he beeped the horn. Khalid was drinking a cup of coffee, he looked like he'd had a rough night.

"Aw man, don't beep the horn! My head is throbbing right now."

"Look at you! Eight years since I last saw yo ass and you're still a mess," Shane laughed.

Khlaid got inside Shane's Range Rover and whistled. "Nice set of wheels, niggero. How much did it set you back?"

"I got Pryze to hook up a decent payment plan. What I

need is a driveway to park this bad boy in. That's where you come in."

"Well you know I'm on my job, dawg. I've got about a half dozen spots for you to peep, so lets get going. Lord knows I can use the commission."

Shane pulled off toward the first house on the list. During the ride, Khalid tried to hip him to every event he'd missed during his eight year bid. Who'd gotten pregnant by whom, who was getting money where. Who got knocked, shot and murdered.

Shane cut him off. "Yo Kha, hear me out real quick. Now you know you my nigga, and I'm not trying ta come at you sideways or nothing. But dawg, can you tell me about any cats from the hood doing some *postive* shit? 'Cause I've got plans...big plans! I need to network, bro."

Khlaid gave thought to what Shane was saying. "So what type of shit you trying ta get into? Stocks, bonds, small business, real estate investments?"

"Well, I was thinking of opening up a recording studio. Ya know, keep it simple, $25 and hour. Pre-production for unsigned artists. I'm shooting to this spot called 'I.A.R.' let them teach me the ins and outs of studio enginerring, post-production, digital audio recording, shit like that."

Khalid instantly thought of Skatz's prior complaints of how unhappy he'd been with Fats interference of Skatman Studios. Khalid figured Skatz's clientele fit in perfectly with Shane's vision. "I might have just the man you're looking for."

Shane nodded. "Good, Kha, good. Like the saying goes, birds of a feather.."

"Flock together," Khalid finished the sentence for him.

They pulled up to the first house on Khalid's list, a Spanish styled Tudor house with stucco siding. Shane didn't even want to look at it.

"Yo Kha, this is hardly what I asked for. Let's save ouselves some time. You got any pictures of the cribs in that briefcase?"

Khalid showed him six photos and he picked out three houses that looked promising. It wasn't until they arrived at the last house that Shane began to show some interest. The house was located in Elmont, right by the highway near Belmont racetrack. *A perfect hideout, but right near the hood,* thought Shane. Khalid didn't even bother to waste a sales pitch on his homie. He knew Shane; either he liked it or he didn't.

It was a three bedroom ranch style house surrounded by a short black iron fence with a two car garage and a spacious front and backyard. The stone facing and wood trimmings immediately caught Shane's attention. He pointed to the satellite dish. "Kha, that comes with the house?"

"Anything you see comes with the house." He smiled.

Both men went around back where Shane inspected a wooden deck with a Jacuzzi built in and a swimming pool sunk in the concrete. A stone barbecue pit lay off to the side lined with the same stone facing as the front of the house. Patio doors made of glass gave a full view from the living room to the backyard. Once the men went inside, Shane instantly fell in love with the place. It had parquet wood floors, a fireplace and the basement was adorned with a bar made of cherry wood with walls to match.

"Do the paperwork Kha, this is it." Shane was already planning his designs and decorating the place in his head. Khalid interrupted his daydream.

"Whoa, daddy-O. Before you jump out the window without a chute, I need to mention, this place is gonna run you $380K?"

"Man listen, write it up, as long as it's still ten percent!"

Khalid left Shane to poke around while he made a few calls to tried amd seal the deal for his homie. After a half hour of Shane going through every shelf, linen closet, cabinet and delight over the kitchen's breakfast nook, he was open!

"Yo Kha, you outdid ya' self this time."

Khalid held up a finger to silence him; he appeared to be having a heated conversation. "Yes cash. Five percent and closing cost?"

He looked at Shane as if waiting for an answer. He nodded. "Yes, closing cost not a problem...Uh huh."

Shane noticed Khalid looking uneasy.

"Phil he's self employed. Owns a record shop ran by his brother. Yes, it's called 'Wax Emporium'... That's good!"

Finally, Khalid smiled.

"No problem. Oh, and Phil, thank you." Khalid hung up."Whew! Had to cut through a lotta red tape for this deal."

"What happened?"

"Your history, son! You've got eight inactive years. That's hard to get around. Your brother's business saved you. Luckily, they ain't sweating ya tax forms. Seems the owner just wants out, and ya brother Ron has good standing with the bank dealing with Wax Emporium so you're in there. He kept you on paper as a silent partner".

"Yes!" Shane pumped his fist in the air.

He'd given Ron the money to start his business over a decade ago. Never in his lifetime did he think the one legal venture he played a small part in jumpstarting would outweigh his numerous illegal deeds when it came time to do something as major as homeownership. This move solidified in his mind that the decision to venture into entrepreneurship, as opposed to getting back into the game was a sound one.

CHAPTER 10
WELCOME HOME, SHANE

Shane spent the rest of the week by himself, shopping for little odds and ends to furnish his newly acquired home. Things were going so smooth for him lately, at times he expected a call from Khalid saying something had gone wrong with the closing on the house. That call never came. He purchased a black leather sofa from Jennifer Leathers, a pool table with red felt covering, and a collection of old blaxploitation movie posters, which consisted of *Foxy Brown*, *Coffy*, *Superfly*, *Dolemite*, and *Shaft*. He purchased a king sized sleigh bed made of cherry wood, and stainless steel pots and pans to accommodate his cooking fetish, a skill he'd perfected during his prison bid. Cooking relaxed him; he'd pretend he was preparing Chauncey's dinner and season each meal with love and patience. It earned him his nickname in prison, "The Chef." "It's all in the seasonings," he would humbly relay to any of the men willing to listen. Shane loaded the posters, pots, and pans in his truck and reserved a date for delivery with the larger items.

He sat in the driver's seat of his truck rolling a bag of 'kind bud', a copycat version of hydro. He dumped the weed into the already split Dutchmaster cigar and expertly sealed it in one deft motion. He lit the blunt and took a deep, long drag, instantly relaxing. He thought of the message he received yesterday from Mia.

"Shane, I need to see you tomorrow night! I'm taking you

to dinner, it's very important so holla at your girl and let me know what's up…Beep!"

Shane had retuned her message as soon as he retrieved it off his cell phone. He decided to call Mia to make sure they were still on for tonight. She picked up on the second ring.

"Hello?"

"Mia, it's me." He smiled, pulling lightly on the weed he was smoking.

"Don't even think about canceling tonight! I just got my hair done."

"Nah Babe, never that. On the contrary, I'm calling to confirm our 'date.'"

"Date?" Mia laughed. "It's a little late in the game for us to be dating, Isaiah being eight years old and all."

"Ha, Ha, you fulla jokes tonight, huh?"

"It isn't tonight yet, Boonk, or we'd be enjoying our date." Mia continued to tease him.

"Ok Mama Mia, I'll see you at nine."

Mia checked her watch. "That's less than three hours. Oh, and wear your best! We are doing it up first class tonight."

Shane blew the weed smoke out. "I'll be sure to pull the classics outta my closet," Shane joked.

"You smoking?" Mia asked. "Doesn't parole check your urine?"

Shane knew when it came to Mia, lying wasn't necessary. "Yeah, I'm smoking, Boonk. As for parole, I'm inactive, no reporting, I get locked up, I do what I owe."

"Well save me some, nigga!" They both laughed.

"You crazy! Nine o'clock, Boonk. Later." He hung up.

As he pulled out of Green Acres Mall parking lot, he reminisced about Mia. *Hearing her call me Boonk brought back sweet memories.* He could tell her everything; she was comfortable to be around.

Shane got to his temporary residence, his brother Ron's apartment, just in time to shower and lay out his clothes for the evening. He had no idea what Mia had planned for him, so he layed out his favorite outfit. He dabbed on a touch of Fahrenheit cologne, *Chyna's favorite,* and got dressed. He wore a cream wool cashmere V-Neck sweater, cream-colored six pleat Armani trousers, a black Kenneth Cole belt and black square toed shoes. After getting dressed, he poured himself some Hennessy. Minutes later he grabbed his coat and headed out the door.

He pulled up at Mia's around a quarter to nine. She came to the window signaling she'd be down in a minute. Shane put on a Maxwell CD and waited. When Mia came down, he was shocked. It had been a while since he saw her put it down like she had that night. She wore a strapless, open-back dress in basic black with a split long enough to show off her chocolate legs. Her breasts reminded him of two mouthfuls of Hershey's Kisses. Her hair was layered in curls and she allowed a pair of diamond stud earrings to decorate her lobes.

"Damn, lady, you clean up good!" Shane could've sworn he felt his manhood twitch at the sight of her.

She rubbed his bald head and smiled. "Is that your way of saying I look nice tonight?"

"No, this is." He leaned forward and kissed Mia on the lips.

He opened the door for her then jumped in the drivers' side. "Where to, Mama?"

"I have to stop at a ballroom on Queens Boulevard to give Boobie her license, it's right near the restaurant." She gave Shane the address and he pulled off toward the highway. During the ride, Mia decided to tell him about Mark. *There's no easy way to do this so I'm just gonna dive in headfirst,* she thought.

"Boonk, there's something I need to tell you."

"Uh-oh, I don't like how you're sounding right now. Is it OK if I light this blunt?"

"That might be a good idea."

"Damn, it's that serious, Mama?"

"I don't know. I'll let you be the judge of that. Anyway, remember the visit in Sing-Sing when I tried to tell you about Mark, and you told me if you don't ask I shouldn't tell? Well, I took your advice and I didn't tell."

Shane nodded and smiled.

"So I'm feeling real grimy right now because me and Mark have been an item since then and to not tell you would make me feel as if I'm leading you on."

Shane started cracking up.

"What's so damn funny?" she asked, unable to hide her irritation at his laughter.

"My bad, Boonk. I don't mean to laugh. It's just that I thought we had an unspoken understanding when I made that comment in Sing-Sing. Even though I never let you finish about your dude Mark, I understood you were no longer mine. Why did you think I just waited outside, or never came by unannounced? I know my position and I'm playing it."

"And that's funny?"

"Naw, what's funny is the importance you've put on yourself." Shane started doing his impression of Mia breaking the news of Mark on him.

"Poor Shane, it's going to crush him to know this fine piece of chocolate has moved on. I have to let him down eaasssy!" He howled, never breaking his laughter.

Mia started laughing too and snatched the blunt from him. "Oh, you got jokes, huh?" she teased, while taking small pulls of choke.

"Nah, I'm fucking with you, Boonk. But on the real, I haven't even attempted to get laid yet. I'm 'bout my business! The quicker I get right, the quicker I get to bond with my boys."

"I feel you!" Mia said, relieved everything went smoothly. She thought she would ruin his mood for the surprise party, but she also knew Mark was there. She had to tell him before they arrived. At the moment, they were exiting the

Queens Boulevard ramp. Mia pulled out her cell phone.

"Boobie? It's Mia, we're five minutes away...huh? OK, I'll tell him." She hung up.

"Boobie said when you get there Khalid has something to tell you about the house?" Mia looked puzzled.

"Aw man, I knew shit was going too good for a nigga!" Shane banged his steering wheel.

Mia looked out the window, using her hand to shield the smile that crept from her lips. When they pulled up to the ballroom, Shane frowned.

Mia patted him on the shoulder. "You'll be alright, Boonk."

They walked through the hallway and made a right toward the main ballroom. Mia motioned for Shane to open the doors. It was pitch black. Shane started to speak.

"What the fu..."

"Surprise!" The lights came on. The huge crowd screamed in chorus, "Welcome Home Shane!"

He turned toward Mia and smiled. "You're too much!" he said while he hugged her. He kissed her on the cheek then whispered in her ear. "Does Khalid really have something to tell me?"

"No silly, that was just to get you inside."

That put Shane's mind at ease as he began greeting the guests at his party. Mia hadn't missed any of Shane's acquaintances it seemed. Everyone he knew was there. *Except Chyna,* he thought, quickly allowing the notion to exit his mind. From the corner of his eye, he glimpsed Pryze and Khalid conversating with drinks in their hands.

Fats' main squeeze Shawnie walked up between the hugs and kisses from the crowd. "Welcome home, playboy!" She handed Shane a bottle of Cristal and took his coat. The DJs for the night were two locals, Rello and Jadel. Mia chose them for two reasons, the first being Shane and the two DJs were tight. The second being they had some of the hottest 'blends' out. Durell a.k.a Rello set things off with a shout out.

"We're requesting the man of the hour ta cut a rug to this dub," he shouted as he blended hip-hop legend KRS-One's "Bridge is Over" instrumental with a classic old school cut. The vocals of The Gap Band's Charlie Wilson bounced off the ballroom's walls.

"Even if the world starts falling, there's one thing for sure..."

The song blared through the speakers. Shane grabbed the nearest lady to him, which was Mia, and began 'stepping'. The blend continued. *'Baby listen to your heart...baby listen, listen!'* The crowd watched Shane and Mia dance for the entire first verse, and then one by one couples joined in. After the song, Pryze walked over with Khalid and they began to talk. Khalid handed Shane a set of keys.

"Are these what I think they are? " he asked Khalid.

"Yep!" Kha winked. "I told you, dawg, I make miracles with the paperwork."

Shane took the bottle of Cristal, spraying it in the air, singing the theme song from the TV sitcom *The Jefferson's*.

"We're moving on up! To the eastside! "

Jadel noticing the show he was putting on and mistook his energy as him releasing the party animal within.

Jadel shouted, "We see you, baby boy. Shake it up ta this cut!" and threw on "I Found *Love.*"

"Sun rises on your face, when I hear that sudden wind blow..."

Shane started doing the Family's dance, reminiscent to the six step,and sang along with the music.

"A picture that's so bright you're my delight and that's why I love you sooo....I've played around with love before, I was foolish, and you know that I played the fool!"

Once Shane started, half the party sang along, dancing, smoking, and drinking. Queens' finest was out in full force.

The crowd started parting as Pryze tugged on Shane's sweater. They'd been partying a little over an hour.

"What up?" Shane yelled over the deafening music. "Ya boy just walked in, looks like he's trying ta steal yo shine." Pryze pointed. Once the crowd dispersed, Shane noticed Fats, fashionably late as usual, making his grand entrance.

"Yo, this nigga walking up in the joint like he lives at the Grammy's!" Pryze gave Shane a nudge.

"Just like Fats, all dressed up and nowhere ta go." They both laughed.

Pryze mumbled, "Which do you think is bigger, his ego or that derby?"

"Chill, nigga, you gonna make me laugh in his face. You know dude is sensitive," Shane whispered out the corner of his mouth.

Fats was truly showing his ass for this particular occasion. He was decked out in a black suit with tan pinstripes, a white shirt with a gold silk tie loosely knotted, and a black derby with a gold silk band. To top it off, he wore a black full-length mink, which threatened to drag on the floor if not for the two females trailing behind him, holding up the tail. He had a black cane with a gold handle, which he tapped against his black Mauri gators. He looked like a cross between a gorilla pimp and a 60's gangster.

"What's up, niggerachi?" Shane greeted him while Pryze grinned at the meaning behind their private joke.

"Ain't shit, my man. Prison's done you some good." Fats referred to Shane's 190-pound frame.

"It is what it is, you spring for all this?"

"Hey! Nothing is too good for my road dawg. *Family Comes First!*"

Fats would run his motto in the ground if given the chance.

"The shows about to start let's cop a seat." Fats clapped his hands and his two female escorts immediately bent over, making it a point to do so in their tight skirts, and picked up the mink's tail.

The seating arrangements had been pre-arranged so that

all Family members had the long table positioned near the
back wall. Everyone else's tables were round and positioned
at the edge of the dance floor.

Shane sat down next to Pryze, immediately questioning
Fats. "Where's Mia?" he asked. "She had Mark meet her
here so I sat them near the front."

Fats' woman Shawnie interrupted. "I think it was real
tacky of her to bring Mark here. Did you know he was
coming, Shane?"

Fats hated when his lady jumped in a conversation
uninvited, but kept his cool because he knew LaShawn a.k.a
'Shawnie' had no problem creating a scene.

"If Mia told me she would have had to ruin the surprise,
but I was told about Mark a while ago."

"I still feel she could've kept him at home. I got mad
girlfriends inquiring about you though, I'll introduce you
later." Shawnie gave Shane a wink.

Shane jiggled the house keys Khalid had just given him.
His mind was elsewhere.

"You heard me?" Fats repeated, snapping Shane out if his
daydream.

"Nah, what you said?" Shane was ready to leave the party.
Two down, one to go, he thought. He reminded himself to
speak with Khalid before he exited the party.

"I said, don't take Mark coming here personal. Fatal said
the dude has a proposition for me. So he's probably trying to
make a business move, not babysit his broad."

Again, Shawnie jumped in, "Stop calling women broads, I
hate that shit!" Luckily for Fats, the comedian for the night
jumped on stage and began his act.

"Good evening people...good evening! Yo, this is some fly
shit here. When I came home all I got was a bus ticket!"

The crowd laughed.

"Who the fuck is Shane anyway?"

The Family started pointing at Shane.

"Nigga, who's you?" The comedian joked on. "I'm about to

jump on stage, so I'm telling one these honeys I'm bout ta go on and I've got the jitters, right? So I'm like, where's the refreshment bar? She points...and I'm off and running..." the comedian ran in place holding his hat. As the crowd starts laughing, he sneaks in another punch line. "I get over there," the comedian whispers "... and there's coke and weed in the punchbowls, ya'll!"

Family members start howling and barking and women start laughing, as the comedian pauses, sits up straight and says, "So I'm stuffing all the weed I can fit in my pockets right..."

Between the champagne and weed from earlier, Shane was near tears from laughter.

"Yo, that's a funny nigga!" Pryze told him, doubling over.

Keisha, Przye's lady, whispered, "I snatched a little something myself."

Shane laughed. "That's what it's there for, Keisha...do you!"

The comedian continued. "So dude's telling me I got ta move the Hyundai, it's double parked. And the damn punchbowl chronic, yeah that's what I call it, anyway that shit's *so good* I'm looking for the car keys to give ta dude 'cause I gotta get onstage and I'm like, I can't find my car keys, so dude says...give me the car keys in your hand until you find the ones you looking for, dumb ass!"

The crowd erupted and the comedian said, "See! That joke wasn't that funny at Manhattan Proper two nights ago." The comedian thanked the audience and exited the stage.

The crowd was still laughing as Mia stepped onstage to catcalls and whistles from the crowd of unruly hustlers and gunmen.

"All right, ya'll." She smiled as they settled down. Shane blew her a kiss. "Right back at you, Boonk," she replied, glancing at Mark who had the sense to maintain his composure.

"Well," she continued, "we've got menus placed in front

of you that consist of three choices, seafood, beef, or poultry. The seafood platter consists of one whole lobster, butter sauce, and jumbo shrimps. The beef's a Porterhouse Steak with side slices of pot roast for the big men." Mia flexed an arm muscle jokingly. "And the poultry's a Cornish hen with a side of Buffalo wings and blue cheese dip."

Someone in the crowd yelled out,"What sauce do we get for the steak?" Everyone laughed.

"A-1 sauce of course," she yelled back, as she exited the stage.

Fats banged his fork against his wine glass signaling a toast. All eyes were on him. The guest list consisted of sixty of Shane's old associates and another forty affiliates of The Family.

Fats raised his glass. "To Shane! A real nigga...'cause we're becoming an endangered species!"

Shane humbly accepted the toast, quickly downing his drink embarrassed by all the attention.

"Speech!" the crowd shouted.

Shane stood up. "Thank you for taking time out your schedule to celebrate my release. This is too much! And again, thank you."

Couples at their respective tables discussed various subjects as they waited on the meal of their choice. Hustlers networked amongst themselves, looking to expand their territories. The women complimented each other on their outfits.

Fats handed Shane an envelope. "Tuck that away for a rainy day."

Shane did as he was told. He had an idea of the envelope's contents.

"We need to talk."

He acknowledged Fats statement with a nod.

The meals came and after everyone ate, the party continued. After the meal, more than a few couples went straight to the *refreshment* bar to get their heads right.

Manny and Fatal sat behind the bar as Fats suggested, insuring no one dipped more than their share of goodies. The refreshment bar consisted of three punch bowls. One was filled with ecstasy, and the other two coke and weed. At the moment, the strippers were hitting the floor in full force, both male and female.

Mia grabbed the mic again. "Ladies and Gentleman, the dancers of Foxy's Den."

Mia looked at the men, and added, "And company... Introduce you to a night of Exotic Elegance." Then she threw in, "Couples are granted immunity tonight, so don't be shy!" A few men looked at their ladies, assuring they had the O.K. to partake in the fun. Most men didn't wait for permission. A couple of women dug in their dates' pocket and peeled off money to tip the dancers. Shane took in the scene with amusement, turning to Fats he commented.

"Ya'll gonna tear the place up!" He shook his head laughing.

"Family comes first!" Fats told him, leaving their table to party with the dancers.

Keisha looked at Pryze. "Don't even think about it!" Pryze handed Keisha a knot of bills.

"Go ahead baby! Have fun, I'm secure. Aren't you?"

Keisha sucked her teeth, smiling. "You just want a pass to act a fool, nigga." She strutted over to the dancer named Mandingo.

"Figures," Pryze mumbled.

Shane laughed. "You ain't grinding, nigga?"

"Nah, I'm gonna wait for you ta open that envelope Fats slipped you."

"Damn, you don't miss shit, huh?" Shane opened the envelope, inside was an invite. It read:

You've been invited to:
A Welcome Home Party
4: DuShane West
By: The Black Rose Family

Date: T.B.A
    8:45 – Until
Admission: $200.00 R.S.V.P
Note: Admission money goes to the 'Man of the Night'
It's how we do!!! (Fam Cum'z 1st!)

Inside the invite was a cashier's check for $25,000. Shane whistled.

"I'll give Fats this much. The Family is organized like a muthafucka! I think Imma go let one of them hoes grind on a nigga now."

Pryze teased him about the comment saying, "I don't see why not, you can afford it now!"

Shane laughed, seeking out the thickest, hottest dancer in the room. Hours later the party started winding down, Folks lined up to say their goodbyes and wish Shane luck. Shawnie's home girl Tarsha stepped to him.

"I been trying to holla at you all night so I figured I'd just slide you the number and see if you call, it being late and all." Tarsha handed Shane the digits folded on a napkin. As she stood hand on hip, in what she considered a sexy pose, Shane noticed Shawnie behind her mouthing the word "no." Or was she saying "ho?"

Shane didn't know, nor did he care. Tarsha was thick and cute, but too loud for his taste. He politely put the number in his pocket, promising he'd call. Shawnie hugged him goodbye, sneaking in a warning.

"She's a gold digger, chicken head and gossip queen, don't do it!"

"I gotcha. Nice to you again, Shawnie."

Shane was exhausted and ready to go home. He noticed Mia standing alone and followed her eyes to Mark and Fats engrossed in conversation. He made his way over to her.

"Hey, Mama!" He smiled. "Great party!"

"Thank Fats Boonk, he footed the bill. But you're welcome!" Mia kissed him on the cheek.

"Fats has an ulterior motive, you did it from the heart."

Before the two could continue, they noticed Fats and Mark walking toward them.

"I hope ole boy Mark ain't doing what I think he is."

"Ya know?" Mia answered, agreeing with Shane.

Mark came over grabbing her hand. "You ready, Babe?"

"I've been ready, Mark."

"This weekend I'm coming to pick up little man!"

Mia felt Mark twitch.

"He'll be ready." She replied.

Fats sighed. "You ready to talk?"

Shane nodded.

"Good, everyone's in the back room." He nodded toward the door at the rear of the ballroom.

When Shane entered, he noticed all the head Family members at a round table. He knew every member with the exception of Gunnz cousin Fatal who came to N.Y. from L.A. a year after Shane had gotten arrested. They knew each other by reputation, though. Shane introduced himself.

"Fatal, right? Heard a lot about you." They shook hands.

"Likewise," Fatal answered, studying Shane. *Strong character, definitely a leader. Humble too,* thought Fatal. He saw Shane as a thinker. *I'll soon find out,* he thought. There was no small talk. Everyone was tired, so Fats got straight to the point.

"Shane, I know you're wondering what this meeting's about. Well, we're planning a heist and need ya input."

Shane held up a hand. "Stop right there! Can't do it."

Before Fats could interject, Shane continued, "First of all, I wouldn't sell a nickel bag of weed right now. *I'm retired!* And if that's what this check is for, you need to take it back." He dug the invite out of his pocket but Fats refused to take it.

"That's you, babybro. I'm just asking for an opinion," Fats told him.

"Well my opinion can be easily manipulated into a

conspiracy charge. Not saying snitches are amongst us, just that I don't know what I'm jumping into. If, let's say Feds was investigating ya'll and this room was tapped. That's all a nigga need! You know what else? Why ya'll still doing dirt? Better yet, I know why, but at least have more legit ventures than illegit."

"You still Family, right?" Manny asked.

"Manny, I got kids my man. I gotta eat, but I'm not a fool, bro. I like nice shit too but I've gotta find a healthy way ta earn."

Skatz nodded his head, thinking of his music and the fact that Shane's philosophy matched his own to a tee. Fats didn't like what he was hearing, but knew better than to challenge Shane, especially in front of the Family. Fats chose to postpone the inevitable.

"Cool, fuck it! Come by the game room later, we'll talk."

Shane was cool and calm as always. Before he left, he turned to Fats and said. "Fats, here's some food for thought. Take it from a man fresh out of prison. I don't know one cat behind bars that doesn't rewind his life to that point in time where he says, I *could've* left the game alone right there. Ego is a motherfucker! Ego will have a nigga locked down for a 'body' with no lawyer fee 'cause he put a rep before a dollar, Fats. You raised 25 grand fa me in one night. That's big, nigga! Change it up! Buy a club, record label, promote parties, and distribute porn. Do it all! And each nigga at this table, make CEO in charge of each venture, but do something! I'll holla at ya'll." Shane closed the door, leaving his old clique to think.

Fats broke the silence for fear Shane words would begin to sink in to the rest of his clique. "Khalid, sometime soon, holla at him. Just ya'll two, you know what to say?"

Khalid nodded at Fats. Everyone exited the ballroom except Fatal and Gunnz. Gunnz knew Fatal like he knew himself.

"Spit it out, cuz!" Fatal uncrossed his arms and legs and

began to speak slow and deliberate.

"He's right, Gunnz! I can see Roscoe laying in the cut waiting for us ta do something major." He twisted his dreads, deep in thought.

"Yeah cuz, I know the man's right, might be time to start thinking 'bout *our* future."

CHAPTER 11
PEACHES & CREAM

Peaches waited for Shane to make an appearance outside the ballroom for nearly half an hour. She didn't mind the wait because she still hadn't figured out how to approach him. Normally, she could strut by a man in the gray, pleated mini she now wore and male testosterone would do the rest. But she had a feeling Shane wasn't like most men. She had given him his first and only lap dance of the night. She noticed a smoothness about him none of the other ballers possessed. His words stuck with her up until the present moment, as she thought back to their conversation. Lucky for the other girls, some fellas weren't willing to wait for her. Shane was willing to wait. She'd ignored the thirsty hustlers copping feels as she walked up on him sipping on a double shot of Hennessy.

"This party is in your honor, so if you're waiting on me, you need not wait any longer." She took Shane by the hand leading him to the stage.

"I figured if I've gotta spend my money, I want the best broad money can buy."

"Well your money is no good tonight, handsome!" Peaches straddled the bulge beginning in his pants and wrestled his zipper with her crotch.

She was jolted back to the present when she finally spotted Shane outside. She smoothed out her mini-skirt and made her move.

"Remember me?" She flashed a smile some models would envy. Straight, pearly white teeth.

Shane whistled. "Shorty, this may sound crazy, but you look better with a ya clothes on."

"Thank you...I think." Peaches gave a deep, sexy laugh, one belonging to a woman.

Shane did a quick appraisal of her wares. She didn't mind; she'd put on one of her best outfits. Shane always peeped a woman's shoes first and Peaches sported a $650 pair of Dior spectator-style stilettos. Her bag was a Marc Jacobs Beverly clutch, at least $750. He'd seen enough to know Peaches had touched a little paper in her lifetime. The black shearling coat that tapered to her waist was a nice touch. His thoughts kicked into overdrive, scanning the hallway for potential stick-up kids. Peaches picked up on his reluctance.

"Listen Shane, I ain't trying ta set you up, I'm trying ta get you up!" She laughed. "I like your style, you just came home, and niggas wouldn't put this party together fa no crab. So Imma get straight to the point – hotel!" Then she added. "My treat!"

She pulled a wad of tens and twenties from her clutch purse. Shane wasn't sure he'd heard her right and swore his luck couldn't be this good. He saw she wasn't joking because she stood, hand on hips, awaiting a response.

It can't be a setup, with all the hustlers that came through here tonight. I'm a li'l nigga compared ta them. Another thought entered his mind.

"Did Fats and them put you up ta this?"

"I don't even know ya man and them. And if I did, I'm not for sale! Believe me, niggas have tried. I step up for what I want, and I'm feeling how you move. You down or what?" Her aggressiveness turned Shane on.

"Say no more!" he said, as the two exited the building.

As the two of them jumped in the vehicle, Shane grabbed the remains of a blunt.

"Mind if I smoke?"

"It's your truck." Peaches held up an Optimo cigar and her own bag of chronic.

"Can I roll my shit? I make it a habit of never smoking anything pre-rolled."

Shane nodded as Peaches used her nail to split the cigar.

"So what city you from?"

"Norfolk, VA. But how'd you know I'm not from NY?" she asked.

"The Optimo cigar gave you away."

Peaches laughed. "You know that's right! I like that, you observant." Peaches liked to talk but didn't come off as silly. Shane saw her as relaxed, and not once had she peeked at any of the truck mirrors as if she was expecting company. He observed Peaches accessories while she smoked.

Shorty's about 28, yet her bag and shoes alone are fifteen hundred. Broad's got on a Cuban link choker thick as my thumb. That's about thirty-five hundred. Fuck a set-up, she should be worried about me. Shane smiled at the thought.

"What you smiling about?" Peaches smiled back.

"Nothing. So what's your story Ma?"

"I'm full of talent but no opportunities, and in search of a man I can fuck with plus make a buck with. If you not the one, cool! But we can still get our shit off tonight." She put the blunt to Shane's lips while he drove.

"You might as well take the 59th Street Bridge into Manhattan and take Seventh Avenue down to the Marriott."

He did as she suggested and soon after parked his vehicle at the entrance to the Marriott.

By the time they checked in, dawn was creeping toward the city's skyline. Once inside the room she poured Shane a drink. He sat on the hotel's plush sofa scrutinizing her every move. He had to admit Peaches played her part just right.

"You sip on this while I go freshen up."

Once he heard the shower come on he emptied his drink, grabbed an unopened bottle and poured himself a fresh glass of Vodka. He removed the .40 caliber glock from his waistband and slid it between the sofa cushions. He'd retrieved the gun earlier from a compartment inside the Range Rover, while Peaches checked them in at the front desk. The present situation reminded him too much of the atmosphere he'd given to many of his prey during his days of robbery. He rolled another blunt, checked the I.D. in Peaches' purse that confirmed she was indeed from Norfolk, Virginia. Being that Peaches told the truth, he felt safe enough to lay back, light up his trees and wait for the fun to begin.

Peaches came out of the shower wearing nothing but a white thong and clear stilettos. As she walked toward Shane, the crevice of her well-shaped ass devoured the thong she wore. Her skin glowed from the laboriously applied mango body lotion. She smiled as she peeped the lust in his eyes, yet admired his self-control. *His ability to stay cool under pressure is sexy.*

She stood in front of him with her legs spread apart in a cowboy stance. She hit the stereo remote, eyes never leaving his as R. Kelly's *"Step into My Room"* echoed softly in the background. Peaches peeled her thong to the side, pulling her pussy lips apart revealing her already moist womanhood. She played with her clit and passed an index finger between her vulva and attempted to stick her finger in Shane's mouth. He gently grabbed Peaches hand and slowly slid her finger down the middle of his chest. She watched as her love juices left a trail leading down to his torso.

"Can't blame a girl for trying," she whispered, admiring how smooth he rejected her attempt.

"I love eating pussy, but only if it's mine to eat," he responded, hoping she didn't take offense.

On the contrary, his actions turned her on more as she took his hands and placed them on her legs. Shane used his fingertips to massage her thigh muscles in firm, circular strokes. Peaches turned around, offering him full view of her magnificent *ass-ets*. He took the opportunity and got a firm grip on each buttock, kneading his thumbs into her ass cheeks. Peaches moaned, the massage felt good after so many hours in her six-inch heels. She turned around and straddled him, she was dying to unwrap the package threatening to burst free of his slacks but reveled in the foreplay. She buried her tits in his face, massaging his bald head. He suckled her breast like a newborn baby, his tongue circling her areolas in light, feathery movements while gently nibbling at her nipples. She gasped.

"Damn!"

He squeezed both tits together, flicking his tongue across her nipples as a boxer would a speed bag. She felt tremors running through her body, something she hadn't felt in years. Men came and went with Peaches, yet none took the time to bask in her womanly splendor. Shane took his time. His hands circled her tiny waist as his lips parted and he gave her a soft kiss on the neck. She reached up placing her palms on his face.

"I want you now!" she said.

Shane smiled, telling her, "Take what you want then."

Peaches fell to the floor already positioning a pillow between her knees and the floor. Shane felt light-headed as blood rushed to his manhood. She savagely jerked his belt, revealing his stiff, wide penis. She grabbed the base of his penis and squeezed. His massive tool twitched as if ready to fight back.

"You got a strong, fat dick!" Peaches told him, licking her lips. "You want me to suck it?"

"Hell yeah!"

Her lips felt warm and moist as she sucked...slowly at first, fluttering her tongue to excite the head of his penis. She traced her tongue down his shaft, stopping briefly to plant big fat kisses on top and gently biting the sides.

Peaches gave Shane the sloppiest, wettest blowjob she could muster, smearing his dick head on her lips as if it was a tube of Chapstick. She started smacking herself with his penis. His dick was so hard it glowed. Peaches realized she wasn't going to get him to cum orally.

Shane picked her up and led her to the bedroom. She pulled a Magnum condom from the front of her thong. "And to believe I wondered if you'd fit this," she said.

She took the condom out, popped it in her mouth, and swallowed Shane whole. When she removed her lips, the penis was fully wrapped and ready for action.

"Nice trick," he said. He grabbed a fistful of hair, spun her around, and immediately began laying pipe. He entered her slowly at first with long slow strokes.

"Oh shit!" Peaches shook her head. *"Yessss!"* she hissed. After a few long strokes, the natural lubrication from her pussy had Shane's dick slamming into her vaginal walls. The harder he hit, the more Peaches carried on. He used her love juices to lubricate his thumb and stuck it in her ass, grabbing an assful of cheek while never missing a stroke. She was in ecstasy. He used his free hand to smack her ass as she squirmed in delight. Shane laid on top of her grinding his massive meat into her as if he was trying to go through the mattress.

"Oh Shane! Damn! Don't stop baby, please don't stop!" Peaches loved it. She'd definitely gotten her money's worth.

They spent the wee morning hours shifting positions. At one time, she had to look back at him, shocked to find he was still fucking her. She could feel his penis twitching inside her signaling he'd spent his load, only for him to pick up the pace again. Peaches's buttocks were stinging and her pussy throbbing. After several hours, they fell asleep drenched in each other's sweat.

Twelve noon was checkout time. She reached across the covers and found Shane was not there. She walked out of the bedroom into the dining area and saw he had already ordered breakfast. She smiled, picked up a croissant, and bit into it. She noticed the floral arrangement centered at the table had a card attached to it, it read:

Had a great time last night!

Call me..............Shane

He had left his cell number. Peaches shook her head and smiled. "Unbelievable!"

Shane spent the weekend decorating his newly purchased house. Delivery trucks came and went, dropping off the large items he had bought earlier that week. Something was troubling him. *I've finally settled down. I've gotta step up and be active in my boys' life or I'm gonna be the same nigga I was before.* He picked up the phone, which had just been installed by the phone company.

"Hello, Mia?"

"Don't act like you don't know my voice," she joked, in her normal sassy way.

"You got that." Shane grinned. "On a serious note, I'm settled in. And I say that to say I'm calling to see if we can start arranging my time with Isaiah."

Mia was ecstatic. "Hell yeah. What you had in mind, Boonk?"

"I wanna pick him up from school starting Monday. How 'bout that?"

"And help him complete his homework, and take him to Karate class on Tuesdays."

Shane laughed. "All that? This house is lonely as hell without my boys, Boonk."

"How's Chauncey?"

"I don't know. Chyna claims he's never home. That's my next call though. I figured I'd make the easier call first."

"And that would be me, huh?"

"Yep!"

"I'll do you one better. I hate to hear you sound so stressed, so if you want, I'll let you come get Pooh Bear now and you can spend the day with him, get him up for school, and the whole nine. Lord knows I can use the rest."

"Mia, you fa real? Don't play with me."

"Chyna must really be giving you a hard time if you think I'm playing. I've dreamed of this day. For you, Isaiah, and me! When you're done doing whatever it is you're doing, come get your boy. I'll have him ready."

"I'll be there, and Mia, thanks. You're the greatest."

"I'm glad somebody thinks so." Mia thought for a moment, and then told Shane, "When me and Mark left the party, I got an earful of lip about me and you."

"How is the dude? He all right? I don't know what him and Fats were discussing and I don't care. But on a personal note, don't go backwards. Ya feel me?"

"More than you know, Boonk. More than you know."

After Shane hung up with Mia, he placed a call to Chyna.

"Hello?"

"Hi Chyna, it's me." Shane hated sounding so stiff and proper, but anything beat arguing with her.

"I know, how are you?"

"Well, I've gotten myself a place and you said once I'm ready to give you a call. I've even got Chauncey—"

Chyna cut him off.

"If you're free next weekend, I'll bring him Friday and if things look up to par I will let him stay the weekend, all right?"

"Cool!" Shane was stunned.

"I'll call you before we leave. You wanna speak to him?"

"Yeah!" Shane was finally going to get to speak to Chauncey. As he waited for his son to retrieve the phone he actually felt apprehension. His son's voice took it out of him.

"Hello?" *He sounds so much older.*

"Hey, Chauncey." He almost choked on his words.

"Hi, Dad." *He called me Dad; that's a good sign.*

He smiled as he absorbed his son's statement, then cleared his throat.

"Mommy's planning on bringing you to see me next weekend and I have so much planned for us I can't wait."

"OK," was all Shane heard. He decided not to push his luck. He wasn't sure how his son felt about him.

"Mommy got my number so you can call anytime. Oh, and try and know what you'd like to do when you get here 'cause it's gonna be all about you! Ya heard?"

Chauncey giggled, "All right, Dad. You wanna speak to Mom?"

"Yeah. See you later, little man."

"I'm not that little, Dad."

"Oh, my bad!" Shane grinned at Chauncey's attempt at putting him in check.

When Chyna got back on the line, he gave her his home phone number. They said their good-byes and he hung up feeling like a new man.

Shane and Isaiah spent Sunday afternoon at the mall picking up small items. Isaiah showed his Father what video games to pick out for the Playstation2 and X-Box that he had at home. He also bought Isaiah one of the newer games to take back with him. They stopped at Footlocker and he brought his son a pair of Timberland boots. He fell right into fatherhood, checking Isaiah's homework and establishing a nine o'clock curfew for bedtime. "'Cause you've got school tomorrow."

Isaiah still had 3 hours, so he and his father made strawberry Quik as they played video games until it was time for him to go to bed.

Shane laid out his school clothes for the following morning, allowing him a choice of which clothes he wanted to wear. This pleased Isaiah and he was real cooperative, even asking his father what he thought. Isaiah showered and then Shane knelt with him to say his prayers and tucked him in. By 9:30 he was fast asleep. He went into the living room and poured himself a glass of Baileys while watching a Mel Gibson movie, *Passion of the Christ*.

"Damn! I'm taking my ass to church next Sunday," he mumbled after the first twenty minutes.

He sat petting a rare 'blue' pit bull he had flown in from Atlanta's pitfall kennels. The dog was one of the five he purchased on-line. The pitbull was actually gray in color. He'd bought a male and female purebred, along with two black Staffordshire bull terrier pups who were now sleeping after an exhausting day of play with Isaiah. The pitbulls weren't quite pups, but were young. In his backyard was Bolo, a huge black mastiff whose sole job was to protect his master's home. The dogs were bred for temperment. Shane loved them. Halfway through the movie, the doorbell rang.

"Who the fuck!" He moved quietly as he clicked the remote to Channel 3 and a video camera showed a view of his front door. Khalid stood at the door with a paper bag in his hand. Shane answered the door, drink in hand.

"What's up, Daddy-O?"

"Kha, you know what time it is, nigga?"

"Go head wit that, son. We night owls!" Khalid walked in without waiting to be invited.

"The place looks good. Can I get a tour?" he asked, admiring the 80 inch big screen television.

"I'll show you a little 'cause Isaiah's in his room asleep."

"Cool! The dogs are a nice touch." Khalid pet the pit, while he playfully snapped at his hand.

"That's Bebo and MacBeth, the black ones are Lady and King."

Khalid threw the bag at Shane.

"We smoking?" He stuck his nose inside the bag and smelled the bud. "What's this?"

"Red haired Ces!" Khalid answered proudly. "I got that from Manny."

"We gotta smoke on the back deck," Shane told him, pointing his thumb toward Isaiah's room.

They went toward the back deck forgetting all about the tour of the house. Shane put his sweathood on and sat on a wooden lawn chair and began rolling.

"It's brick out here. Them must be some heavy ass sweats, you ain't cold?" Khalid asked, shivering.

"Nah, you get use to it up in them mountains. Use that blanket."

Khalid turned to grab the blanket Shane was referring to and almost jumped out of his skin.

"Oh shit!" he yelled, falling to the floor.

"I see you've met Bolo." Shane started grinning, licking the cigar closed.

"Fuck, Shane! You coulda warned me! That fucking bastard's huge! He bite?"

"Like a motherfucka!"

"You got him around Isaiah?"

"That's his little homie You safe long as you don't get on my nerves."

Khalid couldn't get comfortable because the mastiff kept leaning against him aggressively. Shane sensed his discomfort.

"C'mere Bo!" The dog came and laid by Shane while he lit the weed.

"So whas up, Kha?"

Khalid was still captivated by the Mastiff's size as he chewed on a steak bone.

"Son, that nigga's better than having a .45 round the house."

Shane laughed at his homie's uneasiness. "You got that right! And he's *legal* to own."

"Word! How's that Ces?" Shane passed the blunt and Khalid coughed on the first pull.

"Shane, you know why I'm here right?"

"I can guess, but won't you just tell me."

"Fats wants me to convince you to look at this jewelry store heist. He just wants to know if it can be done."

"Oh, that's easy, tell him yeah cuz any spot can get got. Showing him how ain't happening... At least not by me!"

Khalid sighed.

He decided to fall back from the subject of the heist and brought up Skatz's dilemma. He explained how serious Skatz was about his music and how Fats only helped finance the recording studio so he could launder the Family's dirty money.

"What's any of this got ta do with me?" Shane interrupted.

Khalid told Shane about his last conversation with Skatman. How he'd decided he was leaving the Family to pursue his career in music, and how being tied into the Family hindered him from capitalizing on the recording studio's full potential.

"To make a long story short, he feels they're taking his shit for a joke. It's a shame too, cause the boy's got decent clientele. I've mentioned your plans to him and he's willing to sit down and talk business witcha." Khalid paused, hoping his next statement would sink in. "Fats is gonna have a fit! That's why I wanted ta throw him a bone by telling him you'll give the heist a peek." Khalid poured himself a shot of Hennessy straight, the Mastiff's eyes never leaving him.

"Leave'em alone, Bolo. Go play!"

The dog instantly obeyed, disappearing into the darkness of the backyard. Khalid had a feeling the Mastiff still watched from a distance.

"Yo Kha, keep it real with a nigga. Why's this jux so important to you?"

Khalid paused, feeling a brief moment of guilt for pushing Shane to go against his principles. He let out a deep breath.

"I get a percentage of the jux ta invest however I please. Since Fats don't care what I do, I use the money to cop foreclosures. I also fence the shit, take a few bucks under the table. Shit, *everything* I get is under the table! Fats and them got about two dozen cars leased under a dummy corporation. I get the cars and pass 'em out ta Family members. If the lease is, say $600 a month for something like Skatz's CLK 430 Mercedes, I'll charge him $800 and pocket the $200. That's $4,800 a month and I doubt anyone cares. I'm the legit link ta everything."

"And when you fence the goods, what's the numbers on that?"

Khalid smiled. He sensed a bend in Shane's morals and intended to take full advantage of it. He learned that manipulation worked a lot better than brute force from Shane himself. So he made it his business to not only tell Shane what he could profit *off* the heist, but *of* the heist itself. He leaned toward Shane and whispered, a habit he'd grown accustomed to in the past few years.

"The spot is on 71st and Continental, some Jews that specialize in old timepieces. We're only grabbing the expensive shit. Rolexes, Patek Philippe, and so on. The fence is giving up 20% on the dollar. I told Fats 10% on the dollar. That leaves me about 30 large on the minimum take."

Shane could see the truth in his eyes. Khalid already had plans for his cut. He decided to sweeten the pot, he knew the clique wouldn't make the move without Shane's expert opinion.

"I'll break you off a third of my 'under the table' cut, and that's not counting Fats showing his appreciation."

Shane knew what Khalid was up to, yet he couldn't fault him. Hell, he'd made him the way he was. *Might as well see how tight his game's gotten since I've been gone,* Shane thought.

"Why should I bother, Kha? You and I both know I can just pull Skatz to the side and make him a proposition."

"But my way you get a clean break from Fats *and* money in your pocket. Shit, that studio won't cost a dime from whatever you're holding now!"

Shane thought about it.

"I aint making no promises. What's the name of the spot?"

"Soffey & Sons, Ltd."

"I'll do my homework on it. You get back to me in the middle of the week."

CHAPTER 12
SECOND CHANCES

A champagne colored S600 Mercedes Benz valued at over a hundred grand was a rare sight to see in the hood, and was definitely a head turner in Baisley projects where Gunnz had just pulled up. The car stopped way before the rims. Gunnz decided he'd waited long enough. It was time to sit down with Ray-Ray and talk. Fats didn't believe in second chances, so when asked what to do about Ray-Ray, he simply replied, "Put that work in!"

Gunnz had other plans. He'd be damned if he was gonna leave Jason's daughter without a mother. He was going to give Ray-Ray a way out. When he spoke to her earlier that day he could hear obvious tension in her voice. He rang her doorbell, patting his right pocket to insure its contents were still there. Ray-Ray answered the door, her eyes bloodshot and swollen.

"What's up Ray-Ray? What's wrong wit you?" Gunnz asked, already knowing.

"Nothing and everything. I just got a bad vibe. Don't pay me no mind."

Gunnz sat down. "I think I know what's wrong Ray-Ray, that's why I'm here."

Ray-Ray started crying harder. Gunnz just sat on the couch shaking his head.

"I know what made you do it, my question is what made you think you could pull it off? Once maybe, but ya'll got too greedy!"

Gunnz was upset that she'd put him in such a position. He was about to go against Fats' orders. Not that he feared Fats, but he liked his position within the Family's structure.

The only thing Gunnz felt was in his favor was when Fats told him and Fatal to put that work in,bodies never popped up, they *disappeared*. So Gunnz figured if Ray-Ray just disappeared, Fats would be none the wiser.

"I told him once was one too many. For some reason he thought he would've gotten more money. I told him Manny won't give the drivers but so much at one time, then they re-up."

Ray-Ray wrung the used tissue in her hand dreading the answer to her next question, but she had to know. "Gunnz, will I see Face again?"

Gunnz looked at her as if she'd lost her mind.

"Nooo! No Gunnz, you didn't have to—"

Gunnz cut her off, he was heated!

"Bitch, shut the fuck up! I don't give a shit about that li'l nigga! You should be shedding tears fa Jay. He's the only reason I ain't here to reunite you with that stupid motherfucka. I owe Jay that much!! And for the record, Fats don't give a fuck! So be happy I woke up wit a conscience today, and shut up and listen!"

Ray-Ray had never seen him that angry, so she shut up and listened. He reached into his right pocket. Ray-Ray jumped, her heart skipping a beat. He sucked his teeth in disgust at the fact she still thought he'd harm her. He threw ten thousand dollars at her.

"What's this?" She asked him.

"It's 'get outta town and start over, before you get ya self killed' money," Gunnz spat.

"And I ain't playing, Ray! Imma tell this fool I took care of you, so you can't ever pop up. It could mean *both* our asses! Find a small town, some shit not even worth putting on the map, and get gone. Don't even pack!" Gunnz snarled, heading toward the door.

Ray-Ray dropped her head, too ashamed to look him in the face. "Gunnz?" she paused. "Thank you."

"Don't thank me! Your lover died for that dough and that's

just my cut! When you get where you're going, write a letter up top thanking Jason!"

Gunnz slammed the door, never looking back.

Skatz couldn't get Shane's words out of his head. He was feeling his speech in the pit of his stomach. He'd often attempted to convey to Fats and other Family members the message that their clique could be doing so much more. Khalid was the only member who'd listen. The others either were content with being ghetto-fabulous or feared the penalty for making any derogatory statement against the Family.

Niggas is so dependent on mawfuckas, they scared ta have an opinion, Skatz thought as he guided the white Mercedes through mid-day traffic.

Today was the day he decided to break off from The Family. Skatz was one of the most together members of his clique. He had a wife of four years, a three-year-old daughter and a legit 24-track recording studio. He kept his marriage a secret from everyone but Khalid, whom he'd sworn to secrecy. Khalid fully understood Skatman's reason behind it. He pulled up to the Family's Clubhouse, a game room located on 224th in the back streets of Laurelton under the Long Island Railroad trestle. Skatz sat in his car contemplating his thoughts and the possible consequences behind what he was about to do. He absentmindedly fingered the handle of the snub-nosed .357 magnum tucked in his waist.

Just in case all hell breaks loose. He patted the chrome ratchet.

The Clubhouse consisted of four video games, each located in a far corner of the wall. The back room had two pool tables, and the pool table nearest to the rear of the club doubled as a craps table. The downstairs area had a round table where Fats held what he called... meetings.

A makeshift bar and Bose stereo system stood in a far off corner. It was still quite early in the day for those engaged in the habits of the life. Hustlers who slept all day and appeared at night were just waking. So the club was pretty much empty with the exception of Fats and Manny, who sat in a corner calculating The Cab Stand's daily profits. Pretty Boy sat at the bar nursing a drink with a chick Skatz figured was a new girl he was on his way to turning out. Skatz greeted his crimees and sat down.

"What's good, Skatman? Got some fire for the speakers?" Pretty asked, figuring Skatz had come from another nightly session at the studio. He was that rare artist who could write, produce, and mix-down a whole song by himself. He was an asset to The Family if Fats ever got the sense to go legit.

"Skatz, what up, son?" Manny mumbled, never looking up from the bundles of cash he was counting.

Fats just gave him a nod. As Skatz sat there, he suddenly had an epiphany. All of a sudden The Family's dealings and everything it stood for seemed very small to him. Not at all the team he'd envisioned them to be a year ago.

"If you were on the outside looking in you'd swear we were them niggas. But this shit ain't what it's made out ta be."

"What you say?" Fats asked, not sure he'd heard him.

Skatz repeated the statement word for word. Fats looked tight. Manny, seeing the look on Fats' face put away the cash he was counting to see where the conversation was headed. Pretty Boy tried to take the sting out of his statement. He was a pimp, and violence was a *final* option for him,

"I think we do pretty well considering the city's crackdown on crime," Pretty drawled.

"Shut up, Pretty.Let the man say his piece! Shit's been inching to the surface fa months, let's get it out in the open!" Fats barked, biceps twitching.

Skatz was unmoved.

"Im sicka this Penny ante shit. I'm 33, Fats. I ain't no kid!

We've got nothing tangible, nothing legit."

"We got the studio." Fats defended.

"*I've* got the studio!" Skatz banged his fist on the table. "And it could be a lot more lucrative if not for the jive-ass kickbacks you expect. That money could go for street team, marketing, promotion and advertising."

Fats calmed down, realizing Skatz wasn't backing down. He knew the man had a point, but he wasn't trying ta hear him.

"Half that studio is mine, you forget that?" Fats reminded him.

Skatman smiled. He knew that was coming.

"You can have yo half, but find another flunkie ta run it. I'm taking my shit and going solo. I'm telling you to ya face, so if there's gonna be a problem, pop off!"

Fats leaned back in his chair. He had to play it cool, *rock Skatz ta sleep*. He knew no member of his Family to be pushovers. He had to bide his time...

"I can't blame you fa growing up, nigga. You've got my blessing," Fats told him, trying to save face in front of Manny and Pretty Boy.

I'll deal with that li'l mawfucka later, Fats thought to himself as Skatz exited the clubhouse.

Skatz was no fool either, he knew he wasn't in the clear by a long shot, but he'd deal with the drama if it came. For now he was free.

CHAPTER 13
THINK BEFORE YOU ACT!

Shane spent Tuesday morning dropping Isaiah off at school for the second time. He'd convinced Mia to let Isaiah spend the week with him. It didn't take much convincing because Mia found herself getting a lot of unfinished business done in her son's absence. Neither of them mentioned Mark's new found acquaintance with Fats, yet Khalid mentioned seeing Manny with Mark on several occasions. Shane shrugged it off when Khalid told him.

He was now at Queens Center Mall picking out some school clothes for Isaiah. Mia didn't pack enough clothing for a week. He couldn't help but think of Chauncey while picking out Isaiah's clothes, so he purchased two of every item. He spoke to Chauncey every night at eight. He'd even put Isaiah on the phone with him. They spoke about video games, Chauncey boasting he could beat anyone at his new *Grand Theft Auto* game. Shane saw that as a good sign.

A lot happened in a short time. Khalid gave Shane the story on Skatz's departure from The Family not even a half hour after it happened. He told him that Skatz credited his wake-up call to Shane's speech to The Family the night of his party. Khalid promised to set up a meeting between the two, not telling Skatz the nature of the meeting. Shane noted that Khalid still pushed the issue of the heist regardless of the recent turn of events. They parted ways, agreeing to discuss it Wednesday.

On his way to the food court Shane stopped in a Barnes & Noble bookstore to pick up a book called *Cashflow Quadrant*, a follow-up to *Rich Dad, Poor Dad*, which he'd read in prison. The book dealt with financial intelligence and he was trying to get his shit together. As he waited in line, he noticed the woman in front of him purchasing the *Rich Dad, Poor Dad* book.

"That's a good book you're buying, sister."

"Excuse me?" the woman pivoted on her heel, facing him.

He was stunned. In front of him stood five feet, seven inches of pure African beauty. Shane quickly got himself together. *Can't fumble the ball,* he thought.

"I was just saying that's an excellent book." Shane flashed his best smile adding, "this is a continuation of the book you're buying. Pardon my manners, DuShane West." He smoothly stuck out his hand attempting to greet the lovely sister decked out in her 9 to 5 business attire. Unfortunately for him, he was 'thugging' for the day. The black thermal shirt, black leather Schott Peacoat, black jeans, and black suede Timberlands clashed in comparison to the dark blue suit jacket and matching skirt the woman wore.

"The name's Mona."

She gave Shane a firm handshake that demanded respect. Shane was too busy checking for a wedding band or any other sign that the cutie before him was spoken for. He saw none. Mona turned around and continued waiting in line. Shane felt snubbed, but took the opportunity to admire her *ass-ets.* Outside the bookstore he caught up to her.

"Excuse me, Mona?"

"Yes?"

"I may be out of line but I believe in taking chances. On the assumption that someone as beautiful as yourself could be single, would you even consider taking my number?" Shane had written his number on the book receipt already. "I'd rather try and get rejected, than to hug my pillow tonight wondering if I would've had a chance."

Mona laughed at Shane's approach.

"That's cute." She put the number inside her Barnes &

Noble bag.

"Well, before I push my luck, I'll keep my fingers crossed and hope for your call."

"You do that." Mona sashayed toward the mall's exit door, never looking back.

"Damn, that's a bad bitch!" Shane mumbled, making sure she hadn't heard him.

Khalid thought Wednesday would never come. He had plenty of time to think about the possibilities of today's meeting. He knew Shane and Skatz would come to an agreement. His focus was on getting Shane to give Soffey & Sons Ltd. the OK. He even thought of telling Fats that Shane gave the spot a thumbs up, but he didn't know anything about alarm systems and knew Fats would want details. He was on his way to Shane's house. He figured if he got there with Skatz by eleven, Shane could see the place by one, the time scheduled for the actual robbery. Khalid figured he would appreciate seeing the actual traffic on 71st and Continental.

When they arrived, he was on the back porch with his dogs. As Khalid and Skatz entered, the huge Mastiff appeared out of nowhere. Skatz began to ease back into the house.

"Don't do that, Skatz. The dog may take it wrong," Shane explained, seeing his homie's confused look.

"C'mere, Bo!" Bolo didn't budge at Shane's command, causing him to ask…"Skatz, you packing?"

Skatman nodded his head. "Ever since I barked on Fats." Statz answered.

Shane called the Mastiff to his side. "Good boy Bolo, Good Boy!" He praised the dog.

"The dog can smell a pistol?" Skatz asked.

"Something like that."

Actually it was a lot more to it than that, but he didn't want to divulge his dog training techniques. The three men sat while the mastiff observed the other dogs' play. Shane initiated the conversation, getting straight to the point.

"Skatz, that took a lotta heart what you did. So what's your plans now? I ask 'cause we've got similar interest." Shane talked while throwing Bolo chunks of cubed beef.

"So I've heard."

Skatz looked at Khalid. He had told Skatz that Shane would make a good business partner mainly because Fats could not intimidate him.

"I need to build another studio and I'm broke. I need an investor, but prefer a partner. Someone with a love for music who'll take an active role in the business."

Shane nodded, as Skatz continued.

"I have a 24 track mixing board, a triple 8 5.1 professional Pro Tools system. Also, an Akai MPC4000. The rest belongs to Fats."

"Well I've got an idea. Hear me out then hit me wit ya feedback. I'm in a position to expand the mixing board to a 48 track, fill in the equipment Fats fronted you and together we can find a new location. I've spoken to Khalid about a few old lofts down near the village that are priced decently. On top of that we put in a pre-production studio for those artists not laying vocals, and a live instrument room for musicians and bands."

Skatz had no idea Shane knew the business so well. He gave him his undivided attention as Shane continued.

"That way we can run multiple sessions turning bigger profits, using those profits that are extra to promote street team management and advertising."

Shane threw in the last part remembering it was a major issue with Skatz when he broke off from The Family.

"Will you be an active partner?" Skatz asked. He didn't wanna just pay out profits and be the only one putting work in the company. He refused to repeat his mistakes.

"I'm scheduled to enroll in the Institute of Audio Research on Friday. I know my way around a studio, but the certificate boosts our credibility and the contacts are unlimited."

Skatz realized Shane had his ideas thought out way before he'd gotten released from prison. He was hardly finished relaying his plans.

"If I'm out by three at the school, I can work a four to eight shift and if you want, my brother Ron can move the records from Wax Emporium into the joint and we can network."

Skatz cut Shane off. "I'm sold! By the way, Fats owns half the name, so we need a new one. You got any?"

"I've got a few, complete with logos." Shane smirked, wiping the juices from the raw beef on a hand towel. "So we good to go?" Shane asked Skatz, extending his hand.

"Yeah, we good ta go." They shook hands and sealed the deal.

Seeing that their business was completed, Khalid jumped into the conversation.

"So what's the verdict on *our* business?"

"I've got you, Kha, but I don't like it, so I've thrown in a few conditions."

Khalid cut Shane short, not wanting Skatz to hear his plans. Since he'd left the Family, Khalid felt it best he also leave him out of The Family business.

"Take a ride with me, Shane. I've gotta drop Skatz off."

All three men rode in silence. Skatz spoke first.

"That's a big house, Shane. Plan on filling it up?" Skatz turned around and smiled.

"I'm working on it, filling it with the boys and the dogs fa starters."

"Shane, I been married 4 years. It's a beautiful thing when you find the right one."

Khalid was surprised to hear Skatman share that information with Shane so soon. At the present moment Khalid had other things on his mind. If this heist worked out as he hoped it would, he planned to gradually distance himself from the Family as well. He knew Fats wouldn't be able to handle two members leaving in such a short time.

"Where to, Skatz?"

"Take me home, Kha." Again Skatman surprised him.

Skatz's residence was his second most coveted secret. Khalid only knew the address because he'd helped secure the modest townhouse located in Corona, Queens. Khalid didn't mind; Corona wasn't far from Soffey & Sons Ltd. Khalid pulled his green Volvo C-70 down MacIntosh Avenue to the front of Skatz's townhouse. Skatz turned to Shane.

"We'll hunt for the loft first, agreed?"

"No doubt!"

They gave each other dap and Khalid bolted off toward 71st and Continental.

"Damn, son, you ain't wasting no time, huh?"

"I want you ta see the traffic at the same time we're doing it." Shane smiled. He knew the traffic at one wouldn't be much different at two.

"So what's your conditions?" Khalid just wanted to get the speech out the way; he knew it was coming.

"One, in return for my info I get Fats' word nothing happens to Skatman, regardless of my news being favorable or not."

Khalid nodded.

"Two, never, and I repeat *never* ask me ta do this again. And finally, my name stays out of this shit."

Khalid agreed. After riding fourteen minutes in silence they arrived at 71st street.

"Park away from the spot!" Shane barked, he did not appreciate the position Khalid was putting him in. He observed the spot with little interest, after a few minutes Khalid asked him his opinion. Shane was eager to give it; he had to pick Isaiah up from school.

"First of all you're in a high-risk area, not far from the courthouse and in a predominately white area. Response time is cut in half due to an eight lane highway. The 110th

Precinct is minutes away, and anyone black will be observed with suspicion. That pretty much kills your element of surprise." Shane was all business now, reminding Khalid of the man he knew eight years ago.

"What's your escape route?"

Khalid shrugged, "Depends on your analysis of the situation. What would you do?"

"I wouldn't do it."

"If you did do it."

Shane exhaled. He saw Khalid wasn't giving in.

"If you got any chance of pulling this off, you've gotta do it like this... you'll need three men and a female. Have the female wait at that corner store enclave opposite the Boulevard, 'cause that's where the cops will be coming from. The female should have a shopping bag with a sweater to cover the briefcase."

"Briefcase?" Shane held up a finger, silencing Khalid.

"Yes, briefcase! Coming out of there you'll need to look like you belonged in there in the first place. On the way out the three men split up. Briefcase man toward the female. She'll be OK. I suggest the three men wear suits, preferably with Velcro so they can peel them off a block away."

Khalid nodded his understanding.

"More important is the security system, and since I'm retired, in the future know that insurance companies dictate the type of alarms a business needs before they'll insure them. So next time you can find out on your own. This company has the standard buzzer for the door. You must be buzzed in and out. They can't sell $20,000 watches behind a bulletproof glass, that's tacky. So their silent alarm is inside the ballpoint pen they'll be holding, most likely a female since the average gunman would secure the male first. Forget the movies, the buttons underneath the counters no longer exist! So we straight?"

"Yeah we straight!" Khalid had gotten more than he bargained for.

"Well take my ass home, Isaiah has a book report due Monday."

Friday was an exciting day for Chauncey. According to his mother, he was not only given the day off from school, but also driving to New York to visit his father. If things checked out, his mother would even let him spend the weekend. He hoped things checked out, *whatever that meant*. That morning Chauncey awoke bright and early packed and ready to go. Chyna rose to brew her morning tea, surprised to find Chauncey dressed with his bags at the door. She spent last evening answering dozens of questions Chauncey had about his father. She didn't feel up to the trip, but she'd already committed herself.

"You need help getting ready, Mom?"

Chyna smiled. "No, I don't need help getting ready. Is that your way of telling me to hurry up?"

Chauncey giggled.

Chyna rented a car for the trip, not wanting to put the extra mileage on her own vehicle. By four they reached New Jersey, by five they were on the highway headed to Queens. By the time she found Shane's address she thought she'd had the numbers written down wrong. Shane told her he lived alone, yet she had doubts when she took in the view of the massive house before her. She rang the doorbell. He answered the doorbell barefoot in a pair of old gray sweatpants and a wifebeater. He gave Chyna a hug which she reluctantly accepted for the sake of appearance. Chauncey stepped out of the rented car with his duffel bag slung over his shoulder. He dropped his bag, giving his father a hug. Shane hugged him for so long, Chauncey felt awkward. He understood since his son was too young to remember him.

"Isaiah's inside. He's been waiting for you all day."

Chauncey ran inside the house.

"Don't run!" Chyna yelled to him.

"Give him an inch and he'll take a yard," she told Shane, making an attempt at small talk.

"I'll try and keep that in mind." Shane looked at Chyna thinking to himself how mature she looked.

"Aren't you coming in?"

"For a minute."

He gave her a tour of the house and she instantly knew without asking, the conditions had been more than met. Chauncey had his own room, complete with clothing. Chauncey led Chyna to Isaiah's room which she noted was identical to his with the exception of color. Chauncey's room was a burgundy color scheme, whereas Isaiah's was tan. Both blended nicely with the wood walls. Shane showed Chyna his bedroom, which hardly looked lived in. She scanned the room for any signs of a woman having been there, but found none. For some reason she found comfort in that. The basement had plush blood red carpeting and eggshell white walls adorned with old movie posters and black and white photos of slain rappers Tupac Shakur, Biggie Smalls and Freaky Tah of The Lost Boyz. Chyna relaxed and enjoyed the tour. She even played with the pups. Bolo was another story. She made Shane promise to keep the dog away from Chauncey. Chauncey and Isaiah immediately got engrossed in Playstation2. Chyna sat in the kitchen observing Shane preparing the boys' dinner. He definitely knew his way around the kitchen.

"I'll be around to pick Chauncey up on Sunday at one." She was impressed. She almost felt guilty for giving Shane such a hard time... almost.

"I'll have him ready."

Chyna went and said goodbye to Chauncey. She had to force him to pause the game just to kiss her goodbye. *Where's the love?* she thought smiling to herself. Shane walked her to the door.

"Don't forget, keep him away from that dog. And I'll be back Sunday at one. I'm at my mother's, so if something happens you know the number. What are you smiling about?" Chyna was referring to the smirk on Shane's lips.

"I was just thinking how much you sound like a mom!"

"Yeah, yeah, one o'clock." Chyna walked toward the rental.

"Chyna!" Shane yelled, as she looked up. "Thank you." He said softly.

As Chyna pulled off she almost wished she were staying... *almost.*

Shane and the boys did everything three people with a weekend together could think of. They went to Long Island's Q-Zar, the video version of a paintball war, where players wear electronic vests that light up when shot by laser guns. Q-Zar had a maze and split the whole group into teams. Shane was proud to watch Chauncey and Isaiah watching each other's back as a team. They lasted longer than most adults, eliminating Shane in the earlier rounds.

They rented more movies than they could possibly watch when they entered Blockbuster Video. It was then that Shane observed first hand how good a job Chyna had done raising Chauncey. When the lady at the register informed them they were one movie over their limit, Chauncey voluntarily returned a movie he'd picked out so that Isaiah could see *Spiderman*, a movie Chauncey had at home. They had pizza at the mall and then went shopping. Shane knew he was spoiling them, but special occasions warranted such actions. He bought each of them a black suit and matching turtleneck. They'd had a fit about the shoes, so Shane compromised, purchasing black suede Hushpuppies.

The next day was Sunday and he hated to see them go. Even Mia said she was missing her baby. *I can still take*

Isaiah to and from school, but Chauncey feels so far away at times, he thought. He'd just tucked them in for bed. He looked around the house and it was a mess. Empty pizza boxes were on the kitchen table, waterguns on the sofa, bandanas on the puppies. Shane smiled.

"Now this house looks like a home!"

Sunday at 12:45, Chyna was pissed!

"I told that nigga one o'clock! I got something fa his ass, though." Chyna picked up her cell phone ready to curse Shane out when she noticed his truck pull up. She jumped out the rental slamming the door.

"I'm sorry, Chyna. My watch says a quarter to." Shane tapped his watch, doubting it was wrong, but trying not to get on her bad side.

Chyna stopped in her tracks. All three had on black suits and bibles.

Here I am bitching and he took them to church! Her mother's words came to mind, *"Think before you act!"* She told Chyna before she had rushed out the door angry.

Her watch was half an hour off. *Must be the battery,* she thought to herself.

CHAPTER 14
FRIEND OR FOE

Gunnz gunned the V-12 engine down the Brooklyn-Queens Expressway dipping in and out of traffic. The scowl on his face alerted Fatal that something was definitely troubling his crimee. Besides, he was driving so fast Fatal couldn't roll his weed.

"Wha yah do, brethren?" Fatal's Jamaican accent surfaced whenever he got angry. And Gunnz causing him to spill half a bag of L.P.'s finest was enough to get him angry.

"Gunnz, pull over and park... we gotta talk!" Gunnz got off an exit early and parked.

"So you gon' tell ya boy what's got you acting all funny style or what?"

Gunnz knew he'd eventually have to tell him, because he needed Fatal to vouch for him. They were on their way to see Fats ,so Gunnz figured there was no time like the present to get the story straight. There was no doubt in his mind that Fatal would back him up. Blood was thicker than water.

"I was supposed to put that work in on Ray-Ray and I didn't."

"And?" Fatal, not much for words just listened and smoked.

"I'm gonna tell Fats it's taken care of."

"OK."

"If she pops back up, we'll have to hear his mouth."

"Uh-huh."

"I'm getting sick of dancing around his ego, telling me ta kill Ray-Ray was like spitting in my face. Next time he tells me some sideways shit like that, Imma remind that nigga who's ratchet it was who made the Family name worth mentioning."

"I think that was *my* ratchet that sung the most high notes, cousin. But, that's beside the point! Sounds like you're sick of answering to Fats' ego. So either take over or we bounce, 'cause the only thing that makes him the man is the fact that he has connections. Never think we don't have options, Gunnz. Shit we can rob the Clubhouse and move to Miami."

Gunnz laughed, giving Fatal a pound.

"Long as we pledge allegiance to each other, everything else is secondary." A seed had been planted between the two.

When Gunnz and Fatal reached the Clubhouse Fats was having another one of his tantrums. Manny sat counting The Cab Stand's profits from the previous shift as usual. Pretty Boy pimped nights; midnight to four AM was his working hours, so he pretty much just hung out at the clubhouse bar during the mornings. The only one who seemed out of place was Mark, a newcomer to the Family. Manny vouched for Mark. He liked the fact that he was about his paper. Mark was a new driver that brought his own clientele to the table. Fatal, as well as Gunnz did not appreciate his presence. All newcomers were suspect as far as they were concerned. Fats raved on about Khalid's message from Shane.

"Who the fuck is he to tell me ta give Skatz a pass? I run this shit!"

Here we go again, thought Gunnz.

"He's lucky I don't have him *and* Skatman hit."

Khalid intervened. "Whoa, Fats you're talking reckless right now. You don't wanna send the wrong message to the hood, that Family would do their own? C'mon, we've got the info, anyone can run the studio. Matter of fact, I'm putting that together as we speak."

Gunnz jumped in the conversation. "Besides, if you want Shane or Skatz hit, you'll have ta find another nigga ta put *that* work in cuz me and Fatal ain't banging one of our own people just 'cause they wanna do right by *their* family!" Gunnz stood firm by his words.

Fats knew he'd pushed too far this time, so he cleaned up the statement.

"OK, I'm talking out my ass! Fuck ya'll all sensitive for?"

Fatal interrupted. "We're here to discuss the Soffey & Sons jux, so let's discuss it."

Fatal knew it was just a matter of time before the Family experienced an inner power struggle. He just wanted to insure him and Gunnz had a little bit of dough stashed in the event of a need for a hasty retreat.

Khalid went over Shane's analysis of the situation. As Fatal listened, he realized Shane covered every hole he saw in the Soffey & Sons heist, but as with any jux, the element of risk still existed. They made plans to rob the place. Afterwards, Manny made plans of his own.

When Shane checked his answering machine, he was surprised to find Mona had called. He hit the button on his machine once more and listened to her sexy voice again.

"DuShane... I like that name! Anyway, it's Mona. The one from the book store? I've been thinking about you. I figured you sounded sincere enough for a callback. If I hear from you soon, maybe we can get together for a few drinks."

The message paused, then Mona continued. "DuShane, one more thing, at first glance you seemed like a player, and I'm too old for games. But my girlfriends told me I shouldn't write you off without seeing what you're about. My number is..." "Beep!"

Shane shut the machine off and had already memorized the number. He called Mona.

"Hello?"

"Hello, this is DuShane calling for Mona."

"Hey... what took you so long to call back?" Mona said in a sexy voice. She was 32 years old, and a dead ringer for actress Angela Bassett. She'd been fooled before, yet she couldn't get Shane's words out of her head. Besides, how many thugs were reading books on financial intelligence? If she only knew!

They talked a little under an hour and made a date for her to come over and enjoy a home cooked meal the following evening. This time, Shane decided, he wouldn't get caught slipping. He was gonna dress the part.

He spent the next day preparing for his date with Mona. From their earlier conversation he learned that she didn't eat red meat, so he prepared blue snapper he'd purchased at the Fresh Fish market. He soaked the fish in lemon juice, then worked his magic with the seasoning by adding razor-thin slices of orange peels to the sauce. By the time dusk settled on New York, he had aired the smell of fish from his home, showered, and prepared for his dinner date.

Mona mentioned in her last conversation with him how every man that approached her tended to be a thug. She told him he seemed like the thug type, but won her over with his pressure-free approach. She said she was attracted to men who were versatile; the type who could make her feel safe and secure in the hood, yet not embarrass her in front of business associates. Shane wanted to show Mona never to judge a book by its cover. He put on a black pair of baggy, cuffed wool trousers with a white shirt and pink tie, topped off with a black vest. Knowing the suit's jacket would be too much, he opted for his 'kiss the cook' apron. Since she was coming straight from work, he had no fears of being overdressed for the occasion. He'd seen her work clothes, top shelf stuff. Mona told him she was an ADA (Assistant District Attorney) for Queens County. He brushed it off, thinking slyly to himself, *Shit, all the times the system fucked me, maybe I can fuck the system!*

The phone rang, it was Khalid.

"Hello?"

"What up, son?" He sounded drunk.

"Nigga you sound twisted!"

"I am... Imma come through."

"Nah man, not tonight you ain't!"

"What, you got some ass lined up?"

"I'll line yo ass up wit da sights on my pistol if you show up at my door tonight, Kha!"

"Yeah, you got some ass coming. Holla at me tomorrow, soon as possible!"

Shane hung up not caring if Khalid was finished. The phone rang again.

"Hello?"

"Hey Babyboy."

"Who dis?"

"Peaches." Shane calmed down.

"What up, Ma? I thought you was my homie calling back."

"Do I sound like your homie?" Peaches teased.

"Not at all, now is not a good time for me."

She sucked her teeth.

"Shane, I'll give you my number and you can call me. If I don't hear from you then I'll know you're brushing me off."

He took down her number promising to call her soon. The doorbell rang.

"Showtime!" he said, rubbing his palms together.

When Shane answered the door Mona stood there with a bottle of white wine in her hand and a sexy smile showing her pearly whites. He told her she looked stunning and took her coat. Truthfully, he just wanted to roll a fat blunt, stick his dick in her mouth and beat her back out! He was going through the motions because he just wanted to be able to say he fucked a DA.

"Your house is beautiful."

"Thank you!" Shane promised himself he'd get her to loosen up, because he wasn't going to act stiff and proper all night. He'd do just enough fronting to show he possessed versatility. *Then it's time ta push up,* he thought.

He brought out an appetizer and Mona complimented the food. He thanked her and promised the meal would be just as good if not better.

"I hope to make some woman very happy someday by knowing my way around the kitchen." Inwardly, he laughed at himself. *I might've laid that on a little too thick.*

Mona asked for a tour of the house. Once the tour was over the two of them ate in front of the fireplace with Miles Davis' album *Kinda Blue* playing softly in the background.

"DuShane, I'm always talking about me, tell me about yourself." By now the two of them were cuddling. Shane stroked her hair, while she sat between his legs enjoying his touch. He told her about his children, his likes and dislikes, dreams, and goals. He skipped his past.

Mona asked what type of business he was in and he replied, "Music, real behind the scene stuff, pre-production, artist development, things like that."

Shane started kissing her neck and she moaned. He got an erection and she ground her buttocks against him.

"Shane, I've got a confession to make." He scooped up Mona's hair and smelled it, placing light gentle kisses behind her ear.

"I'm listening." He stuck his hand between her thighs, feeling the moist warm heat emanating through her panties.

"I did a background check on you. I know about your time upstate. I couldn't help it I've had bad luck with men—."

Shane cut her off. "If most women were in a position to

learn up front what they were getting into, I'm sure they would. So after you found out, what made you still come over?"

"If I held your past against you without knowing your situation, I could be doing us both a disservice. Even Malcolm X started as Dirty Red." Her words caused him to smile.

"So everything's cool with us?"

"Yeah." Mona turned her head and started kissing him.

"I like how you feel, Shane, but it's only fair I warn you not to get yourself worked up 'cause we're *not* having sex!" He smiled, causing her to ask, "What are you smiling about?"

He pulled out a bottle of scented oil. "I did have a Plan B."

Shane gave Mona a massage that rivaled some health spas, starting at the insoles of her feet working in between her toes. She appeared so relaxed he thought she'd fallen asleep. His hands firmly massaged her calves, working the oil into her skin. He massaged her thighs, slowly lifting her skirt until her buttocks were exposed. Mona refused to take off her clothes even though Shane promised to leave his on. She said she didn't want to start something she couldn't finish. His hands didn't want to leave her firm cheeks. As she lifted her ass in the air, he kissed her clitoris, rubbing the tip of his tongue across her love button. Mona backed her ass fully into his face as he marinated in her sweet, fresh scent. All the while, his fingertips massaged her lower back in circular motions. His penis stretched the fabric of his pants to the limit as he climbed on top of her, purposely resting his rock-hard penis between her ass cheeks. He twitched his manhood between her buns, dry-humping her. Shane was hoping to break her willpower. Her breathing had gotten heavy by the time he'd reached her shoulders.

He whispered in her ear. "Can I just rub my dick on your ass cheeks?"

Mona nodded consent, sucking on Shane's bottom lip. He rubbed his stiff, blood-gorged shaft from the crack of Mona's ass to her clit, occasionally slapping his heavy organ against her wet snatch. He pulled off his tank top and rubbed his bare chest against Mona's back, cupping her breasts while teasing her nipples.

"Touch it," Shane whispered. And Mona squeezed.

"Oooh, it's so fat."

"Lemme put it in...just once. Look how wet you are, don't deprive yourself...just once."

Mona spread herself wide, giving him the go-ahead. He guided his dick in, sloshing the head of his penis around the entrance of her pussy, slowly entering her so she could feel every inch of him when he did. He ground into her far as he could in circular motions

He whispered, "Mona Baby, I've gotta make this one pump count, OK?"

"Yes, baby, make it count, *make it count!*"

"Can I get another one?" Shane asked, adding..."Can I get a few?" He was already stroking her.

"Just fuck me, DuShane, and stop playing!"

He drove it home, plowing into her with lustful vengeance. In his mind, he fucked her on the defendant's table in the same court he blew trial in.

Mona was horny! She bucked like she hadn't had any dick in years. He grabbed her hair, purposely being rougher than necessary, yelling. "I want you to cream all over this dick!" Mona nodded, gasping for air. Shane smacked her on the ass till each cheek glowed red.

"I'm cumming," she screamed.

"No more, Shane! Please, no more!"

He was banging her until she jumped with each thrust. As he felt himself about to explode, he asked, "Will you suck it for me, baby?"

All the proper etiquette left Mona, and the freak within took control.

"Yes baby, Yesss!"

His nuts were about to explode as he spun her around, never letting go and came all over her designer clothes. To

Shane's surprise, Mona smiled and kissed the head of his dick.

"I thought you didn't eat meat." They both laughed at his comment.

"I'm wiling to give what I get." She smiled, slighty blushing.

Shane sat in his living room reflecting on Mona and their previous night together.

Damn, I wilded out on her last night. He was shaking his head in disbelief. *I'm lucky if she ever calls me back.Fuck it, I needed ta relieve some tension. Mona's crazy, making a nigga get all dressed up fa nothing!*

A car horn sounded and Shane grabbed his house keys and exited. Khalid leaned on the horn longer than necessary. Shane paused, looking at him as if he'd lost his mind. The last thing he wanted was to bring unnecessary attention to himself, and Khalid's constant horn-blowing was a surefire way to cause his new neighbors to stop by and complain.

"What the fuck is you doing, Kha?"

"C'mon, get in, we've gotta talk." Khalid was hyped.

He jumped into Kha's Volvo, and they immediately hit the highway heading toward Manhattan. Khalid had done some inquiring and stumbled across a loft for rent in Soho, perfect for Digimon Studios, a name Shane and Skatz had finally agreed upon. He couldn't understand why Khalid was so hyped over a loft they hadn't even seen yet.

"You watch the news last night?" Shane shook his head.

"They did it!"

"Did what?" Shane asked, getting bored with Khalid's game.

"The heist. What else have I been hounding you about all week?" Khalid tossed him an envelope. When he looked inside, he saw what he guessed to be about ten grand.

"That's the dough I promised you. Don't expect shit from

Fats, though. You put a real monkey wrench in whatever he had planned fa Skatz. I think he'd rather give you the dough than give Skatz a pass. Whole lotta words were exchanged between them behind that shit!" Khalid referred to the tension between Skatman and Fats at the clubhouse. He did not ask Khalid to elaborate, so he took the hint and changed the subject.

"That's more than enough to rent the loft and get the studio started, huh?"

"Was it clean?" Shane asked, ignoring Kha's question.

"Was what clean?"

"The heist, everyone get away? Anyone get hurt? Was it clean?"

"You would've been proud son. Shit went smooth, real professional!"

"Kha, don't call me son."

"My bad, everything all right?"

Shane sensed that Khalid was feeling uneasy and decided to put his old friend at ease.

"Kha, easy babyboy, it ain't nothing you did. It's just that when you say 'son' it reminds me of the boys. I shouldn't be setting up heists, I should be hounding Mia and Chyna to death to spend time with my little men."

Khalid nodded agreement.

"You right, son...I mean Shane." Khalid smiled in embarrassment. "But don't sweat it. Right now you need income coming in or you'll eat away your stash. So after you set up shop you can get on your job with the boys, but it ain't like you bullshitting. By the way, how'd it go with the chick last night that caused you to give me the bum rush off the phone?"

Shane laughed, pulling out a bag of smoke. He shook the twenty sack.

"Kha, I *gotta* roll up fa this story!" Shane leaned forward and in a conspiratorial whisper, said, "Nigga, last night I laid an Assistant DA!"

CHAPTER 15
COPS & ROBBERS

It had been three weeks since Shane had hidden himself from the rest of the world, with the exception of his calls to Chauncey and Isaiah each night before their bedtime. He explained to both his kids that Daddy was hard at work making a living so they could spend many more weekends together. He felt good knowing they understood and that for once in his life he could honestly say he was telling the truth. Digimon Studios was finally open for business. Shane and Skatz did the majority of work by hand. Skatz during the day, and Shane at night. The school Shane attended taught secrets even Skatz was unaware of. Digimon Studios catered to the "unsigned artist." They'd pooled their money together and rented a Ford Excursion and shrink-wrapped the vehicle with Digimon's logo and handed out posters and flyers in the tri-state area, limiting their resources to each borough's hot spot: Harlem's 125th Street, Jamaica Avenue, Flushing's Main Street, and Queens Center Mall in Queens, 3rd Avenue and Fordham Road in the Bronx and Downtown Brooklyn.

The loft they'd rented was a spacious two story duplex with spiral steps leading to the second floor where a soundproof studio held live instruments and a queen-sized bed for times when a session lasted so long it made no sense to go home. The first floor held a mini-bar, refrigerator, pre-production room, and 48 track mixing console complete with acoustic foam. The waiting area boasted plush leather couches and a 60-inch television equipped with Playstation's latest video games and complete surround sound. All for $30 an hour. The two of them made the studio so comfortable an artist would hopefully not want to go home. The front area flaunted a half moon receptionist desk. Shane had given Peaches the job.

The first week the phone rang off the hook with inquiries from Skatz's old clientele asking if the Digimon complex was ready to be broken in. Shane took to business like a natural. One artist named Fantab had a CD cover that resembled the book cover of the lastest street novel, *A Hustlers Handbook* by Tracy Thomas, but was called *A Hustler's Life* with their artist leaning on the same type of car as the guy on the original book cover. The back of these CD mix tapes had the artist's black and white photo where the author's photo would be, and instead of a synopsis, Shane put the artist's bio. They even sent champagne baskets of Cristal, the CDs, and Digimon turntable mats to dee-jays, radio execs and record labels. Every artist coming through was cracking for Digimon's Promotional Package.

Shane kept Peaches busy typing up various production contracts giving Digimon artists the right to independently shop their own deal. Skatz admired Shane's business savvy. Digimon was run legit and practiced good customer relations. No one left feeling cheated. Ron had a room to himself and acquired the dream job of spending his days digging through Wax Emporium's vinyl records–now located in the back room of Digimon Studios—listening for old basslines and rifts.

Business was in full swing, life couldn't be better...*or could it?* Shane felt empty without his boys, as if his happiness was a lie. *Time to call Chyna.* He knew Mia would be no problem as far as Isaiah was concerned. Getting Chauncey for a weekend was his biggest challenge. Shane noticed Peaches bent over the reception desk talking to two artists.

When she noticed him watching she winked.

I'll call in the morning, tonight Imma treat myself ta some of that snatch, Shane thought, smiling.

"Detective Rogers. This here's McCullem, 110th Precinct." McCullem didn't bother to greet Shane.

"Can we come in, Mr. West?" McCullem spoke in an authoritative manner as if he wasn't really asking Shane's permission to enter his home. He blocked the detective's path.

"Fa what?"

"We've got a few questions," McCullem snapped.

"Well I ain't got no answers, so kick rocks!" Shane went to slam the door, but Detective Rogers' foot prevented him from doing so.

"Bolo!" Before Shane could finish, the Mastiff was by his side. The dog didn't even bark; he just stood showing his teeth. If Shane gave the order, Bolo would go for the kill or die trying.

McCullem stuttered. "Boy, if you release that dog we not only reserve the right to shoot it in self-defense, but to also charge you with aggravated assault on an officer."

The detective's threat instantly brought Shane back to his senses. He nodded toward his backyard and Bolo instantly disappeared.

"Whatta ya'll want?"

Rogers gave his partner a look that suggested McCullem let him do the talking. The Irish detective figured his partner may have a better shot at getting through to Shane being that they both were black. While Rogers talked, McCullem took in Shane's house with contempt. They'd ran a check on him and McCullem knew he'd been recently released. He'd gotten a look at the house and knew Shane had to be dirty.

"We've got some info you may want to hear," Detectives

Rogers told Shane.

"About what?" Shane asked, wishing the detectives would find another black man to harass.

"Soffey & Sons, Ltd."

If the officers were looking for any sign that Shane knew of the recent heist performed on the Jewish jewelers, they found none. He kept a straight poker face and even feigned agitation when the detectives tried to give him the silent treatment, hoping he'd give up a sign he was lying.

"That name suppose ta ring a bell?" he asked, playing dumb.

"Can we discuss this inside?" McCullem asked. He wanted to see the inside of Shane's house.

"No." Shane stood his ground. "Ya'll finished?"

Rogers continued. "We got an anonymous call that you were in on that job." Rogers held up a hand to stop Shane from interrupting. "Of course we don't believe every tip we get, but we did run a check, and you're no angel, Mr. West. Eight years for armed robbery, priors for gun possession too. Computer says the Soffey job is your Modus Operandi, but I say this is too easy. Somebody's trying to set you up, West. But bet this, you know who did this, and when they see we wasn't dumb enough to do their dirty work for them, they'll come at you direct. Until then, know we're watching you." Rogers handed Shane his card.

"Just in case things get too out of control for you to handle."

Just what I fucking need! I knew shit was going too smooth for a nigga, thought Shane as he threw the officer's card in the trash can.

"I'm too old ta be playing cops and robbers."

Chyna spent the morning with Dana and Sherry going about their morning ritual of getting the shop ready for business. Chyna was in the process of updating her girlfriends on the recent events concerning Chauncey's weekend with his father.

"So let me get this straight." Dana interjected. "Not only was the man bringing the kids from Church, but he wasn't even late?"

Chyna nodded, signaling she had the facts right.

Sherry jumped in the conversation. "Chyna haven't you run out of reasons for hating this man yet?"

The question was unexpected from Sherry. Dana, maybe, but Chyna didn't expect Sherry to come at her so hard.

"What do you mean by that?" Chyna was ready to defend her actions when Dana quickly put in her two cents.

"Please, first you think he told Chauncey not to tell you he was coming home, and found out you were wrong about that. You told him Chauncey wasn't home when he was, until you got a conscience about that. You set conditions that the man seems to have more than met. And screamed on him or was ready to before you had all the facts. Girl, you ain't sick of fronting? You still love him!" Dana had finally put out in the open what Sherry long suspected, but Chyna would never admit.

Chyna attempted to downplay Dana's words by laughing them off. "Dana, you're bugging. Talking out your ass is not a good look for you."

Sherry, the most sensible of the three, chose to stay neutral, but Dana wasn't having it.

"What you think Sherry? She might listen to you."

Since Dana put her on the spot. Sherry being the oldest of the three, came with her usual diplomatic approach.

"From a person's point of view that's on the outside looking in, yes, it looks that way to me."

Chyna refused to be put on the spot. She knew if she made too much of a fuss about what her friends were saying it would make them seem right, so she played it cool.

"Ya'll got a right to your opinions, but you know what

they say about opinions, right?" Chyna asked, as all three
women laughed, repeated the saying in unison.

"Opinions are like assholes, *everybody's* got one!"

Shane was surprised to hear Mona's voice on his answering
machine.

"Hi DuShane, remember me? It's Mona, I thought I'd hear
from you by now. I hope I didn't scare you off." Mona's sexy
laugh echoed through his empty house, she continued. "You
really brought me out of character that night. Next time
we'll make love, *if* there's a next time. Call me, stranger."
Beep!

The next call was from Chyna. It was actually good news
for a change.

"Shane! It's Chyna, Chauncey couldn't stop talking about
his weekend with you. Call me! We'll make plans for him to
spend Thanksgiving weekend. Um, take care." Beep!

Khalid called. "Call me, we gotta talk, urgent!"

The last message disturbed Shane. He poured himself a
drink and rolled up a spliff. *Something's up! Them detectives
aren't smart enough to know what they know. There ain't
that much intel in the world. Feds maybe, but two washed
up detec's from the 110th, I don't think so!'.*

He looked at his situation from all angles. Who could
benefit from trapping him off, and why? Definitely not
Khalid, Fats would simply have him hit, and he figured
Gunnz and Fatal most likely participated in the Soffey &
Sons jux so his thoughts were stuck on Mark.

*Would he think me, and Mia's convos have been about more
than Isaiah? I guess if a nigga's insecure enough, but Khalid
said only certain members knew of the jux and Mark wasn't
one of them.* Shane wondered if he could get Khalid to run a
family 'field test' on Mark, so he called his cell phone.

"Yo?" Khalid answered.

"Kha, I got your message. Can you come through?"

"Yeah, I'm on my way, we gotta talk, son... I mean dawg."

"Hurry up! The door's open."

Khalid arrived fifteen minutes later. He and Shane wasted no time getting to the point. He told Khalid about the detectives' visit. They agreed that there was a fungus among them. The Family field test was agreed upon. The test, invented by Shane, consisted of putting a member in a position of extreme pressure to see if he'd crack. Khalid would immediately put a scenario together. Now he was informing Shane on a new turn of events.

"I guess when it rains it pours, 'cause I fucked up too!" Khalid sifted through the details of the Soffey fence, a jeweler named Bailey who made the mistake of not dealing with Khalid directly. He explained to Shane how nervous Bailey was about carrying a substantial amount of cash, causing the jeweler to make out a cashier's check.

"So what's the problem? They're good as cash," Shane pushed, trying to get Khalid to make his point.

"Will ya let me finish?" he yelled. Khalid was obviously stressed cause he rarely raised his voice. He poured himself a drink and continued his story.

"I was supposed to get ten percent of the take, $6,000 for me, $54,000 for the rest of the clique to split. For some reason this time Fats wants to go to Bailey with me to collect the dough, so I'm like, 'I'll bring you 54 grand this afternoon cause Bailey's the cautious type.' But Fats wants to give me six thou out of his pocket and I sign the check over to him."

Shane interrupted. "But you can't let him see the check 'cause its more than sixty grand right?" Shane smirked.

Khalid gulped down his drink, reluctant to finish the tale.

"Yeah, you right, but I'm telling this dude I'll get him 5 grand for each watch. A half dozen Patek Philipes, and a half dozen Rolex masterpieces. Anyway, I come out the spot with the check stashed thinking I'll smash him wit the dough later. Gunnz and Fatal rush Bailey, talking 'bout why was he playing games wit their cash. Bailey cracks, telling Fats 'I just gave Mr. Cosgrove a hundred and twenty large!' If looks could kill we wouldn't be having this discussion. Fatal fished the check off me."

"Damn, Kha, so you would've taken 66 grand from them! What was you thinking? That's *more* than half. Fats probably knew you pinched, but accepted it. Over half though..." Shane let the words trail off, he didn't know what to tell Khalid.

Khalid wasn't finished. "Fats got Manny checking the books on the sneaker store, the used car lot and what's left of the studio. Rasta Paul left me that car lot when he went upstate. Fats don't even have a right to that kickback he charges for the lot."

Shane shook his head. "Kha, you ain't in no position to give Mark no field test, nigga *you* may become his initiation into the Family!" Shane disappeared into his basement, he came back and threw a roll of bills in Khalid's lap.

"There's the ten grand you gave me. If I were you I'd scrape up some coins and bounce!"

"You really think it's that serious? He's got a hundred and twenty gees ta calm himself down wit."

Shane looked at Khalid like he was stupid.

Mona stayed true to her word. The evening was her treat and Shane finally saw her dressed down for a change. She wore tight-fitting Dolce & Gabbana jeans with a white matching D&G mockneck sweater with a black leather jacket and boots. Shane wore a tan suede Nubuck jacket with matching Timberlands and light blue denim jeans from The Gap with a tan V-neck Gap sweater. Their simple ensembles complemented each other. They'd just finished eating at BBQ's in the village. Mona looked up at Shane, who seemed deep in thought as they walked toward Mona's parking spot.

"What's on your mind, Shane?" She asked, leaning him against her silver BMW X-5 and sliding her hands underneath his sweater to keep warm. Shane stroked her hair with his fingertips.

"Mona, I'm trying to do the right thing but it feels like my past is going to snatch me up in some bullshit any minute and I can't do shit about it!" He felt frustrated. He wanted to share with Mona the recent events in his life that led up to his feelings, yet her job prevented him from doing so. He knew if Mona knew of a crime, it was her sworn duty to report it. Mona fingered his dog tags. Unbeknownst to Shane, she knew the meaning and circumstances behind the inscription "People vs. West 752 N.Y.S.2d 070." She'd even gotten the files from a colleague and read up on the details of his case file.

"People, places and things, Shane," she mumbled, leaning into him.

"Huh? I didn't catch that."

"People, places and things. Change the people around you, the places you're hanging around, and the things you're doing. It's the only way to *truly* change. Do you think a recovering addict goes to bars or drug spots to hang out? No, they go to non-alcoholic bars with other recovering addicts. Spend time with your boys, your lifestyle is addictive Hon, change it!"

Shane fingered the dog tags absentmindedly as Mona continued. "People vs.West. The defendant was standing on line to purchase a sweater when the officer, observing he was wet, merely suggested he had recently been outside. No reasonable suspicion or probable cause existed for a full blown arrest, therefore judgement is reversed as a matter of law."

Shane smiled. It didn't surprise him that she knew his

appeal word for word.

"You could still be in those mountains another decade, babe. You could be coming home to two grown men with a grudge instead of two young boys who need their father. Make it count. If not for you, for those upstate not fortunate enough to get a second chance. Or better yet for your mother and father whom I know did not raise you that way!"

Shane nodded. "For myself, Mona, *and* my children!".

She smiled. "I can drop you home or you can come to my house, but this time we're gonna make love."

"In that case, I'm going to your place."

Shane took Mona's advice. Since he'd known no other people but ex-cons and felons, he immersed himself in Digimon Studios and stayed to himself. He found himself spending more time with Mona. Since neither of them was committed to the other, Shane took Peaches for an occasional night on the town, followed by their occasional romp in the sack.

Instead of heading straight to Digimon after his hours at the Institute of Audio Research, Shane would drive to Queens and pick Isaiah up from school, taking him along to Digimon.

Peaches often helped with Isaiah's homework while Shane worked. Thanksgiving was right around the corner so Chauncey was due any day now. *So much happened in such a short time,* thought Shane. It felt as if Isaiah mentioned Mia cooking Thanksgiving dinner only days ago. He decided to get a head start on his own holiday cooking. He and Isaiah left the studio early to go food shopping while Peaches tagged along. After dropping Peaches off and putting Isaiah to bed, Shane fed Bolo and the pups. He had his nightly conversation with Bolo then headed off to bed.

This was going to be Mia's first Thanksgiving without Isaiah. She knew he wanted to spend the holiday with Shane, so she gave in. Mark had been non-existent in the last two months, and without it being actually said, she knew the relationship was over. Her only regret was that Mark hadn't left earlier. Maybe then she could have been available enough to see where she and Shane stood.

Peaches hardly worked Foxy's anymore, so Mia figured Digimon Studios clientele was in full swing. Mia and Peaches remained cool since Peaches had the decency to ask if she was OK with her seeing Shane. A courtesy, considering Mia was still with Mark at the time. *Mark, what a waste of time he was,* Mia thought to herself. Although Khalid laid low since the incident with Fats and the cashier's check, he did relay to Mia that Mark was now pushing a platinum gray Cadillac Escalade. *Khalid handled the paperwork so he should know. Well, Isaiah's got his Daddy,* she thought to herself, looking at the brighter side of the situation.

Shit, I oughtta hit Miami for Thanksgiving weekend, go soak up some sun.

After thinking about it for a bit, Mia picked up the phone and dialed an airline.

This time Chyna flew Chauncey in instead of driving. Shane and Isaiah met them at the airport. He helped her with her bags while the boys ran wild through the airport.

"Cut it out!" Chyna told the boys.

Shane was surprised to find Isaiah listened too.

"You've gotta teach me that," he joked. Surprisingly, Chyna's whole attitude seemed to have changed for the better.

"It's all up in the throat, you gotta bark at them! Let 'em

think there's repercussions for being hardheaded." Chyna flashed Shane a smile.

"Am I dropping you at your mom's house?" Shane asked.

"You can just drop me at a hotel outside the airport."

Shane thought for a moment at the fact she was willing to spend Thanksgiving held up in a hotel so he and Chauncey could be together.

Chyna's not the monster I make her out to be, he thought, as he spoke without thinking.

"Why not stay with us?"

"Yeah Mom, stay with us, you can show Dad how to make stuffing." Chauncey gave Chyna his best 'don't say no' face.

"Your father's probably having guests, and I don't want to intrude." The truth was, Chyna didn't feel like bumping into any chickenheads Shane may be involved with. Shane spoke up.

"Whoa! Hold up, wouldn't that be a violation of one of your *conditions?*" Shane teased. "Seriously Chyna, it's just me and the boys." He leaned closer whispering, "Besides, you can teach me the proper techniques to active parenting." He winked.

Chyna knew she'd accept the invitation. She often wondered how Shane interacted with Chauncey. She didn't want to seem thirsty and jump on the invitation immediately. Shane just drove toward his house. It had been a while, but he still knew his *Chyna doll.*

"I've gotta stop at Petco."

Chauncey looked up from the PlayStation him and Isaiah played on the Range Rovers flip down television, asking, "Bolo's gotta get his grub on, Dad?"

Isaiah giggled, but Chyna missed the humor in Chauncey's statement.

They arrived home by early evening. Shane told her she could sleep in his room and took the belongings he'd need to the basement. Chyna observed him for the first few hours. He helped the boys put away their clothes, then she watched them play well into the night. When it was time to feed the dogs, Chyna had a chance to see the humor in Chauncey's earlier statement. First, they fed the pups their lamb and rice mixture, then Shane went to the back deck. Chyna couldn't help but admire his house, but wondered what he was into to afford such luxuries. Chauncey dragged his mother outside to observe the show. Chyna smiled.

"What's all the fuss about?" Shane gave her a mischevious grin, dangling a side of beef and motioning her to come by his side. She shook her head.

"What, you don't trust me?" Shane dangled the meat over the edge of the deck by his fingertips.

"What are you?"

"Shhh! Watch...don't even blink." Chyna watched and saw nothing, she just saw Shane drop the meat. Chauncey and Isaiah clapped excitedly.

"Our turn!" Isaiah yelled.

Chyna had a look of confusion on her face.

"What is wrong with ya'll? This is what ya'll do for fun, throw good meat on the floor?"

Her statement cracked them up. Shane handed her the next strip by the fingertips and stood behind her, as she mimicked what she saw him do. A few seconds went by and Chyna began feeling silly, as she went to draw back the meat she heard a slight pitter pat then, *swoosh*! Bolo jumped in the air, snatched the meat, and disappeared into the darkness.

"What the...?" Chyna checked for all her fingers.

"They're all there! He only likes dark meat," Shane joked.

"Very funny." Chyna nodded toward the kids. "And you're telling me you let these boys do this?"

Shane and his boys nodded affirmation with big cheesy smiles on their faces.

"Didn't you promise me you'd keep that dog away from Chauncey?"

"I kept my promise! You never said keep Chauncey away from the dog." Chyna gave Shane one of her famous 'you played me' looks. Chauncey jumped in before things got heated.

"It's my fault, Mom. Bolo's trained and I used that to get to him, I'll show you." Chauncey called out.

"C'mere, Bo!" The Mastiff appeared out of the darkness and stood in front of Chauncey.

Isaiah told Bolo to sit, and the dog obeyed without question.

Chyna smiled. "OK, but does that work for everyone?"

Shane introduced Bolo to Chyna and explained the process to her. By the next day he assured her the dog should obey her basic commands if he felt that it was his master's wish. By midnight, the boys went to bed.

Shane was waiting for a moment alone with Chyna, and after almost a decade he had his chance. She had other plans, though. She was going to retire for the night. Since the moment Shane invited her to stay, Chyna decided she'd be cordial and stay out of his way. Shane had other plans.

"Well, it's been a long day. I'm turning in." Chyna yawned and stretched, signaling more exhaustion than she actually felt.

Shane turned serious. He was not about to let her off the hook. He needed to talk to her. He gently grabbed her arm telling her, "Wait a minute."

Chyna turned. She found it hard to look at him directly, so she averted her eyes from him.

"Chyna, I may never get a chance to really sit down and talk to you again and I've got some things I need to get off my chest and if you've got some things to tell me I need to hear that too. Whatever it takes to come to some sort of understanding. If you hate me, I still find myself needing to know. Call it closure, call it what you want. But I've got to get my feelings out before they eat me up inside."

Chyna wasn't sure how to react. She wasn't even sure if

she was ready for a confrontation with Shane. One thing she did know was that it was long overdue.

He sat her down on the sofa and started a fire in the fireplace. He made them some hot chocolate, adding double shots of Bailey's liqueur to give it some kick. He put on R. Kelly's *TP2.com* and sat down. After a few minutes of silence, Shane began to talk. He wasn't sure where to begin, but his feelings had been bottled up for so long that once he began he found his thought's flowed freely and fluent.

"Chyna, anytime I fuck up I have a tendency to retrace my steps to the point of origin of where I went wrong and it always leads me back to the day we parted. From there my life took on a domino effect. I pushed the things that mattered most in my life to the back of my mind because it hurt too much to think about. For the record, when I left you, at the time I would've sworn my reasons were legit enough to back my conscience. A decade later I realize how selfish my thoughts were. I wanted to do the right things, get a job, be a father. But I also wanted things, a nice house, a car, money stashed for a rainy day. And a job couldn't get me those things. I had two felonies and no real skills."

To Shane's surprise she hadn't attempted to interrupt. She made herself comfortable, propping her bare feet on Shane's table.

"You mind?"

Shane shook his head, momentarily thrown off by the sight of her pedicured feet. Shane recalled how she'd rub her feet against the crotch of his jeans and he'd instantly swell-up.

"You were saying?"

Shane snapped out of his thoughts.

"Yeah, I was saying, a job couldn't cut it, so after we parted, I hit the streets twice as hard. Coming home to you and Chauncey kept me grounded, forced me to set limits on how far I'd go. Without ya'll, I had no limits. I was outta control. Anybody could get it! Anything could get got! I used material possessions to dull the pain, to convince myself I was right all along, it was *you* holding me back." Shane paused, then added in a whisper, "I was a fool."

It dawned on Chyna that he wasn't telling her anything she hadn't figured out herself. What surprised her was how much insight he had when he expressed his past mistakes and the sincerity each statement held as he talked. He hadn't even begun to convey his thoughts into words. He waved his hand around the house, telling Chyna.

"Now that I am where I always felt I could be in life, it's empty and lonely. It reminds me of that movie *Mahogany* when Billy Dee told Diana Ross ..." Chyna knew the movie Shane referred to as well as the quote. They repeated it together.

"Success is nothing, without someone you love to share it with!" They both smiled.

Chyna expressed things to Shane she'd been denying for years.

"DuShane, I can't say I've hated you all this time. The truth is, by being a bitch I was allowing myself the luxury of not having to deal with you, your incarceration, your second child, or Mia. I went through a lot when you left, physically and mentally. And I got my strength from a determination to one day make you regret leaving me and Chauncey. When I look around and see what you've accomplished, despite the obstacles, I am not surprised! The man you've become is the man I've always seen. I admit I feel cheated. When I was pregnant with Chauncey, I remember repeatedly asking you, are you sure this is what you want? Because I don't wanna wind up another baby's momma. Remember that?"

Shane nodded. He remembered as if it were yesterday. Chyna poured her heart out. Shane poured them another shot of hot chocolate. This time he doubled the Bailey's as Chyna reminisced.

"I remember reading an *Ebony* magazine one night in our bed and it showed DMX and his wife. I said 'I thought she'd be prettier.' And you told me you respected him because he stuck with his high school sweetheart once he hit it big, while so many other rap stars and athletes got themselves, as you put it, a *showcase broad* or a *trophy wife*. You said if you had millions you'd want to spend it on the ones who was there for you when you ain't have shit. Based on that statement alone I thought my spot was secure." She lowered her voice adding. "I guess I thought wrong." She took a sip from her mug.

Shane decided it was best he let her statement go unanswered. He was content with the fact they were communicating like adults. Chyna was just relieved to vent her feelings; now she felt she could move on.

"So can I get a tour of the house?"

"Of course." Shane showed her the basement, because she'd pretty much seen everything else. They shot a game of pool and continued to talk. She told him of her job at Simply Styled and dreams of opening her own nail salon sometime in the future. She asked him how he planned on managing his mortgage, among other expenses, and he told her all about Digimon Studios. He promised to take her by to see it before the weekend ended. Every time Chyna tried to break the balls Shane had racked on the pool table, she scratched.

"I see your game's a little rusty." Shane was referring to the billiard hall on Queens Boulevard he and Chyna had frequented in better days. He crept up behind her, holding the stick while adjusting her grip.

"You're holding it wrong. You've gotta wrap your fingers around the stick. You remember how to do that don't you?" he whispered in her ear.

"How's that?" she asked, breaking the sexual tension between them.

"You still got game." He smiled

"I ain't the only one around here with game," she shot back at him, smiling.

Chauncey and Isaiah were the first to wake up. When they entered the living room they noticed Shane and Chyna had fallen asleep on the couch. The boys woke them up. Chauncey was grinning from ear to ear. Isaiah did the same, not knowing why, just following his brother's lead. Chyna freshened up while Shane used the boys' bathroom to do the same. He made everyone breakfast then seasoned the thawed-out turkey, prepping it for Thanksgiving.

Later in the day the four of them went to Manhattan to play video games at a virtual reality arcade, then to the Disney Store. Shane purchased two Looney Tunes varsity jackets for the boys along with Mickey and Minnie mouse hats for him and Chyna, which he persuaded her to wear as they walked through Manhattan. All the while the boys pointed and snickered. They all ate franks and drank papayas while they window shopped. Their last stop was Digimon Studios.

From the outside it didn't look like much. Shane rented the loft in SoHo's warehouse district. The walls and doors were covered with graffiti. The entrance had a wrought-iron gate and an intercom with a camera. He used his key to gain access. Once they walked in it appeared they stepped into a technological wonderland. The place was empty with the exception of Ron, who was working the track board tightening up his latest project. He was surprised to see Chyna with Shane... *smiling* at that! Seeing her in such a good mood lifted Ron's spirit. He knew his brother needed peace with her before he'd get peace for himself. Ron gave Shane a pound.

"What's up, Bro?" Ron added. "Hey Chyna, it's been a minute." He kissed her on the cheek.

"Hey Ron." She winked, playfully punching his arm.

"Uncle Ron!" the boys chimed. They rushed Ron, trying to pin him down.

Shane laughed. "What's good, Ron?"

"For starters, that technique you showed me cut my

deadlines in half. That school you're in's the truth!"

"School?" Chyna caught Ron's last statement and realized Shane was truly trying to turn his life around.

He gave her a tour of the facility, pointing out the functions of each instrument. He even let her and the boys cut a demo. Chyna was impressed, she was flattered to see how much her opinion meant to him. He truly wanted her to see the changes he'd made with his life.

Shane and Chyna let the boys run wild through the backyard with Bolo and the pups while they debated recipes and prepared Thanksgiving dinner for the following day.

"Are you sure they're safe back there alone?"

He put her mind at ease, telling her, "The lights from the deck illuminate the backyard and the neighborhood is good. And Bolo won't even allow a stranger to come near them boys' circumference."

"But won't the dog listen to anyone? What good is that?"

Shane laughed, breaking it down to Chyna.

"Baby, you've got it twisted."

Chyna smiled. When he referred to her as Baby it stirred up old memories, although she was sure he wasn't aware it slipped out.

"Bolo understands plenty, especially being bred from such an aggressive breed of dog. But he mostly goes off body language and actions. He knows I love Chauncey and Isaiah and sees the affection that I have for them. We feed him together. That all plays a big part. If I tell Bolo to sit and then Chauncey says, 'Come here, Bo,' he won't listen. But then I say, 'Come here Bo.' It's like saying to him, he should've listened to Chauncey in the first place. But he won't attack for Chauncey because Chauncey doesn't know the order. Now if Bolo sees a stranger he'll protect Chauncey regardless. So if an associate comes by, Bolo notices there's no affection so he stays on point. Dogs sense these things."

"Since we're not affectionate, he's liable to flip on me, huh?" Chyna pointed the spatula playfully at Shane, hand on her hip.

"Although we don't show it, he can feel my love for you. Hear my heart flutter when you're around…"

Chyna blushed, brushing off Shane's statement as game and returned to her cooking.

That night they talked more, this time the conversation consisted more of a question and answer type of format. This time Chyna prepared the drinks, hitting Shane with the first question of the night.

"Where do you see yourself ten years from now?"

He didn't even have to give her question much thought, he'd had eight years of asking himself the same thing.

"Pretty much where I'm at right now, with the exception that how I feel now I know to be temporary and I need it to be permanent. I need my kids and my woman by my side so this house can be a home. Until then I can never call myself a wealthy man, and I don't mean dollar wise. 'Cause 'Family comes first!" Shane shot Chyna a question.

"If you could change one thing in your life what would you change?"

"Your eight years of incarceration and how I chose to handle it. I still think it affects Chauncey in ways I'm not aware of and I feel the way I dealt with things play a major part in that."

Ouch! Shane thought. *That shit hurt. I'm not feeling this twenty question thing at all.* He elaborated on her reference to his incarceration.

"Chyna it may sound crazy, but maybe I needed that shit to happen. If not, I wouldn't be the man I am today. Besides, the way I used to be, what good would I have been as far as raising Chauncey? I'd rather have done that time and learned something, than to have stayed in the street the same man I was."

She was surprised to hear his statement. "When we were together, did you cheat on me? And if so, why? And if we were together now what would prevent you from doing the same thing all over again?" Chyna knew the answer to the first part of her question; she was more concerned with knowing if Shane had given any thoughts to the reasons behind his past actions. In her mind, the first step toward change was for Shane to identify with his faults. He spoke slowly, deliberately, as if he and Chyna had all night... Actually they did.

"Yes, when we were together I cheated. Why, we started mad young, Chyna, and at that age I guess I looked at love as knowing who wifey was and putting her above the other broads who'd connive and plot for a piece of dick. Age doesn't excuse my actions, but in our younger years, we men are filled with lust, and if you're a street nigga you're measuring manhood by how many women you've ran through. I remember once when we were in our early twenties, Dru said you gave it up to Van." Shane smiled at the fact him and Chyna's memories could trace back as far as High School. "Remember that?"

Chyna nodded, a smirk formed on her face at the thought of such an old memory.

"You denied it to the end! I made a fuss about it to minimize the chance of it happening again rather than having an insecurity issue. I figured you proved long ago where ya heart was. Even if I caught you slipping, I figured it was payback for all my indiscretions you suspected but couldn't prove. That's that 'teenage love' Slick Rick was talking about."

Shane's mood got more serious, his tone was sincere. He answered the final part of Chyna's question. "As we get older, we grow up. We get more responsibilities, which lead to larger stakes. As a man you lose more for acting like a teen. Married men get caught cheating, they have to answer to their children in the long run. Risk their wife's health, their own health! Maybe lose all he's built with his spouse over some ass... Plus child support! Marriage is a partnership, an investment of trust between two people. A spiritual bond. I'm a man and that's why I wouldn't do the same dumb shit I did as a teen."

Chyna and Shane both knew that somewhere along their nightly sessions the questions jumped from being asked in general to becoming personal. The questions ran into the wee hours of the morning before they decided to call it a night.

"We've got a lot to do tomorrow, so I'm going to bed." She downed the last of her drink, kissing Shane on the forehead.

"I'm starting to feel we've called a truce," Shane told her, smiling.

"Joke's on you. The truce began after the first night we talked." Chyna began walking toward the bedroom.

"If you can behave yourself, I'm willing to share the bed with you."

Shane jumped up causing her to laugh.

"Can I snuggle?" Shane asked with a boyish grin on his face.

"Yeah, we can snuggle." Chyna pointed to Shane's crotch, adding, "No poking! I know your tricks." She switched into the bedroom letting her robe drop, exposing a cream colored teddy.

Thanksgiving Day, the boys attempted to bring them breakfast in bed. Attempted, because Shane's eggs were runny and Chyna's were burnt. They looked at each other, laughed then switched plates. Isaiah pointed to their glasses.

"Chauncey made the eggs, Dad. I made the orange juice for you and Ms. Chyna. It's fresh squeezed!" Isaiah commented proudly.

Fresh squeezed was an understatement; amongst the seeds and pulp Chyna could've sworn she'd seen an orange peel rise briefly to the surface. The two of them forced down what they could. By afternoon, Ron and his woman for the moment, Angie, arrived. They brought baked macaroni and cheese. Skatz and his wife arrived shortly after. Their daughter played cops and robbers with the boys.

Shane hollered at them from the bar, "Ya'll find another game to play."

Ron and Skatz smiled at the hidden meaning behind his statement. At dinner Shane said the prayer: "Lord, I thank you for this day. I thank you for this food. I thank you for bringing my loved ones and friends safely to this gathering. For showing me and my boys the importance of *real family!* In the name of Jesus, thank you. Amen!

"Amen!" everyone at the table chorused.

"A little rough around the edges, but we get the point," Ron joked, causing the whole table to laugh.

After dinner the boys taught Skatz daughter Brianna how to work the Playstation2. Ron and Shane played chess. Chyna whispered strategies in Shane's ear and he shook his head no while pointing to one of Ron's pieces. Ron jokingly asked if he was playing two people. Skatz made everyone drinks, music played, and the mood was festive. Isaiah danced with Brianna while Chauncey's main focus was watching his parents getting along. Everyone had a nice time.

Sunday morning everyone seemed to be in a somber mood. Isaiah seemed to be the only person whose spirits were up. Chyna was pleased to note how efficiently Shane got his boys dressed and ready for church. After the service, he pulled up to Mia's place, honked the horn, and watched as she took Isaiah upstairs waving goodbye to the rest of them. Chyna noted to herself how cordial Mia and Shane were to each other, realizing their relationship must be strictly platonic.

Once home Shane helped her and Chauncey pack, and they helped him straighten up the house. He pulled into the airport terminal a half hour before their flight was due and Shane hugged Chauncey goodbye, kissing him on the forehead. Chyna surprised Shane pecking him on the lips. He smiled.

"See you at Christmas?" he asked Chauncey. Chauncey looked at his mother, who nodded her affirmation.

"Yeah, Dad."

They turned to catch their flight, it was 6:20. They had 25 minutes until boarding. Shane noticed Chyna removed her cell phone placing a call as he pulled off.

Shane reached home around the same time their plane took off, when he entered the house his answering machine blinked. MacBeth, the pitbull pup aggressively shook the bottom of his jeans.

"Get 'em girl!" Shane joked, hitting the answering machine. The message read 6:20 pm, it was Chyna.

"Right now you're probably sneaking a look at my butt 'cause I'm walking away from you as I speak. We had a nice time and I just wanted to leave my cell and work number."

Shane saved the message to write the numbers down later. He sat down on the couch stroking MacBeth. The puppy relaxed through half squinted eyes.

"I know girl, I miss them too," he mumbled to the pup.

On the plane, Chauncey couldn't stop talking about the weekend they'd spent at his Dad's house.

"I'm glad you had fun too, Mom."

"Yes, it was better than I thought it would be."

"And you and Dad got along great!" He smiled.

Chyna thought she read something in her son's smile. "Don't get all worked up 'cause we're communicating and start seeing something that's not there." Chyna shook her head, smiling. "Kids."

"Well at least I don't have to feel guilty for loving Dad."

Chauncey's statement troubled her. She looked into her son's eyes and gently asked, "What do you mean?"

Chauncey shrugged his shoulders, feeling as if he'd said something wrong. She cupped his face in her hands, coaxing him to explain himself.

"It's OK, talk to Mommy, Chauncey."

"I just knew you didn't like Dad, so I felt guilty when we had fun together, you know? Like I was betraying you or something. But it doesn't matter now, right?"

"That's right baby, it doesn't matter. And no matter what, it's OK with me for you to love your father."

Chyna kissed him on the cheek, laid back, and closed her eyes. She felt ashamed of herself for confusing her son because of her personal feelings. All these years she promised she'd keep her opinions of Shane to herself, letting Chauncey form his own opinion. Obviously, she'd failed at concealing her emotions. *This weekend has definitely been a wake up call,* she thought. Already it felt as if a burden had been lifted off her shoulders.

CHAPTER 16
WHAT'S BEEF?

Fats sat at the Clubhouse round table nursing his drink. He'd been there for over an hour in silence with a scowl on his face. Gunnz observed him in a disinterested manner while toying with the toothpick in his mouth. Fatal sat in the corner appearing to be sleep, nestling his trademark MP5 in his lap. Gunnz couldn't stand the silence nor Fats' funky mood any longer.

"What's eating you?" Gunnz asked him.

Fats immediately answered as if he'd been waiting for the question.

"Everything! Shit's falling apart. This nigga Skatz not only bounces, but has the balls ta tell me ta pop off. Shane's got the nerve ta take our money but when a nigga asks for a favor it comes with conditions. And to top shit off, Khalid's stealing from us. No telling how long that's been going on!" Fats threw his drink against the wall and stood up, knocking his chair over.

"Gunnz, them niggas working together. I put money on it! Skatz just happen to wanna leave when Shane comes home, and they both are conveniently interested in going into the same business? Get the fuck outta here! Ain't that much coincidence in the world. I wouldn't be surprised if Khalid was stealing that money ta partner up wit them dudes. I want 'em hit, Gunnz, all of 'em!" Fats slammed both hands on the table, looking Gunnz directly in the eyes. He wasn't taking no for an answer.

Gunnz, seeing Fats was serious, took his eyes off him to glance at Fatal. Fatal shook his head, signaling he'd take no part in executing their own peoples, former members or not.

"Can't do it, Fats," Gunnz smoothly replied. Never one to lose his cool, even Gunnz admitted Fats' theory seemed plausible. He knew firsthand that Khalid was the one who'd gotten Shane and Skatz to have a sit down in the first place, but principle wouldn't allow him nor Fatal to murder their own.

"Fats, I feel where you're coming from, dawg. Skatz? He's got a right to want out if you're not giving him what he needs from the Family. But I admit the way he did it was fucked up. Not fucked up enough to kill him, but fucked up nonetheless. Shane ain't done shit really, but jump on an opportunity any cat fresh out the joint would take. Besides that, you're fucking wit a thinker. Remember that nigga Freedom he had beef wit back in '92? Rumor has it Freedom stuck his key in the door and the leaves from the yard sounded off two shots into that dude's chest and out of the pile steps a nigga in all black fatigues and ski mask. Cops found no shells. They claim it was a *professional* hit. Shane never mentioned it Fats, but ya know that's his handiwork."

Gunnz let his words sink into Fats thick skull before asking, "You want beef like that for this family?"

Fatal spoke, never opening his eyes. "Tell him 'bout Curly."

Gunnz nodded. "Oh yeah, you remember the Curly situation, Fats? The nigga swore on his kids to have Shane in a pine box by the end of summer. Curly was found dead in his bed. They said the killer entered the home and had a sandwich, waited for Curly to call it a night, and blam!" Gunnz pointed his finger like a gun, while Fats clenched his teeth in anger.

"Again, no prints, alarm system untouched. And the nigga might be trying to change, but trust me, let him be!"

Fatal chimed in, repeating "Let him be."

Gunnz continued. "You're asking us ta kill our peeps, Fats. That's crazy, think about it. Wasn't Ray-Ray bad enough?"

Fats decided to pull his ace card, hoping to pull Gunnz back toward his way of thinking. Fats tilted his head, pouring himself another drink.

"Bad enough? Fuck it, let's talk about Ray-Ray. Just to show ya'll I ain't the monster ya make me out ta be, we'll talk about Ray-Ray. The same Ray-Ray you gave money to ta leave town. The Ray-Ray I knew you didn't get rid of, but I figured as long as the hood *thought* she disappeared then the Family would've been sending the same message as if she *had* disappeared. I ain't say shit 'cause your way Gunnz, everybody's happy!" Fats downed his drink, slamming the glass on the table and pouring himself another. "How bout ya'll put the work in on Khalid, and I keep ya'll out of whatever plans I have for Shane and Skatz?"

Gunnz glanced at Fatal, already knowing his response.

Fatal was still shaking his head when Gunnz spoke. "We're not fucking wit it, Fats."

Fats couldn't believe two cold-blooded killers could have the nerve to set moral standards to their jobs. "What the fuck? Would you gentlemen mind if I sought an outside alternative to my problems, or would that also be a breach of scout's honor?"

"Do you, nigga. You feel it's yo world anyway! But I'm warning you, don't fumble the ball 'cause ain't nothing sweet about them two cats! You'll get Kha, but watch Shane and Skatz!" Gunnz got up to leave, Fatal trailing closely behind him. He turned back toward Fats, flashing him a grin.

"Strap up scrappy!" he said, closing the door.

Fats paid him no mind, he'd already begun making calls.

Redrum was on the come up! He'd put in his tenth year with the UBN (United Blood Nation). The set he was in, GKB (Gangsta Killer Blood) ran deep in Queens. He took his leadership seriously, enforcing the rules he'd sworn to live by religiously. He had finally acquired his own spot to hustle out of. The spot wasn't much to some hustlers, but to Redrum it was his sole source of income.

The spot really was a colonial house that belonged to Mr. Roberts. Mr. Roberts was a retired postal worker who enjoyed female company. At his age, female company consisted of middle-aged crackheads willing to give the old timer sexual favors in return for a test of Redrum's product, which at the present time was crack cocaine. Redrum extended Mr. Roberts an unlimited supply of work until the government sent him his monthly check. Most times, he received most, if not all of the old man's money. The old timer stayed broke, though by the end of the week he had one of his lieutenants distributing work from inside the house. Soon the traffic consisted of more than just the females Old Man Roberts freaked off with. His house was the only one that never used the Cab Stand. Rum pulled in about a thousand a day. A decent amount for himself, but hardly enough to feed the rest of his homies, Y.B., Bee Lover, Woo, and Mumbles.

His spot had been running now for three months. He had a few young homies hustling 'off the hip' by bike, but their profits hardly compared to the Roberts house profits. *If them greedy ass Cab Stand niggas was outta the picture, I'd be caking enough for all my damus ta eat.* He called his homies Damus (Swahili for Blood). Y.B. walked up with Face's sister, Dee-Dee. Ever since Face's disappearance, Dee-Dee played their clique close. Rum knew Face was catching a 'lick' occasionally, but never knew the details. They kept Dee-Dee close to them constantly picking her brain for details since she was the last to hear from her brother. They stood at the entrance of the car wash, on 220th and Merrick waiting for Woo to come through.

The trio did a double take of the black Hummer H2 coming out from a fresh wash and wax. Skillz stood observing the workers apply the Armor All to the interior and tires.

Dee-Dee squinted, focusing on Skillz as she tapped Redrum, whispering excitedly, "That's him! Rum, that's the nigga right there!"

Redrum had to stop Dee-Dee from pointing.

"I see the dude, Dee-Dee, but what about him?" Rum asked, trying to calm her down.

"That's the dude that had Glen on the phone the day he up and vanished."

Rum and Y.B. approached Skillz just as he was tipping the car wash workers. Skillz peeped Dee-Dee the moment she ID'd him.

"Yo homie, lemma holla at you!" Rum yelled out.

"Be 0-50 blood, he might have a ratchet," Y.B. mumbled, telling Rum in code to stay on point. Skillz didn't need codes; his instinct warned him to stay alert. As Rum stepped within range, Skillz pulled out the AMT Semi-Auto 9MM mini from his pocket, cocking back the slide in one smooth motion.

"Pop off or step off! Your choice."

Rum stared at the gun unafraid.

"I ain't repeating myself! Now bounce!" Skillz jumped in the Hummer, cruising toward the Clubhouse.

"Rum, you ain't gonna follow him?" Dee-Dee asked hysterically.

"Fa what? That's one a dem black rose niggas. He going ta they li'l hangout." He added, "Its official, Dee-Dee. If you last heard from Face through them cats, you can stop stalling and have your momma pick out a casket."

Dee-Dee's eyes began to water as Y.B. tried to comfort her. He whispered, "We'll get them niggas, Dee. For Face, we'll get 'em!"

Rum watched the Hummer turn off Merrick Boulevard

adding, "Sooner than you think, homie ...sooner than you think!"

Shane was walking Bolo down the avenue back toward his house when an unmarked car rolled slowly beside him. The dog's ears shot up.

"Easy, boy," Shane cooed to the dog.

Detective Rogers stuck his head out the window of the vehicle, while McCullem kept his eyes on the road.

"Evening, West! Just want you to know we're still watching you. Notice you've been keeping some interesting company lately."

Shane figured the detectives were bluffing, fishing for a lead regarding the Soffey & Sons job. He stopped and faced the car. He knew he'd been laying low for weeks.

"Officers, how are you?" Shane knew they were detectives, but decided if they wanted to pick at his nerves, he'd return the favor by downplaying their rank.

"Did I forget to pick up some dog poop or something? I know your caseload is much too busy for little ole me. Am I jaywalking?" He mocked the detectives by asking the mastiff, "Bo, did we double park the truck?"

Rogers had enough of his sarcasm.

"The offer's still open, West, 'cause the calls keep coming. Snitch won't leave a name, though."

"Don't you got a ticket quota ta make?" Shane continued to taunt the detectives. "Fucking beat cops... beat it!"

"Why you listen here, smartass..." McCullem jerked the door handle.

Shane shook Bolo's chain, and the dog stood on his two hind legs, snarling at the detectives.

McCullem got back in the car and pulled off.

"We'll wait for your call, West." Rogers shouted sarcastically as they sped off.

Redrum focused on the task ahead of him. Thinking back on the day's earlier event, his knuckles turned white as he gripped the steering wheel of his recently acquired red Lincoln Aviator. He sat patiently in his truck, cloaked by the blackness of night. His homies were 'blooded out' wearing their war colors... *red*! The truck held an arsenal of automatic weapons as they scoped out the entrance to the Family Clubhouse laying for their prey to surface.

Mumbles lowered the tinted windows of his late-model Lexus, pointing down the street toward the hangout. Fats and Skillz were leaning on the Hummer. Skillz engaged in a heated conversation on his cell phone. Rum and Mumbles pulled off.

"Showtime!"

The carload of gunmen masked in red bandanas sped toward the Clubhouse. As soon as YB stuck the barrel of the SK Rifle out the window, Skillz reacted, spinning behind the SUV out of his line of fire. YB let the rifle cut loose.

"Blak, Blak, Blak, Blak, Blak, Blak, Blak, Blak!"

Woo was firing a series of bursts from the rear window when Skillz took two carefully aimed shots, blowing out the back window of Rum's truck.

"Blam, Blam!" The force of the magnum caused the truck to swerve.

Fats fired three shots into the side of the truck. "Blaka, Blaka, Blaka!" the gun barked.

"What the fuck? Ya'll niggas want it? Come and get it!" he screamed.

Fatal, hearing the commotion, kicked open the Clubhouse door just in time to see the late-model Lexus coming up. He emptied the sixty round clip into the sedan. The occupants of the second vehicle never got a chance to shoot. The vehicle smoked and screeched as if it wouldn't even make it across the intersection. When Skillz saw the bullet holes in his truck he was ready to pursue the masked bandits. Fatal stopped him.

"We'll get 'em later, it's them Blood niggas. Any fool knows that!"

Skillz was tight, screaming, "*Ooo* dem niggas gon get it! They done shot up the TV's in da truck!" He jumped up and down in the street making a scene, still brandishing the .44 magnum in his hand.

"Will somebody calm that fool down? We need ta bounce before the pigs come." Fats put the guns inside his car's stash box and told Fatal to get Skillz inside his truck. Skillz continued raving.

"Get in the truck, Skillz!" Fatal had the door to his Hummer open, motioning for him to get inside.

"I shoulda killed them bitch-ass niggas at the car wash! *Ooo*, I'm hog-tying them little dusty-ass niggas and branding my name on they ass! Fucking grimy little dirt bomb motherfuckas! *And* I know where that bitch live."

Fats and Fatal could hear police sirens in the distance forcing them to shove Skillz in the truck.

"C'mon, nigga, we can't get at 'em if we locked up." Fatal pulled off, following Fats.

Meanwhile, somewhere near the Queens borderline Mumbles flashed his headlights, signaling Rum to pull over.

"What's up? We gotta get these whips off the streets before we get pulled over."

"Woo's hit real bad. I don't think he's gonna make it. I don't even think the whip'll last another block!"

Mumbles shook his head in disbelief as he looked at the holes in his Lexus. "What the fuck was dude in the trench packing?"

Mona called Shane around midnight. She'd gotten his message hours earlier, but decided to shower and prepare herself for bed before calling. She wanted his voice to be the last thing she heard before dozing off. When she called she was disappointed to find he was in a melancholy mood.

"What's wrong, DuShane? You don't sound like yourself."

"I've got shit on my mind and you may be the perfect person to discuss it with."

"OK, what's up?"

He told her about his visits from Detectives Rogers and McCullem, what they'd told him about Soffey & Sons Ltd. and the anonymous call they received. He was careful not to mention anything about the robbery that the detectives hadn't.

"I hate to ask, but this is my career we're talking about, so I have no choice. Before I stick my neck out, did you have anything to do with that crime?"

"No, Mona, and I'm not asking you to go out on a limb, I just need to know if I should start stacking my paper for a mouthpiece. Things are going good for me now and I just like to prepare for the rainy days."

Mona sighed, feeling his pain. With Shane's past, an anonymous call was enough to throw a monkey wrench in everything he'd accomplished thus far.

"Give me a few days to poke around and I'll get back to you."

"I appreciate it, Mona."

"No problem. You can make it up with dinner... talk to you later." Mona hung up.

A clever rabbit has three hiding places, thought Shane.

Gunnz and Fatal wanted to wait a few days before retaliating on the Bloods, but Skillz wasn't having it. He wanted retribution! By morning he'd concocted a plan for revenge. It hadn't been 48 hours since the drive-by incident, and Fats had already fixed the Clubhouse entrance as well as Skillz's vehicle, hoping that would calm him down. He wanted everyone to keep a cool head for their next move. Skillz still wasn't trying to hear him. As far as he was concerned, 'Any blood would do!' Fats decided it best they get someone who wouldn't be expecting it, but at the same time deserved it. They'd decided on a pimp named Cadillac Slim, a.k.a Caddy. The Family picked Caddy for two reasons. First, Caddy funded Redrum. They wanted to hit Rum where it hurt, his pockets! Secondly, Caddy was the getaway driver that got cold feet on Shane during the robbery that got him his eight year bid. Fats secretly had a third agenda, the hope that a chance to finally get back at Caddy would bring Shane back where he belonged: with the Family.

On this particular morning Fats sat in the Clubhouse with Gunnz and Fatal discussing how they planned on getting hold of Caddy. The Family didn't believe in drive-bys; kidnapping was their M.O. The trio noticed Skillz was running late, which was unlike him. A half hour passed before Manny strolled through with Mark right behind him. Another ten minutes passed and Skillz came through with a wicked smile as he plopped down in one of the round table chairs.

I hope this dude ain't go off and do some crazy shit, Fats was thinking.

"Had ta pick up a package." He smiled. "It's upstairs." His smile grew even wider.

Gunnz asked him, "What was so important about this package that it couldn't wait?"

"I needed to make sure he didn't skip town."

Fatal smiled, sliding off to retrieve his tools. Fats slapped his forehead with his palm.

"Unbelievable! What'd you do, Skillz?"

"Caddy's in the truck!" He smiled.

As the half dozen Family members walked up the stairs, Mark realized that the Black Rose Family was more than living up to his expectations. He also knew the time would come for him to 'put that work in' to officially become a member, earning his black rose.

Skillz opened the trunk of the Hummer H2 and sure enough Caddy was in the cargo area, bound with duct tape covering his whole head. Skillz had the decency to cut a hole near his mouth, keeping him alive long enough to kill him. Gunnz noticed Caddy was handcuffed from arm to ankle with the chains interlocking each other. Cadillac Slim looked as if his spine would snap at any moment.

"Are you comfy?" Skillz taunted, although the duct tape prevented Caddy from hearing or seeing anything that went on.

"Bring 'im downstairs," Fats ordered. "I need a drink!"

Skillz and Fatal set up shop. Fatal placed his tools before him preparing to inflict pain upon their prisoner. Skillz didn't waste no time; he punched Caddy in the face, breaking his nose. The duct tape caused Caddy to choke on his own blood.

Skillz savagely ripped the duct tape, causing Caddy as much discomfort as possible. Once the tape was removed he sat shackled to the chair, choking on his own blood and phlegm.

"Aw man," he sputtered. "What'd I do?" Caddy asked, pleading.

"You decided to be Blood, that's what the fuck you did! Your little homies did a drive-by." Skillz paused. "Correct that, *called* themselves doing a drive-by! All they did was shoot my fucking truck up!"

"Son, I ain't have nothing ta do wit that!" Caddy said, copping a plea.

Fats dimmed the lights, not wanting to see whatever sadistic torture they had planned for him. The last time Fats witnessed Fatal's work, he woke up in cold sweats for a week.

"Gunnz, turn the radio on, I don't wanna hear this nigga's screams." Fats turned to Fatal.

"Keep him alive. I've got a visitor coming ta see him." Fats got on his cell phone and called Shane.

"Talk to me." Shane answered, he'd just finished dropping Isaiah off at school.

"Long time no hear from, Dog."

"Fats?" Shane asked.

"The one and only. I need you ta come through da Clubhouse."

Shane heard faint screams emanating from the background. He immediately thought about Khalid.

"Come through, fa what?"

"I've got something you should see." Fats enjoyed toying with Shane. He hung up. Fats knew he would be at the clubhouse in a matter of minutes.

"Got him!" Fats grinned.

Sure enough, Shane arrived five minutes after he'd hung up. Gunnz answered the Clubhouse door with a blank expression.

"What up, Gunnz?"

"Ain't nothing, Fats downstairs."

Gunnz stood outside taking a cigarette break. Torture didn't turn him on like it did Fatal. Just kill'em was Gunnz motto. The kidnapping and torture was too risky in his opinion. Gunnz took a deep breath, savoring the fresh air. Caddy had pissed and shitted himself and the basement smell had become unbearable. The smell was the first thing to hit Shane when he entered the basement. With the lights dimmed he couldn't make out the shackled prisoner in the corner. Shane could see whoever it was; they were too skinny to be Khalid. Relieved, his eyes scanned the room meeting Fats. Shane brought a .357 Desert Eagle along, what he referred to as, 'the one-hitter quitter,' since one shot usually did the job. Fats spoke first.

"That was quick, Want a drink?"

"Hell nah, how can you down anything wit that smell?" he asked, causing Fats to laugh.

"See, that's why I love this nigga, ya'll! We got a dude damn near dying in the corner, and he ain't one bit phased by it."

Shane felt a chill run through him as he realized that he didn't trust his old comrades anymore. "Whatta ya want Fats?"

"You mean what have I got." Fats pointed to Caddy, snarling, "Get'im boy!"

At first Shane didn't recognize him. Skillz had cut his ear off with a scalpel, and his face was covered in blood.

Skillz joked, "You might wanna talk to his good ear."

When Caddy looked up and saw Shane he felt sick. The whole scenario made sense to him as he pleaded with Shane. "Please son, you ain't gotta do dis..."

Shane recognized the lisp his voice carried.

"Caddy?" he asked, still unsure of the man's identity.

Caddy nodded weakly, affirming Shane's suspicion. When he tried to speak, it came out in a hoarse whisper. "I wasn't built fa da robbery. I...I..."

Shane had to lean in to hear him.

"Tried to stop you...to tell you....but you'd already did it."

Caddy smiled as bloody snot ran off his chin. "...never did waste time, did ya?"

At that point Shane wanted to leave, more concerned with police running up in the Clubhouse at that exact moment. *Be just my luck*, he thought. Fats interrupted those thoughts.

"I figured wit ya'll history I'd let you put the sorry bastard

out of his misery. Kill two birds with one stone since he
fucks wit them Blood niggas. They shot up the Clubhouse a
coupla days ago."

"And my truck!" Skillz added, snuffing Caddy with a right
hook.

Shane looked at Caddy, shaking his head at the bloody
mess they'd made of him.

"Sorry ta disappoint ya'll, but I came ta terms with this
situation years ago. I've got no beef with this man. I put
myself in jail!"

His words gave Caddy hope, as he quickly spoke up.

"C'mon Fats you heard 'im, can I go now?"

Skillz cut Caddy on his cheek with the scalpel. "Shut the
fuck up! He ain't calling the shots, nigga!"

Shane looked at Skillz and turned to leave. On his way
out, Fats shouted, "That turn the other cheek shit's gonna
wear off sooner or later. When it does, you've still got a home
wit us!."

Shane kept on walking up the stairs. Caddy knew it was
over for him. Shane shocked him, cause had the shoe been
on the other foot, Caddy would've killed him right then
and there. Even facing sure death, Caddy hadn't learned a
thing.

When Shane stepped outside, Gunnz was on his cell
phone. He covered his phone asking Shane, "Feel better?"

"About myself....Hell yeah!" He pulled off playing Jay-Z's
"D'evils."

*"The closest of friends, when we first started. But grew
apart as the money grew, soon grew black-hearted."*

CHAPTER 17
STREETS IS WATCHING

Christmas was right around the corner. Since Cadillac Slim's disappearance, the Bloods had declared an all-out war on the Family. Mark had finally earned his black rose tattoo by slicing Dee-Dee down her left cheek to her neck. She had needed 160 stitches. Skillz talked Fats into it, claiming that since Bloods tend to initiate their own members in the same fashion, it would be sending GKB a message. Mark got his tattoo on his right forearm and had been showing it off ever since.

Khalid was still laying low. He hadn't been around since he got caught stealing. Grateful that the Bloods kept the Family too busy to think about what he'd done, Khalid had been reduced to earning his money the old-fashioned way— by working for it!

Mona was able to put Shane's mind somewhat at ease by informing him that although the detectives had nothing on him, they felt he knew the identity of the perps. He was just happy to know he wasn't a suspect. He was convinced Mark was the anonymous caller, but Khalid wasn't in a position to suggest a field test on anyone. Although he occasionally called Shane, Khalid pretty much went to work and came straight home. Shane did the same. Gunnz would drop off paperwork to Khalid every now and then, telling him to give Fats time to calm down. Gunnz's coldness gave him the chills.

Shane continued to speak to Chyna and Chauncey every night and take Isaiah to and from school. Often, Isaiah spent days at a time at Shane's. Mia traveled back and forth to Miami. Shane never asked her business. He was too grateful for the time with his son.

Skatman's CDs were making quite a buzz in the industry, and he pretty much had his foot in the door. All he needed was distribution. He still spoke to Pretty Boy and learned that he and Mia had something in the works. When Skatz informed Shane, he just shook his head.

"I hope she knows what she's doing."

He also informed Shane of rumors that Fats had an outside hit put on them and Khalid.

When Shane told Khalid, he replied, "Yeah, Mia told me. I panic everytime Gunnz drops off paperwork. I'm on borrowed time right now, Shane. How can Mia deal wit Pretty Boy knowing who he's dealing wit?"

Shane laughed. "Gunnz ain't out ta getcha, Kha. And if Mia knew something solid, she'd tell ya, and she'd definitely tell me, at least I'd like ta think she would. We should be glad she's on the inside, besides Fats went outside the Fam for a reason. So somebody's on our side! Just lay low and do the right thing nigga, we'll be aight."

"I spoke to Mia. She said most members are telling Fats ta leave us be."

Shane felt his temper rising.

"Fuck Fats, aight? Man up, nigga. He *ain't* that dude! If shit pops off, it pops off. He should worry bout me if he pushes shit too far." He hung up on Khalid.

Shane went to the studio early. He had a few projects he wanted to catch up on. Before entering, his eyes surveyed both sides of the street in one quick glance. The Glock 21 felt light on his waist, but he was conscious of its presence. He hated carrying it, but ever since hearing of Fats' attempt at finding a hitman to kill him, he felt the gun was necessary.

As he walked into Digimon, Peaches was at her desk taking

care of business. Shane was amazed at how proficient she'd become. He originally gave her the job just so customers could be greeted by some eye candy, but Peaches proved to be more than just pretty face. Shane had even stopped double-checking her work. This particular morning she had been the first to arrive.

"Hey lady, how are you this morning?"

"Fine. Oh, the noon session with Ambush was cancelled."

Peaches handed Shane a cup of Nescafe Frothe. He added a shot of Bailey's as he talked business with her.

"Yeah, Lotto said the group is trying to get signed. They meet with 'The Inc.' today. I wished 'em luck. What's that you're working on?"

"Just trying to think of a hook for Skatz new joint 'For Da Love of Money.' Actually, the hook's an O'Jays original, I'm just learning the song. He said I could sing the hook if I sound good... *And I sound* good!" Peaches smiled, showing off her pearly whites.

"Why you never told me you sing, Peaches?"

"'Cause I want to be taken seriously up in here. And telling you I sing makes me sound like a groupie." She laughed.

She's definitely got the looks, thought Shane, as he snuck a peek at her notebook.

"What're these?" He pointed.

"My songs!" He saw over a dozen songs written and began taking her even more seriously.

"Come in the booth, Peaches." Shane explained the concept of ad-libs and a studio engineer's job to Peaches. He asked her to blow a few bars and was taken aback by her raw natural talent. The girl could sing!

By the time Skatz arrived, Shane had laid her vocals down on one of his unfinished songs. He walked in just as Shane was talking to Peaches. His hands were animating the points that his words could not.

"Peaches, Skatz has a rapid flow, sorta like a Kool G Rap

sound. You try and picture his words as a gun on fully auto, 'La da da da bam, la da da bam!' And your voice would be the massage to the ears after all that rapid flow. Sort of like, 'slow down baby, slown down baby.' But draw it out slowly." Shane hadn't even noticed Skatz standing at the door.

"Ahem!"

"Oh, my bad, Skatz. Have a seat, you need ta hear this!" Shane fiddled with a few knobs and one of the songs Skatz was working on filled the room, only this time the song sounded complete. The song, "An Oldtimer's Twenty Bars" was twenty bars of freestyle Skatz threw together for Jadell and Rello's next mixtape CD. It was unfinished, but Shane had sampled an old Culture Club record called "Time" and spiced up the beat to bring the sound up-to-date. Peaches' vocals added a new flavor to the song. Skatz listened to her acapella intro blending into the medley.

Time won't give me time, 'cause time makes brothers feel
That though this cold hard steels between you and me
You know we've got nothing but time, but time won't give me time
(Won't give me time)

All of a sudden Skatz's lyrics and the beat came in right on time.

In my prime I took flicks wit chicks in Latin quarters
But now I'm old and niggas think them chicks is my daughters
Cuz I been down on this Quarter enough years ta cop ta manslaughter
Fa trying to be the next Rich Porter.
And it's a shame when ya 45, and named Bo peep
And ya call yourself an OG, but they call you OT
I hit tha streets for the bread and meat, like shit is sweet
Hand ta hand selling 'leak', but I can feel my bones creak

It's arthritis!....and youngblood, the way police ride us..
It's time fa me ta get it in weight or give it a break!
But I never did listen to my common sense, or my first
instinct
But I'm the first ta think. I'm thinking, Skatz if we stack
A couple of Gee packs, before they have me in a max
Niggas pointing like...he's back?
I could invest like monopoly in properties
And probably cop a proper piece of something proper
overseas
And though the clocks ticking, I move and stick and go fa
mine
But it's the blind leading the blind, so now I'm doing the
time!

Peaches's voice returned singing the soulful hook:

Put your head on my shoulder, touch me in the visiting
room
It could be that we lust for cheese, but our love overcomes
our tears
Oh and time, if you had been so much more...but time is
precious
I know this and...
Time won't give me time, and time makes brothers feel
That through this cold hard steel, you and me know
We've got nothing but time...but time won't give me time...
won't

Shane cut off the song. "What you think?"
Skatz nodded. "It's a lot better than what I had in mind.
Kind of sends a powerful message without me sounding like
I'm preaching, I'm all right with it. Let's press it!"
Shane knew that was the most props Skatz was giving
up. He was a perfectionist, and felt as soon as he gave
Shane credit, his production would get lazy. Skatz sat

contemplating what he'd just heard.

"What?" Shane asked him.

"You trying to make me tha next Ja-Rule or something?" Skatz grinned.

"Shit, we could use some Ja-Rule money round this joint!" Shane cracked.

Skatz gave him a pound. "You got that right" They laughed at the truth in the statement.

"On a more serious note Shane, what we gon do 'bout Fats? I ain't Kha, my nigga. I ain't wit sitting around waitin to be a vic."

"I feel you on that. I've been thinking." Shane told Skatz they needed someone on the inside to infiltrate the Family. Shane stared at Peaches. She was singing into a dead mike, itching to lay a few more vocals down.

She'd be perfect! What man is turning that down? Shane thought.

"Yo Skatz..." He nodded toward Peaches.

"Think she'll go for it?" Skatz asked.

"Only one way ta find out." Shane called Peaches over to talk, she sat in his lap.

"What's up?" she asked.

Shane explained the situation and she listened intently. The whole time Skatz appraised her from head to toe. Both men knew Peaches had more than it took to snag a baller like Fats. *The trick is making sure he keeps her around,* Shane thought. He explained the details of his plans to Peaches. She wiggled in his lap and felt him starting to rise.

"And what happens to this dude if I can pull this off?" she asked.

Shane and Skatz glanced at each other, Skatz spoke up, "Look, for your own safety, we think you should let me and my man worry about that."

Peaches leaned over and pecked Shane on the lips. "Say no more, I'm in, when do we start?"

Skatz began rolling a blunt. Once Peaches agreed, he

knew Shane would want to smoke as he plotted. During their months together, they'd practically learned to read each other's minds.

"After Christmas," Shane mumbled.

Skatz passed him the blunt and while he and Peaches smoked, Skatz laid an old skit in front of the song they'd just heard and stored it under a new name. "Time (An Old Man's Memoirs)."

Chyna and her girls sat discussing her plans for the week. Ever since she told Sherry and Dana about her spending Thanksgiving with Shane, the girls had been hoping the two of them would get back together. Chyna had informed them that Shane would be picking them up for the trip back to New York. As Chauncey ran around the shop soaking up all the attention the older women were giving him, Sherry touched up Chyna's appearance. Not that she needed it, but Sherry felt her appearance reflected the shop. Dana talked non-stop as Sherry braided her hair.

"Girl, you wearing that outfit..fa real!" Dana referred to the tan nubuck-suede capri pants Chyna wore with the brown leather bustier and brown leather six inch heels supporting her petite, yet muscular frame. The boots laced up on the sides, matching her top. Sherry gave her two long braids flowing down the front of her cleavage. Intertwined with the braids were brown leather straps, giving Chyna the look of an Asian Pocahontas. The women in the shop occasionally glanced in her direction, envying the attention Sherry gave her homegirl.

"These hoes are ready to kill you up in here, girlfriend," Dana giggled, speaking loud enough for the women to overhear.

"Cut it out, Dana," Sherry spoke in a low tone, so only Dana could hear her.

Chyna noticed Faye, a thirty year old woman, hand Chauncey a dollar.

"Give Faye a kiss baby." Chauncey turned his head just out of Faye's reach.

"Chauncey! Give her back that money." Chyna noticed his expression as he returned Faye's dollar. She called her son over, handing him five dollars, smiling. She spoke loud enough for everyone in the shop to hear.

"Give mommy a kiss, the five is on me."

Chauncey kissed his mom, as Dana whispered, "You taught him well. No telling where Faye's lips been."

The trio cracked up, causing unwanted attention from the customers. Faye felt snubbed by Chyna's action. Trying to save face, she spoke up, defending her action. She walked over and said to Chyna, "I didn't mean no disrespect, Chyna, he's just such a cutie."

Dana held in her laughter, knowing it took all Chyna's strength not to answer Faye sarcastically.

"It's nothing, Faye. Chauncey knows better than to take money from people, and especially not to be letting just *anyone* kiss on him."

The women who overheard Chyna's statement started snickering causing Faye to blush out of embarrassment.

"Chyna baby, it's me Faye. I ain't just anybody. Don't be so hard on ya little man. Soon he'll have all the honeys chasing him."

Chyna held up her hand signaling Sherry to stop braiding, and stood up facing Faye.

"Faye, that's *my* son over there. And yes, them hot-ass little hoochies will be all over him scheming and making babies, and I ain't having it, so I'm schooling him early!" She turned to Chauncey who was now playing cards with Stacey.

"Chauncey, tell Faye what Mommy taught you 'bout women."

Chauncey giggled shyly.

"Uum…" Nervous with all eyes on him, Chauncey repeated what his mother told him, "Quality is more important than quantity?" Chauncey asked, hoping he'd repeated her words correctly. The women in the shop hooped and hollered, clapping. "That's right, baby!"

Chyna wasn't finished with Faye. "Does my baby look like he needs for anything Faye?"

Faye didn't need to look, 'cause Chyna had Chauncey decked out in the finest threads.

"No," Faye answered.

"Then please don't hand my baby no money. He ain't no pimp."

Faye caught the meaning in Chyna's last statement, and felt slighted by it, but she knew not to push her luck. Chyna was in rare form.

At that moment Shane pulled his Range Rover up in front of the beauty shop.

"Baller alert!" One of the women hollered. He walked in and a few women threw catcalls playfully his way. Chauncey's eyes lit up and he ran toward his father, pulling him.

"C'mon Dad, Mom's waiting for you." Once the women heard Chauncey refer to Shane as Dad, Chyna smiled as their excitement wound down at the realization he wasn't available. None of the women wanted a repeat performance of the tongue-lashing Faye had just gotten. Shane walked up on Chyna, checking her out from head to toe.

Flawless, not a stitch outta place, thought Shane as he hugged her.

Chyna surprised her girls as she kissed him full on the lips. Shane took advantage of the situation, sucking on her bottom lip before she could back away. She smiled, whispering, "That's right, make me look good!"

She smirked, as Shane came back at her. "I'm too late ta make you look any better." He twirled her around as she modeled for him. Faye ran up on Shane in an attempt to steal Chyna's shine, since all eyes were on them. She held out her hand, flirting. "Name's Faye, handsome. And you are?"

"Taken!" Shane responded, eyes never leaving Chyna's.

Chyna loved how he smoothly shot Faye down, she was ready to reward him on the spot with some good loving, but still had some issues they needed to iron out. Chauncey was ready to go. He lugged the bags toward the entrance of the shop. Shane teased him.

"What's the rush? I got Santa hog-tied in the truck."

Faye walked away in a huff, trying her best to keep her head held high amongst snickers and jeers. Dana pulled Chyna away from Shane.

"Girl, you ain't gave him none? You crazy!"

Chyna gave Dana her 'button it up' look, introducing him to her and Sherry. After introductions, Shane asked Chyna if she was ready. They exited the shop. Chyna was sure everyone had enough news to talk about until she returned.

Shane had the house adorned with Christmas decorations. The windows were trimmed with lights and the front door held a wreath. Inside, he had a pine tree that sat bare. He decided he'd give himself the pleasure of decorating the tree along with Chauncey and Chyna. He assumed they'd be tired after the ride, but Chauncey jumped right into the task. They gave him the privilege of placing the star atop the tree. They also took the time to scatter Kwanza décor about the house. By the time the fireplace and candles were lit, Chauncey was roasting marshmallows. Chyna and Shane were lying on the sofa underneath a quilt. By midnight everyone was ready to call it a night. Chyna noticed Shane headed for the basement and stopped him. She stared at him with her *bedroom* eyes.

"You don't have to sleep downstairs," she whispered softly, taking his hand in hers leading him to the bedroom.

Shane treated Chyna like a queen, catering to her every chance he got. He wasn't sure where they were headed, but he was just happy they got along. He decided months ago to let her dictate the pace at which they'd go. He gave her a massage, working her calves.

"How come you haven't tried to sleep with me yet?" she asked.

"Because I'm hoping we have all the time in the world to reach that stage where you feel comfortable enough. I'm not trying to ruin our progress by risking a thirsty move or rushing you."

Good answer, thought Chyna. She placed her face in the pillow and enjoyed her massage.

That week Shane did it all. He taught Chauncey to bake cookies, making them from scratch. Him and Chyna debated everything in the kitchen from recipes to seasonings. Since Shane couldn't sleep with her, they did everything but sex, at times still giving each other orgasms. At night they would express their feelings to each other, each comparing how the other had grown. At times, feeling as if their ten years apart never existed.

"Have you had unprotected sex since you've been home?" she asked. Lately her body yearned for his touch.

He knew where her question was leading and he was tempted to lie, but he wanted to start things off with her correctly. He told the truth as he thought about that night he'd shared with Mona.

"Yeah, I have."

Chyna looked at him disappointed. "Why'd you put yourself at risk like that?"

"Because I had her hot and bothered and felt if I went to get a condom she would've came to her senses by the time I got back. I didn't wanna break the mood."

Chyna shook her head. "If you wanna be with me Shane,

you need to get tested."

"Would you be willing to do the same?"

"Yes, I get tested regardless and I haven't done anything since Tim." Chyna's reference to Tim reminded Shane how close he'd come to losing her to another man.

"Chyna, are we working toward getting back together?"

"I would like that." Chyna smiled, knowing she'd turned his question into a statement.

Christmas morning Chauncey woke his parents at 6AM. Shane rolled over sleepily, looking at Chyna.

"He can't be serious?" he moaned.

"Does it every year. You remember Christmas morning as a child. That boy probably didn't even sleep last night." She laughed, jumping out of bed excitedly.

For a minute she reminded Shane of the young girl with braces he fell in love with at first sight. He smiled at the memory; a teenaged Chyna, working at Mickie Dees. As Shane placed his order, he couldn't take his eyes off her. When she handed him his change, he allowed his hand to touch hers a little longer than necessary. He asked for sweet and sour sauce for his fries and young Chyna thought he was hitting her with a lame-ass pick up line.

"What are you smiling about?"

Her question brought him out of his daydream, back to the present.

"Nothing, just had a flashback that's all."

"Well come on." She grabbed his hand pulling him out of bed. "I want to see Chauncey's face when he opens his presents."

When they reached the living room Chauncey had already placed everyone's presents in piles according to name. They all took turns opening a present at a time. Chyna opened Shane's present first. It was an 18K rose gold, heart-shaped locket trimmed in baguete diamonds on a 20-inch snake chain.

"It's beautiful!" she exclaimed.

"Open it!" Shane and Chauncey said in unison.

"Knock on wood!" Chauncey added, grinning.

When Chyna opened the locket there was a black and white photo of her son in a black pinstripe suit. Shane placed the locket on her neck. Chauncey went next, tearing into a gift Shane gave him. His present was a virtual reality headset, and an assortment of Playstation games and accessories. Chyna smiled, Chauncey was ready to end the gift-unwrapping session and test out his new software. Shane opened his present from Chyna and Chauncey, jokingly shaking it and listening for clues to its contents. It was an oil painting of the three of them. Shane already had a place for the painting picked out above his fireplace.

"How'd you get it done?" he asked.

"We posed for the picture and gave the artist an old picture of you."

Shane kissed her on the lips. Chauncey tore into his next present. Even Bolo and the pups had presents. Shane bought them a silver water and food bowl with paw prints engraved on it. And to his surprise, Chyna and Chauncey bought Bolo a black leather collar with his name and address engraved on a single dog tag. Her and Chauncey gave the 'blues', the two pitbull pups, gray collars. And the terrier's collar was the same as Bolo's.

"Now I know who's who." Chyna joked.

Chauncey jumped in the conversation, "Mom, the female pup have nipples and the males don't. That's how you tell them apart."

"Excuse me?" Chyna playfully responded, then whispered to Shane, "Now he wants to be a veterinarian."

Chauncey peeked from behind the television, where he busied himself hooking up his Playstation 2 accessories.

"I heard that!"

Shane and Chyna laughed. Chyna had to admit, she definitely saw a different man emerging from Shane. She liked the *new* him.

CHAPTER 18
STRATEGIC ALLIANCES

Two weeks had passed since Christmas, and Shane couldn't help but feel a sense of loneliness. Once again the house felt empty without his boys, but even more so he missed Chyna. They'd gotten closer than ever in the last few weeks. As dusk settled in, Shane took Bolo for his nightly walk. Like any other night they walked from his block up to the Boulevard and back, while Shane puffed an L. As they rounded the corner of the service road leading to the highway, he noticed a man walking toward him with his hat suspiciously low and a hood drawn tightly around his head. His instincts caused him to quietly set the Mastiff in defense mode.

"Watch 'em, Bo!"

The Mastiff's ears shot up. Shane, conscious of the glock tucked inside his sweats, stooped down pretending to tie his sneaker. As the man got closer he asked Shane, "Yo, my man, you got the time?"

"Nah, I ain't got the time!"

The aggressiveness of Shane's response caused the man to hesitate.

"Yo name Shane, right?"

The question immediately put him on point, as his peripheral vision caught a glimpse of a dark figure closing in on his right. The man before him made his move.

"Got a message fa you from Fats!" Before the man could

reach his gun, the Mastiff had been given the command.

"Get 'em, Bo!"

Bolo launched into the gunman, knocking him off balance. With a vicious twist of his head the dog's jaws locked onto their intended target, crushing the man's throat. Before the second gunman could realize what was happening, Shane spun, firing two shots hitting him square in the chest. He stood over the hired thug as he coughed up blood. Delirious from pain, the man mistook Shane for his partner who now lay dead on the pavement, a victim of the bull Mastiff's killer instinct.

"Cal?" the man sputtered. "This was suppose to... an *easy* hit." That was all he managed to say as Shane bolted through the trees utilizing the darkness to shield him from sight.

As soon as he got home he stripped his clothing, burned them, and called out for Bolo in his backyard. The Mastiff didn't follow him home, but Shane knew he was there. The dog appeared out of nowhere. Had Shane not known better, he could've sworn the dog knew the severity of what they'd done by the way it slowly emerged from the darkness. He thoroughly washed Bolo, knowing the police would know the first victim died of an attack by a dog. A *big* dog, and Bolo fit that description. He was also aware of the fact that Detectives Rogers and McCullem knew when he took Bolo for his walks.

"Time to get gone," Shane whispered to himself.

Shane arrived in Bethesda during the first sign of daybreak. He dumped the gun, free of fingerprints, right before he hit New Jersey. He was now as clean as he could hope to be. He had called Khalid and told him to keep an eye on the house and feed his dogs, which was nothing new to Khalid, so he didn't suspect any trouble. He told Skatz of the need to push their plan with Peaches ahead of schedule.

Skatz simply replied, "I heard."

Shane knew that to mean he had already gotten wind of the attempt made on his life. Shane told him he'd be returning to New York in a few days with some 'friends' and to be ready when he returned.

He pulled into a cheap motel in hope of some much needed sleep, and decided he'd kill two days with Chyna and Chauncey and then meet up with his friends. Shane called Pryze first.

"Speak!" Pryze answered.

"I need a favor, my nigga."

"I'm listening."

"Me and Fats done come to a head. I'm up two, but I'm outnumbered. He done gone outside the line of scrimmage."

"Say no more. Who's quarterbacking?"

Pryze knew Shane's codes well; the situation was not new to them.

"I am," Shane answered.

"When?"

"In a few days... be ready!"

Shane hung up and dialed Dru's number. After a few rings Dru picked up.

"Dru," he answered.

"Dru, what's up? Imma need you in a few days," Shane told him, straight to the point.

"Not a problem, should I bring luggage?" Shane knew he meant his own artillery.

"Naw, just be ready!"

"Will do, Daddy O." He hung up.

Shane slept until noon, knowing Skatz would immediately update him on any events of importance. He dipped his black Range Rover into an IHOP parking lot and went inside. After his steak and eggs breakfast he drove to Simply Styled hair salon. He needed to see Chyna.

"Unfucking believable!" Fats couldn't believe his luck after receiving news on the failed attempt on Shane. Actually, he couldn't believe Shane's luck.

"Can somebody explain ta me why that nigga's still breathing, and two niggas is dead?"

"I can, my man." Fatal teased, with his index finger pushing his fitted LA hat off his eyes. "The answer is simple: you done fucked wit the wrong man, Fats."

Gunnz jumped in right behind his cousin. "Fatal's right, Fats. Every nigga in the hood gun goes off, but it's the way a dude *thinks* that makes him dangerous. And you done started a war with a thinker!" Gunnz smiled at Fats' discomfort of finally biting off more than he could chew.

"Now you can have the comfort of wondering if that's really the UPS man delivering a package when your doorbell rings." Fatal jumped in the fun, taunting Fats at his own expense. "Or if that's really the telephone man up on that pole." Fatal pointed upwards.

Gunnz laughed.

"Ay yo, Fatal, why is that homeless squeegee man holdin a ratchet?"

"Cuz that ain't no squeegee man, Gunnz. That's that nigga Shane! Duck Fats!!"

Fats slammed his fist into the table, shaking his drink.

"What the fuck ya'll find so funny, huh?"

Fatal wasn't used to being screamed on. He snarled at Fats through clenched teeth.

"*You* motherfucker! That's what. You done put us all at risk. And don't think for a second I ain't thought about sending your head by courier ta Shane just ta squash this shit you started. So if you don't like what I said, nigga, speak up now!" Fatal banged the table, only this time the force caused Fats' drink to spill over.

"Fatal be easy babyboy, be easy," Gunnz said. "Fats,

stop yellin. The last thing we need is to start some internal shit within the Fam." Gunnz mediated while Fats calmed himself down after Fatal's statement that trust no longer existed between the two men. Gunnz talked strategy, giving Fatal and Fats time to cool down. Gunnz came at Fats with a more diplomatic approach.

"Everybody aight? Good, now hear me out... Fats, I feel the same way Fatal does. You done fucked with Shane for no reason and started a mess. Now knowing him he'll lay low for a couple of days, then try and get at you. Unfortunately, me and Fatal gotta guard you so now we're in the middle. And although *we should*, me and Fatal will only try and look out fa your well being, but *we won't* seek out Shane! And that's awkward 'cause if we're letting off ratchets to hold you down, then we are in this shit like it or not. And I don't like it."

Manny interrupted Gunnz. "Since you've put the hit out, you might as well lay low and hope some ambitious young thug on the come up gets the drop on Shane ta collect that ten grand. That way your problem gets solved. And by laying low you're not putting Gunnz and Fatal in the awkward position of guarding you. You can stay at my place." Manny's eyes never left the money he counted as he gave Fats the suggestion.

"Cool, I'll stay at your place Manny, and I'll relieve Gunnz and Fatal of the burden of holding me down. But I ain't staying held up in the crib like I'm a rat or sumthin'."

"Whatever," Manny answered, counting The Cab Stand's profits.

Fats looked at Fatal. Troubled by his silence, he spoke up. "Fatal, you ain't have ta shit on me son, I got love fa you. Shane don't know you, so why I get the shitty end of tha stick?"

Fatal thought carefully before he spoke. "It just upsets me Fats 'cause this drama could've been avoided. And of all the cats who deserve ta get hit, you pick Shane? Shane ain't try ta steal sixty grand from this family. I mean don't get me wrong, I ain't wit hitting our peeps, but I can think of a few dudes who deserve it more than him."

Fats nodded at the truth. He knew he needed Fatal to ride with him and the Family. So Fats did something he rarely did. He explained his actions to Fatal.

"Fatal, you're 100% right. But I figured if I hit Khalid or Skatz first, or even simultaneously, Shane would be on point and I'd never get him. So I went for the hardest target first." Fats threw in as an afterthought, "I didn't consult with you or Gunnz 'cause ya'll said ya'll wanted nothing ta do with it."

"I'll give you that Fats, we did say that, *but,* I figured with all these little Blood niggas acting up, you'd hold off. We need to know when and where the beef is coming from. And we can't determine that if we're out here fightin two wars at once," Gunnz reasoned.

Manny also threw in his two cents. "Ya'll need ta calm ya boy Skillz down! That fool tries ta pop a Blood with each day that passes. The nigga done lost it, probably out there now starting some shit."

Everyone in the room nodded their heads in agreement.

When Shane pulled up in front of the beauty salon, Chyna's face lit up at the sight of him. She greeted him at the door with a kiss. It had only been a couple of weeks since they last saw each other, yet for them it felt like an eternity.

"What brings you out here, stranger?" Chyna asked hugging him.

He fished a piece of paper out of his pocket, handed it to her, and flashed a smile. Chyna, unsure of what she was reading, started smiling when she realized exactly what it was he'd handed her. She put her hand on her hip, waving the paper at him.

"So you think you're gonna get you some now, huh?" she teased him. Shane had shown her papers from his doctor giving him a clean bill of health.

"I know you didn't drive all the way down here to get laid?"

Shane laughed along with her.

"Nah baby, I brought the papers along; the papers ain't bring me."

He found her straightforwardness amusing. Laughter seemed like a good antidote for the last twenty-four hours' events. He knew he'd soon have a lot to deal with. *No telling what might happen when I head back home, so I may as well live the next two days as if they were my last,* he thought. He hadn't arrived in town with a plan, but at the first sign of trouble, Chyna had been the first person to pop into his mind.

Looking into her eyes he asked her, "Can you take the next two days off? We can take Chauncey to Disney World or something."

At first she thought he was joking, but she knew by the look in his eyes he was dead serious.

"Your for real, aren't you?" Although her schedule was flexible, she had inhibitions about taking Chauncey out of school for any reason other than an emergency.

"Chauncey's got school," she told him, fighting her own indecision. "When?" she asked.

"Right now! You only live once." He knew he had her.

"You want me to rush our son out of school and pack our bags now?"

"No, I want you to rush our son out of school and just hop on a plane with me. We'll buy what we need when we get there."

Chyna walked into the shop, grabbed her bag, and headed out the door.

Even as they boarded their flight, Chauncey couldn't believe his parents were taking him to Florida—Disney World at that, and on a school night too! He kept thinking he'd wake up in the school cafeteria, the victim of his own daydream. After exiting their flight, it finally dawned on him that he was not dreaming. They strolled into a Holiday Inn and checked in, then Shane took his family shopping. They bought all the things they needed. They even bought luggage.

After dropping off their belongings to their room, they went straight to Disney, hitting every ride they could. Chauncey picked the scariest ones. They bought souveniers for everyone they could think of. Chyna bought coffee mugs for Sherry, Dana, and herself. Shane bought Chyna a stuffed Minnie Mouse. She bought Shane the Mickey Mouse, and by the time they reached their hotel room Chauncey was exhausted. He talked himself to sleep out of sheer excitement. Shane finally had Chyna to himself; he had a lot he wanted to get off his chest and hoped she wasn't ready for bed herself.

"Are you ready for bed?" Chyna asked in her most seductive voice. She'd decided she waited long enough. She admitted to herself that she could no longer find reasons to deny herself the pleasures he *patiently* longed to give her.

"That boy really loves you," she told Shane, causing him to blush. Then she whispered shyly, "And I love you too."

His heart fluttered, his stomach twisted into knots... she had finally said the words he had been longing to hear.

"You love me?" He stepped closer to her. "Are you sure? I mean..."

"Shhh!" Chyna placed a finger on his lips silencing him.

"I've been fighting the truth ever since Thanksgiving at your house, probably way before that." She let her robe drop, revealing her La Perla undergarments. She smiled, whispering, "I'm ready."

Shane's thoughts were jumping all over the place. He wanted to share with Chyna the recent change of events in his life. At the same time he wanted to forget his troubles and luxuriate in the love she had to offer. He opted for the latter, kissing Chyna as she rubbed his crotch whispering, "I've missed you so much..." Before she could finish Shane began sucking on her tongue, kissing and nibbling on her neck causing her nipples to stand erect. She palmed his face in her hands, staring intently.

"I don't want no jail dick. You took your frustration out on them freaks, you gonna make love to me!"

Shane nodded. That's exactly what he had in mind. Chyna began to step out of her six inch heels, but Shane stopped her.

"Leave 'em on!" He squeezed her breasts as her nipples jutted forward, teasing his lips, inviting him to taste her. The sight of her two-inch nipples caused his penis to stiffen. He sucked greedily while fondling her other breast then sucked in as much of her 36C's as he could, circling her areola while stimulating her nipples simultaneously with his tongue.

Chyna threw her head back. Hissing through half slanted eyes, she shoved her unattended breast in Shane's mouth. He savagely sucked on it, massaging and kneading the saliva soaked breast in his hand. Chyna's panties were moist with her love juices, as Shane gently kissed his way down her stomach, trailing his tongue down to the neatly trimmed 'V' of her pubic hair then back to her bellybutton. His tongue playfully danced in and around her mid-section causing her to arch her back and push her pelvis toward him. He tilted his head. Stiffening his tongue, he ran it slowly between her pussy lips, then entered her as if his tongue was a penis.

"Oh God, yes! Don't stop, baby. Uumm, that feels so good!" she cooed. Shane used every ounce of saliva at his disposal to lubricate her sex. He loved the fragrance she gave off. He reveled in it, thinking to himself, *Damn this pussy's good, I could eat it for days!*

He puckered his lips, sucking in her already erect clitoris and gently catching it between his teeth giving it a tongue massage. Chyna grabbed fistfuls of hotel bedding as she rode into his face, grinding into his mustache. She trembled as she climaxed and Shane took every drop. He continued his tongue bath, using it to trace down her pussy to her ass crack and back. Chyna tensed up when he reached her ass, surprised that he licked that spot, but she was too hot to object.

He felt tonight must be all about her as he nibbled down her thighs to her calves, kissing the soles of her feet. Shane devoured her feet sucking on her big toe as he massaged her calves, making sure each leg received equal attention. Chyna reached up, grabbing him by the head kissing him roughly. It turned her on knowing he found no part of her body off limits.

She stripped Shane down to his bare skin, and when she looked at his penis she couldn't believe her eyes. His dick looked ready to burst! She got moist just looking at how fat and shiny it looked. She threw him on the bed and licked her juices off of his face while sucking his earlobe. When she stuck her tongue in Shane's ear, he stiffened up, moaning.

"Umm..." Shane's chest vibrated from the pleasure Chyna gave him. She smiled, pleased with herself knowing she hadn't forgotten what pleased her man. She sucked on his chest, adding gently placed love bites on her way to his nipples. She glanced at his ever erect penis twitching at attention begging for its turn of affection.

Chyna trailed her way down to his stomach, giving as good as she got. She allowed her tongue to play in his bellybutton as her juices flowed in preparation for the main event. She gripped his penis, squeezing it to test its girth. She puckered up and rubbed her lips between the head of his dick, while gently massaging his balls. Her tongue traced the vein going down his manhood, then back up as she took him into her mouth as deep as she could. On her way up she'd shake her head back and forth, stimulating the sides of his shaft. Chyna couldn't take it no more, she wanted her pussy *stretched.*

She straddled him and whispered, "I want you inside me, now!" She grabbed his penis, positioning it to enter her. She placed her manicured hands on his chest as she rode him. She was twisting and turning her hips in a circular motion as he held her ass cheeks squeezing her into him. By the time they'd switched positions, Shane was pounding into her pussy doggy style. The sight of her round ass teasing him as it bounced with each thrust was too much. He watched as the sweat dripped of his body, splashing her ass. He stuck his thumb in it while she was too horny to object. The headboard banged against the wall adjacent to Chauncey's room. They didn't stop; they were too much into each other to notice any of the ruckus they were causing.

Chauncey couldn't sleep with all the noise going on in his parents' room. He didn't know much, but he knew enough to know what they were doing. He smiled, placing the covers over his head. *That's right Dad, come home, where you belong.* Chauncey prayed that night that his parents would get back together so they could be a *family* again.

Shane laid in bed stroking Chyna's hair, his mind deep in thought, wondering if he should tell her what transpired in New York or just savor the moment. Chyna stirred in her sleep. *I know I ain't mentioning the two bodies, so why bring it up at all?* he thought, struggling to convince himself which course of action he'd take. He knew once he headed back to his hometown all hell would break loose, 'cause if Fats didn't plan on bringing it, he knew his own intentions. Chyna lifted her head off his chest.

"You OK?" she asked.

"No, I need to talk to you about something."

"You're not gonna hit me with the 'we made a mistake'

line, are you?"

"Chyna, believe me that's the last thing you gotta worry about me saying."

"OK, what's on your mind?"

Shane sighed, not knowing where to begin. He decided he might as well start at the beginning.

He explained to her how he and Skatman partnered up, which led to him speaking on the Soffey & Sons heist and the visit from the detectives, Khalid's stealing, and Fats putting out a hit on him. When he finally brought up the failed attempt on his life, he downplayed his part in it, claiming he believed he injured one of them. Chyna was surprised that he was able to keep such a straight face and such an uplifting mood with so much drama going on in his life.

"So what are your plans now? Why not relocate and start over?"

The thought had crossed his mind, but he knew Fats would take his retreat as a sign of weakness. The world was a small place, and he didn't want to spend his life looking over his shoulder. He'd already decided he was going to see his problem through to the end.

"I've gotta handle this, Chyna. I don't want no gunmen knocking on our door a year from now talking bout retribution and shit."

She noticed that his statement included her and Chauncey in his future.

"Promise me you won't do nothing crazy."

He figured getting Fats before he got him wasn't crazy. But he made the promise, just to put her mind at ease.

"Me, Pryze, and Dru plan to have a sit-down and work this thing out."

Chyna was no fool, but decided to trust that he'd do *the right thing.*

"Chyna, I need you to promise me some things... I need you to promise me you won't tell me not to go, and that you'll keep a pleasant aura around Chauncey. I don't want him catching on that something's wrong."

She nodded her head, acknowledging she'd given her word. Chauncey knocked on the door.

"So where are we going today?" he asked. It was 6AM and he was fully dressed.

Shane looked at Chyna and laughed.

They arrived in Bethesda, Maryland by 11PM. By midnight Shane was saying his goodbyes. Chauncey begged him to stay, as Shane gave Chyna a look that suggested she do what she can to make leaving their son easier on him.

"Chauncey, let Daddy go handle his business so he can hurry back home."

Chauncey nodded, none of them missing her emphasis on the word *home*. Chauncey hugged him.

"Thanks Dad, you da man! The kids at school will never believe this!"

Chyna kissed him as Chauncey ran inside to call his friends and brag about his trip.

"Yeah, Dad, you da man!" Chyna joked. Her tone turned very serious. "You be careful."

Pryze and Dru met Shane at a hotel as he updated them on his situation, telling them of Fats' transgression, the failed hit, as well as his plan for the downfall of the Family.

After their meeting he looked at his two homies telling them, "Aight, ya'll, all my cards is on the table. Ya'll don't owe me shit. So I'm asking, is you in or not?"

Pryze had a silly grin on his face as if he wouldn't miss this type of action for anything in the world.

"If we run into any paper, it's ours to keep?" Dru asked,

business like, as always.

Shane knew Dru's question was more of a statement. He and Dru were childhood friends. He didn't know too many dudes that put in work like Dru, but Dru was known to strip a victim of all his valuables once the 'work' was done.

Shane nodded. "Yeah Dru, what you find, you keep!"

"Count me in then," Dru said blandly.

"You know me nigga," Pryze said rolling a blunt.

By the time they finished smoking the weed, Shane's cell phone rang. He checked the screen and recognized the number from the studio. He hurried and answered.

"What up?"

"Yo Shane, it's Skatz."

"Yeah, what's good? We're on our way back now."

"Shane, I've got bad news."

Shane braced himself for the worst. "Spit it out, Skatz!"

"Khalid's *dead*!!!!"

CHAPTER 19
WAR!

Shane, Pryze, and Dru wasted no time. Once they reached New York, Shane contacted Skatz, advising him to round up Peaches and Mia and meet him at the Digimon office. Shane took his comrades to his home long enough to drop off their bags and strap up. They'd already discussed their game plan. Pryze was to get at Fatal, Dru would take care of Gunnz, and Shane would take on Fats. Since Pryze knew Fatal to carry a 60-shot MP5, he opted for a Mach-11 submachine gun. Dru brought his two .45 calibers and Shane holstered his Desert Eagle .357. They headed to the studio, anxious to hear the details of Khalid's death.

As soon as Shane entered the studio, he could feel the somber mood emanating through the room. Mia stood up, hugging Shane, her eyes red from crying.

"They killed Khalid, after all they'd been through together. I don't care, Boonk, that shit is foul! Fats would never have gotten where he is without Kha washing his dirty ass Cab Stand money. They could've given him a pass, Boonk." Mia put her head in Shane's chest and started crying.

He stroked her hair, feeling awkward. He spoke to Mia, but was addressing the whole room.

"I know how you feel, Boonk, but that's why we're here. We're all gonna make this shit right. I'd be lying if I said I'm here strictly because of Khalid. I'm risking everything I've

built 'cause I'm not waiting around for Fats and the Family
to try me a second time."

Skatz nodded. "I feel what you're saying, dawg, cuz Fats
been laying low ever since you got the drop on them dudes,
so expect some retaliation. Until then, what's the plan?"
Skatz was ready for action, as he spoke, he felt himself
getting amped up.

Shane sat down and looked around at everyone seated.
Mia was being consoled by Peaches. Skatz, Pryze and Dru
were expressionless, waiting for war. He finally spoke after
several minutes of thought.

"I've decided to break this plan up into three stages. The
first being Peaches meeting Fats. That's where you come
in, Mia. You're gonna contact Fats, tell him to meet you at
the club. Once he shows up at Foxy's, Peaches will meet
him. Peaches, I know how Fats is; he'll definitely holla at
you. From there you've gotta do what it takes to get him
to wanna make you his mistress. Meanwhile, me, Pryze,
Skatz, and Dru are gonna sit down wit them Blood niggas
and see if we can form some sort of alliance."

Skatz was ready to question Shane's decision on forming
an alliance with Redrum and the GKB, but Shane raised
his palm.

"I know what you're thinking, Skatz. One, why would
the Damus trust former Family members? Two, what could
they do to possibly help us achieve our goal? The answer is
simple; they'll trust us 'cause they've probably heard about
the failed attempt on my life and Fats' ten grand hit on me.
Second, they can help us by providing a distraction for us to
pull off stage three of my plan. We've just gotta teach 'em
how ta do they shit right. If they cause enough problems for
the Fam, we can sneak in and out handling our business!"

At hearing Shane's plan Mia calmed down. The chance
to avenge Khalid's unnecessary death seemed within her
grasp. She fixed everyone drinks at the studio's mini bar.
After passing around the drinks she asked Shane what was

stage three.

"That's when each of us sneak in, hitting the three strongest elements to the Family."

Fats, Gunnz and Fatal," Dru said, answering Mia's question for Shane.

"We've only got one chance to do it right," Shane added, knowing his old clique wouldn't be sitting ducks for the gunmen. Mia sat down, thinking of any holes she could find in their plan. On a whole, she figured it to be as good a plan as any.

"And what do I tell Fats if he asks what I want to see him about?" asked Mia.

"Tell him you've heard rumors pertaining to me and him, and you have a message for him from me." Shane paused in thought. "If he comes, the rumor is we have beef, and that you asked me about it and I danced around a straight answer. My message will be I wanna sit down and talk." Shane rested his chin on his fist, let out a sigh and continued.

"Whatever he says will be bullshit, but try and remember it anyway. He's really just there so Peaches can meet him." He took a swig of the cognac Mia had given him before asking if anyone had any questions.

"When is this going down?" Peaches asked.

"Tonight! Shit is real, and we all are at risk until we handle this."

Peaches panicked.

"What's wrong wit you?" Shane asked her, hoping she wasn't getting cold feet.

"I gotta go home and change outfits!"

"Dru, do me a solid and go wit her?"

Dru followed Peaches out the door without question.

"Son, this is you? Shit is banging!" Pryze referred to the studio complex.

Skatz saw Shane was into deep thought so he left him alone, giving Pryze a tour of the Facility.

"Come check the place out, Mia." Skatz tilted his head,

motioning for her to give Shane some space. Mia took the hint, joining Pryze and Skatz for the tour.

Shane poured himself another drink, allowing his mind to reminisce on the last few months. *I'm finally where I want to be in life and I'm risking it all right now for no real reason. If niggas wasn't trying ta body a nigga, I'd leave this shit alone. A nigga couldn'ta told me this time last year that I'd accomplish all that I have and it would be my own peeps that would cause me to jeopardize that. I've got a home for my boys, I've got my own business, a fat bank account and a hot whip.*

Shane tried to think to himself what he would've done differently if he could turn back the clock. His mind couldn't come up with a logical alternative. He thought about the things that mattered most to him and how he was risking his freedom for revenge. *No, not revenge. Peace! What am I gon' do? Fats put a hit out on me! Shit, I done caught two bodies! Premeditated when you add the fact I kept the burner on me for just that type of situation. Throw in my record and self-defense is not an option. Who am I kidding? Self-defense isn't an option period,* he thought, as he reflected on when he'd first met Fats.

Fats, the world is very different now, my nigga. I remember when we first started this mess we call the 'Family.' I remember when it was just us two little niggas wit big plans.

Shane laughed as his thoughts of the Family's origin came into place. He had taught Fats the art of allowing your enemy to be overconfident by playing humble. How 90% of our communication comes from body language. And Shane remembered things that Fats had taught him.

"Shane, you'll head security cause that's your area of expertise. Me, I'm gonna get us a clique of live wires, but what's gonna make us worse than the average cats is that we're gonna be organized."

Shane laughed at the irony of the situation. After downing his drink, the laughter turned to hate.

Fats arrived at Foxy's Den around midnight with Gunnz riding shotgun. He was 'gripping the grain' doing seventy on the BQE when he finally exited the highway. Gunnz advised him to park at a distance so they could watch the traffic in and around the popular strip club. He had a bad vibe about Fats meeting with Mia. He smelled a rat.

Fats' instincts were telling him to turn around and head back to Manny's crib, the spot he was currently calling home. The two men chose to drive Manny's BMW745, figuring the Bentley would cause them unwanted attention. Gunnz offered Fats a hit off the trees he was smoking, but Fats turned him down, knowing he needed to be on point in case Shane appeared.

He laid his head back, thinking about Shane and how he'd pushed him to his limit. *Should've left well enough alone, now look at me! My biggest problem is one of my closest friends. Scratch that, I can't even call him a friend 'cause you don't do a friend like I did Shane. I'll never admit it directly, but I tried to hit 'em out of fear. Fear that he'd come home and take over what I broke my back ta build. Fear that niggas would follow his newfound humbleness over my ego. That Shane's change would show these niggas there's more to life than being ghetto fabulous. Shit, I was right to; the motherfucka caused Skatz ass ta do a 180 on us. Skatz!... I could've taken his music more serious, and still had him on the team. I can't believe I've broken every rule I gave myself when I chose to be the leader of something as special as the Family. Had I stuck with the original rules, I wouldn't be in this mess.'*

Fats remembered the day he and Shane wrote The Family Code. He still knew it word for word, as he mentally checked off their by-laws.

1. Any punishment carried out must first be voted on by each family member.
2. Every member has an equal vote, regardless of status.
3. None of us will involve ourselves with another member's woman.
4. Family comes first, outsiders last.
5. No fighting amongst each other.
6. All members in charge will kickback a percentage of their earnings to keep 'Stash' growing in case of emergency.
7. Emergencies are as follows: bail money, lawyer fees... etc.
8. If we cannot decide what constitutes an emergency, we vote.
9. No stealing.
10. Members pay a fine for breaking a minor rule. Infraction of a major rule results in punishment being voted on.

Fats had a headache. His thoughts began playing on his conscience. *I've broken so many rules over the years, I might as well scrap the code. I broke rules one, four and five with just Shane and Skatz. I broke three every time I tried to holla at Mia. And Khalid..Aw man, Khalid! That nigga brought us to a whole 'nother level. I played myself! And this nigga Shane was suppose ta be my nigga. I waited eight years fa this? Ta get in beef wit my man? Fuck it then! I know your sneaky little tactics mawfucka!'*

"Strategy my ass!" Fats accidently said out loud.

"What happened?" Gunnz asked, thinking Fats spotted something suspicious.

"Nuffin, I'm sick of sitting here, let's go inside!"

Mia spotted Fats as soon as he stepped into Foxy's. She noticed that he had downplayed his dress code for a change. *This nigga must be ready for war*, thought Mia, referring to the green army flight jacket Fats wore along with insulated green fatigues and a matching cap. Fats had nothing but a thermal long john shirt underneath. She remembered

Shane telling her to try and notice if Fats was wearing a bulletproof vest. She saw none. He was dragging his feet in a new pair of tan Timberland construction boots as if he was in no rush to talk to her, she noticed his eyes scan the club focusing for anything out of place. Gunnz gave Fats distance, positioning himself in a corner where he'd notice any potential threat heading in Fats' direction. Mia noticed Gunnz was also dressed for war. Fats approached her, seating himself at the bar.

"I'm here, whatta you want?" Fats snarled, causing Mia to notice the platinum 'fronts' in his mouth. It was the only jewelry she saw, which was unlike Fats so she knew he came expecting trouble.

"I wanna know if the rumors I'm hearing are true," she said to Fats with the same attitude he was giving her.

"I don't know, what rumors might that be?" He smiled a sinister smile as if he knew the game she was playing.

"I'm hearing you and Shane got beef."

"Did you ask *him*?" he fished. He knew the answer; he just wanted to see how well Shane had schooled her.

"He danced around the question," she answered just as Shane instructed her to.

Fats looked at Mia through half-slanted eyes. "You're playing a dangerous game, shorty. What's the message you got fa me?"

Fats gave Mia the chills, she only knew his good side. She'd never dealt with his bad side before, she only heard rumors. She glanced at Gunnz, noticing he too was strictly business. Mia kept calm, relaying Shane's message.

"Shane wants to have a sit down with the Family to see if ya'll can call a truce while things are still at a point where everyone can work things out."

"So you already knew we had beef then?" he said, feeling her out.

"I know something's obviously up between you two, yeah!" Mia glimpsed Peaches working her way toward Fats and quickly tried to wrap up their conversation.

"I'm not sure I can trust Shane right now. I'll get back to you." Fats threw a hundred on the bar.

"Lemme get some Nyak," he ordered.

She stepped away from him to get the drink. Peaches stepped up to the stool next to his. She was dressed in regular street clothing.

"This seat taken?" she asked in a mildly seductive voice.

"I don't know, ask the chair!" Fats snapped back.

"Excuse the fuck outta me!" Peaches sat on the bar stool wiggling her fat ass, hoping to break down Fats' funky mood. *This nigga not gonna be easy,* she thought. She was looking exceptionally sexy this particular night, she had a mission to complete! Peaches had her Alicia Keys' hairdo going strong, and sported a short leather black snorkel type jacket and knee–high Petit-Peton boots with six inch heels. The plaid wool mini she wore showed off her curved, smooth caramel skin. Peaches took off her coat, revealing a black Baby Phat laced tee, threatening to burst from the strain of her cleavage.

Mia walked over, handing Fats his drink. Shane knew if Fats found out that Peaches and Mia were cool, he'd never approach her, so he instructed them to show a dislike toward each other. Both women put up a good front.

"Lemme get a glass of Hypnotiq!" Peaches crumpled up a twenty, throwing it on the bar and glared at Mia.

Mia huffed, faking agitation as she rolled her eyes at Peaches.

Peaches remarked, "Bitch, go blow in ya man's ear. Better yet, *blow on his dick!*"

Peaches' little outburst caught Fats attention. He glanced at her from the side admiring her ass, then her physique. Fats turned on his barstool until he faced Peaches.

"Miss lady, if I knew you had a mouth like that, I wouldn'ta dreamed of coming at you sideways earlier." He stuck out his hand, introducing himself. "Fats, and you are?"

"Pretty sure yo mama ain't named you Fats." Peaches' smile removed the sarcasm from her statement.

Fats laughed, sipping his Nyak.

"My name's Peaches."

At that moment Mia returned with Peaches drink and Fats' change. Before she could leave, Fats barked at her. "Bring us both another!"

"Same tab?" Mia asked, pretending to have given in.

Peaches turned toward Fats, making sure Mia heard her. "These hoes ask the dumbest shit sometimes."

Fats copped a feel on Peaches, rubbing her thigh he said, "Be easy, baby, it's not that serious." Fats was enjoying the two women's verbal catfight.

Mia stared Peaches down, pointing at her. "You've got one more time, bitch!" She stormed off as another barmaid served their drinks.

"What's with you two?" asked Fats.

Peaches shrugged. "I don't know, never did get along, some bitches are just born haters. Fuck her! So, where you from, Fats?"

Redrum sat on the steps of Old Man Roberts' house surveying the streets at each end of the block. Ever since shooting up Skillz's Hummer, he'd come by at least once a day to take pot shots at the Roberts' crib. Because of this, the house which doubled as a 'spot' wasn't seeing any money lately. Rum had enough of Skillz fucking up his paper, and for the past two days, him, Y.B., and Yellow camped out on the old man's steps, strapped, hoping Skillz had the nerve to show his face. Rum scanned the corners, noticing two Mercedes CLK coupes turning the corners at both ends of the block.

"Be O-50 ya'll, shit don't look right." Rum noticed the cars moving at a slow pace, inching at a speed no more than ten miles an hour as if looking for someone. Rum slowly stuck his hand in his sweatpants, gripping the butt of his revolver. Y.B. was the first to notice the black Range Rover turn into the back streets.

"Yo, that shit is hot!"

Rum got agitated at Y.B.'s praise of the vehicle. "Y.B., insteada drooling over that truck, yo ass should be watching ta make sure no shit pops off."

"Be easy blood, I'm on point." He screwed his face at Redrum.

The three vehicles stopped in front of the house. The tension grew as Y.B. began to reach for the Tech-9 he had stashed near the front stoop.

"Chill, someone's getting out," mumbled Yellow.

Mumbles jumped out of Shane's truck and the tension left the men on the steps. He walked toward his peeps, 'threw it up,' and began explaining the visitors he had brought along.

"Yo Rum, I think you might wanna hear these dudes out. They've got something to say worth listening to." He pointed his thumb toward the three car caravan.

"Who are they?" Rum asked.

"Shane, Skatz, and two other dudes."

Redrum got hype, yelling at Mumbs. "What!" You brought them Family niggas here? You fucking stupid or what?"

Mumbles waved his hands. "It ain't like that Rum, they got a little sumthin brewing wit Fats and 'em too!" Mumbles waved them over as Shane and his crimees hopped out their whips.

Redrum didn't know what to make of the situation, but he ordered his homies to do nothing. He knew Mumbles wouldn't have brought anyone to the spot that meant to do them harm. He still didn't appreciate him not telling his intentions ahead of time, but he'd decided he'll deal with him later. At the present time he decided to hear Shane and his men out... Mumbles not leaving him much of a choice. Shane spoke first, noticing how tight Redrum was at Mumbles.

"Don't be too upset with Mumbs...like I told him earlier we knew where to find you, I just felt him bringing us would show more good faith than us coming alone."

Rum nodded.

Shane continued, as Rum listened. He had a feeling the group of men before him held the answer to his dilemma. Shane sat down on the stoop beside Redrum.

"Do you think you can win this war against the Family the way your fighting 'em right now?" he asked, already knowing the answer.

"I think so, and if not, I'm willing to die before I let them niggas take food off my plate!" Rum answered.

Pryze rolled a blunt that Y.B. lit for him. Shane took in the scene as he watched the tension dissipate, realizing Rum and the GKB may be willing since they shared the same goal. He spoke to Rum, bruising his ego as he made his point.

"Rum, your strategy's the only thing holding you back. For every drive-by ya'll do, the Family will kidnap one of your homies. The only reason they haven't done it yet is because Fatal killed Woo, so they're one up on ya'll. At the rate Skillz is going, they'll be two up any day now."

Shane thought for a moment, then whispered, "I can show you how to go up against the Family, an eye for an eye."

"So basically, you want me ta fight your battle for you while you lay in the cut?" Rum asked, ready to reject Shane's offer.

"Actually, my guess is your mob'll be nothing more than a distraction since Fats and them are expecting you. That's where we come in." Shane pointed to his three crimees, continuing on, as he explained to Redrum how each of his partners and himself had an advantage over Fats being that they'd yet to surface. He explained how he and his boys had a better chance at blindsiding Fats if they kept their alliances amongst themselves.

Rum smiled, stroking his goatee. *Shit, we just might pull this off,* he thought.

"OK homie, what's our first move?" he asked.

You mean our last move, thought Shane, as he put Redrum on to the third and final stage of his plan.

Khalid's funeral was held on a dark gloomy Sunday. Puddles of rain covered the ground. Shane held Mia as she fought to control the tears streaming down her face. He hated funerals and was reluctant to attend Khalid's. He knew if it were him in that casket he would want Khalid to pay his last respects. His parents stared at the coffin in disbelief. All his life Khalid's parents believed him to be a law abiding citizen, never once causing them any problems.

The good die young, thought Shane. Khalid had a closed casket funeral, who ever did him made sure it was overkill. Shane knew it wasn't Gunnz nor Fatal for the simple fact Khalid's body had been recovered. *Not their style,* he thought. What really had him tight was the fact that Fats and the Family had the nerve to show up at Kha's funeral. After services were over Shane stepped right to his business, approching Fats and his crew.

He whispered to Fats, "Ready for the showdown, Ty?" Disrespecting Fats by using his *government* name.

"Whatever nigga!" Fats snarled, not wanting to make a scene.

Shane pointed to his neck at his black rose tattoo he'd recently gotten altered.

"Like my new tattoo?" he asked, smiling.

Fats looked at Shane's tattoo. He'd added a slash through his black rose.

Shane turned back and looked at Fats, screwing his face as he told him, "See you soon, nigga."

Then he walked away with his hands in his pocket fingering the Snubnose.

It was on! Between the GKB and Shane's people after the Family, it was just a matter of time before the drama unfolded. Shane had noticed Peaches at Fats' side at Khalid's funeral, which was taken as a good sign. She'd successfully infiltrated the enemy. All he waited for was a phone call from her giving him Fats' location.

Meanwhile, GKB was giving the Family hell. At Shane's advice Redrum switched tactics. He had each Family member tailed, successfully locating Gunnz's and Skillz's crib. Now that the GKB knew where the two of them rested their heads, they decided to turn up the pressure. Shane and Pryze sat in Dru's Benz adjacent to Dru and Skatz in his own white Benz. They'd been waiting a week for Peaches to call. Shane's cell phone rang. Peaches sat waiting for Shane to pick up his cell phone. She sat on the bed in Manny's spare bedroom while Fats went to handle some *unknown* business.

"Hello," Shane answered.

About time thought Peaches, as she quickly brought Shane up to date on Fats' movements. She explained that Manny's place was like a fortress and that two vicious dogs patrolled the grounds at all times. In short, she assured him if they were to get at Fats successfully, it couldn't happen at Manny's crib.

"Me and Fats are going out tonight. I've promised him something special." Peaches broke down her plan to him. She explained the promise she'd made to Fats: a threesome involving her girlfriend Poison.

Shane interrupted her, prepared to punch holes in Peaches' plan.

"Can we trust Poison?" he asked, not wanting to leave

any unnecessary witnesses.

"I guarantee we can trust Poison. I even introduced Fats to the real Poison just to ensure this 'date' goes down. Be at the Radisson at midnight, the one in the Bronx, near Parkchester." She hung up.

"Was that the call?" Pryze asked, passing Shane a freshly lit blunt.

He nodded. "Yep!" We're on...tonight at twelve, we all make our move! I hit Fats, you hit Fatal, Dru takes Gunnz."

At 10PM, Digimon Studios resembled a shooting range as Shane and his crimees prepared for war. Since Fats gave Gunnz and Fatal the night off, they knew this would be their only chance to hit the trio while they were isolated. Shane, outfitted in a Kevlar body armor vest made by Point Blank shot questions at his partners to ensure they were focused.

Shane pointed. "Pryze, what's your job?"

"Fatal! Go through the adjoining blocks backstreet, second floor window is the house's weak spot. In and out, make it look like a blotched burglary," he answered.

Again Shane pointed. "Dru, your job?"

"Catch Gunnz slipping, put three in 'im. Take his shit so it looks like a robbery."

Shane nodded, pleased his boys had their shit down pat. Shane added, "Fats' shit ain't looking like nothing but what it is .... *Murda!*" For a split second Shane hated how he sounded, but quickly shook it off. He had work to do, as he focused on the task ahead he turned to Skatz.

"Stay by the phone, expect a call from each of us around 12:30. If things are successful, we'll call in for a 1AM session. If we fail, we'll call in canceling a session."

Everyone nodded. Shane headed out the door first since his ride to the Radisson would be the longest.

"What do you want?" Mia yelled through the half-opened door. She'd left the chain on the door, refusing to let Mark in as he swaggered on her front steps apparently drunk.

"I asked you a question, are you fuckin P.B.?" Mark slurred, referring to all the time Mia spent with Pretty.

"What do you care, huh? You're out there doing you, hanging with the same niggas gunning for Isaiah's father. If they'll flip on him, then you're definitely expendable, dumb ass. And no, I'm *not* fucking Pretty Boy. I ain't dumb enough to go through the whole crew, OK Mark? Now kick rocks!" Mia slammed the door in his face.

"Guess what, bitch? I kick ass better!" Mark kicked in Mia's front door as she shielded her face from the splintering wood that flew forward...

CHAPTER 20
POLI (TRICKS)

As Shane drove down the Bruckner Expressway, his conscience fought with what he was about to do. He flashed backed to him and Fats playing 'skelzies' as kids. How they used to use the caps from the 'push-up pops' as tops, to how they'd steal the Play-Doh from Woolworths to put in the tops to give them the proper weight. Fats and Shane would take turns, one distracting the sales clerk while the other boosted the Play-Doh. Shane smiled, as he reminisced on the day him and Fats ran away from home with a bookbag full of tuna sandwiches. With five dollars each they swore to trek their way to Hollywood, only to head back home by midnight, not even making their way past midtown Manhattan. Shane sighed.

There's gotta be another way. Although he had doubts about his next move, he went against his better judgement, still heading toward his destination.

Peaches laid out two sexy lace lingerie sets on the foot of the hotel's bed.

"Which color do you want me in Daddy, the red, or the black?" she asked, stroking Fats ego as she waited on Shane.

"The red one; ya girl Poison can wear the black. Where is

she anyway? I'm ready to get the *jumpoff* jumping off." Fats grinned at the thought of sexing not one, but two hoes the likes of Peaches and Poison.

"Fats, lemme go freshen up, I know that girl's due any minute now." Peaches slid into the bathroom and dialed Shane's number. He picked up on the first ring.

"What's up?" he answered.

"Where you at? This nigga getting restless," Peaches whispered into the phone, using her foot to flush the toilet.

"I just pulled into the lot. What's your room number?" he asked, as the adrenaline rush took control of his body.

"Room 112," Peaches answered

"Peaches this is no time for games—"

"Nigga, this is Fats were talking about. He specifically asked for room 112. He asked for room 69, but they don't have one. Now hurry up! I'm coming downstairs." Peaches stepped out the bathroom carrying her cell phone. Fats had jokes.

"Girl I hope you ain't take a shit spoiling my plans." He stuck out his tongue and flicked it at her. "Cause a nigga's licking all ya'll assholes ta night!"

Peaches twisted her face. "Very fucking romantic, Fats. Don't embarrass me wit yo bullshit when I bring Poison up here." Peaches headed out the door twisting her fat ass, leaving him salivating. She stuck her head back in the door telling him. "I want you butt naked and standing at attention when we get up here, don't spoil my fantasy!"

Pryze had on all black as he moved quietly through the backyard of Fatal's house. He'd parked his car on the corner and moved through the shadows with the grace of a cat. He took notice of the second floor window he would use to gain entrance. *Doesn't look like ole boy home yet. Guess I'll have ta wait for'em inside..*

Pryze tested the pipe alongside the house for sturdiness before effortlessly climbing to the second story level. Pryze stuck a pocket size mirror toward the corner of the window peeping inside without revealing himself. He knew from his cat burglar days with Shane that the moonlight would illuminate his black silhouette even in the dark. He went into the side pocket of his black fatigues, retrieving a pocket glass cutter and cut a half moon around the window lock. Afterwards he placed a wad of clay against the window's cut to muffle the sound. He tapped the clay and lowered it inside the house. He stuck his finger in the half moon, turning the lock and lifting the window while gently making his way into the house.

Gunnz sat in the driver's seat of his Mercedes Benz fiddling with Skatzman's CD in his hand. He looked at the production credits one last time. *Digimon Studios, catchy little name.*

It had taken him some time but he'd finally tracked down the address for Shane and Skatz's studio. He noticed the traffic was pretty heavy in and out the spot. He also knew he couldn't get past the wrought iron gate without being detected. The studio was secure.

Gotta go with Plan B.

Gunnz exited the vehicle and headed toward the studio's entrance. Gunnz rang the buzzer and stood under the camera. To his surprise, a buzzer sounded, clicking the gate open and allowing him access. When he reached the first floor, Skatz stood about a foot from him. Gunnz looked around whistling.

"This is a nice set-up, Skatz." He tapped the wood on the reception area's desk. "I always told Fats you was our way out the hood. He should've took you as serious as Shane did." Gunnz walked closer to Skatz, still talking. "And you know Fats can't admit he fucked up, so he starts a war over nothing." Gunnz nodded toward the chair facing the couch. "Can I sit down?" he asked.

Skatz began to realize that he came to talk. He remembered how Gunnz spoke up for him in front of Foxy's Den and how he was always the first to diffuse the tension between him and Fats. Skatz sat down opposite him. "So whatta ya want, Gunnz?"

"All this bullshit ta come to an end," he answered. "The walls are closing in on me, son. GKB knows where I live, and lately them cats seem a lot more smarter. You know, nowadays these young kids are either real smart or real dumb. I'm tired, Skatz....I'm not feeling this shit anymore."

"You want a drink?" Skatz knew Gunnz wasn't trying to con him, he *looked* tired!

Gunnz shook his head. "Nah, I'm good. Besides, your troops will be back soon." Gunnz sat up, looking Skatz dead in the eye and said, "Skatz, ya'll ain't gotta hit me and Fatal. Your problem is Fats, cut off the head and the body can't function. Me and Fatal will just retire and find us a hobby." Gunnz got up to leave, turning toward Skatz he said, "Oh yeah, when Peaches is done setting up Fats, she ain't gotta leave town. She can continue working for ya'll."

"You know?" Skatz asked, surprised Gunnz knew the inside scoop.

"Yeah, I remembered her from Shane's party...did my homework from there." Gunnz tossed Skatzman's CD at him. "Your spitting has stepped up too! Number three's my favorite song." Gunnz walked out the studio, humming the baseline to Skatz's song. Skatz sat back took a deep breath and sighed. All of a sudden he jumped up from his seat. *Oh shit!*

He ran to the phone, quickly dialing Dru's cell phone.

"Gotta stop this nigga Dru," he mumbled to himself getting only a voice mail message.

He had his cell phone turned off. So did Shane and Pryze.

Standard Operating Procedure, thought Skatz, as he shook his head, slowly rubbing his temples. He felt the beginning of a headache forming.

Peaches came downstairs, bumping into Shane on her way out the elevator. He grabbed her by her elbow. "Wait in the truck, the door's open. Keep it running and jump in the passenger seat." He took the elevator up to the first floor and checked the staircase doors to make sure they opened. As he crept toward Room 112 he pulled out the key card Peaches handed him at the elevator. He pushed the card into the doorlock then pushed his way in. "Don't move!" Shane pointed the 357 auto toward the lump in the bedsheets and fired twice. "Blaka...Blaka!"

The sound of the Magnum was enough to make Fats panic, he sprung out of the bathroom door, firing wildly. "Brap! Brap! Brap!"

Shane dropped to one knee, firing once. "Blaka!"

The force of the bullet knocked Fats into the wall. Shane went to put another slug in him just *to make sure,* when he heard screams, followed by the static of security radios. Shane stuck his gun in the doorway firing one high shot and jetted down the staircase. When he reached the parking lot Peaches had done exactly what he told her to do. They pulled off slowly, ignoring the sirens in the background. Peaches hugged his arm, placing her head on Shane's shoulder pretending to be two lovers enjoying each other's company. A mile later Shane ripped off the stolen license plate he'd stuck over his real plate, while removing the double-sided plumbing tape.

Dru began to get restless waiting on Gunnz and decided he'd carry out the orders his own way. He scouted the circumference of Gunnz house, arriving at the window he considered the weak spot of the structure. Gunnz's first floor window had a screen facing the outside. Dru stuck two toothpicks in the holes outside the frame, wiggling the screen off its track. Sticking his index finger inside, he used the proper levers to push the screen up. He used a mini-screwdriver to open the window, then returned everything to its proper position. He sat inside Gunnz house waiting for him to enter.

No need to waste gas waiting on this dude ta show up, thought Dru, as he sat with his two 45's facing the front door.

Pryze crept around the squeaky baseboard in Fatal's house. As he passed the hallway he noticed a door halfway open. As he neared it he heard a voice, "I've been expecting you."

Fatal sat in the corner chair of his bedroom with the MP5 resting in his lap. They could see each other through the mirror on Fatal's dresser. Fatal had an advantage since Pryze's eyes hadn't had a chance to adjust to the darkness and Fatal knew his own house. He spoke to Pryze through the door.

"That Mach you're holding will slice through this door like rice paper. Same goes for my baby." Fatal patted the Heckler & Koch submachine gun, "If you're here then you're unaware of the fact that Gunnz is talking with Skatz as we speak. You've got two options, Pryze. Bang it out right here and now, or go get the facts before you fuck ya'self!" Fatal's face was contorted with anger. Pryze knew he couldn't kill him without possibly killing himself. Pryze was no fool. He opted for the latter of Fatal's *options*.

"Gunnz speaking to Skatz right now, huh?" Pryze was kneeling behind the door, just in case Fatal had a change of heart. "In that case, I think Imma go hear the message... you walking me to the door?"

Fatal cocked the MP5, answering. "Nah, nigga, go out the way you came in, and expect a bill for my window." Fatal waved Pryze away with a motion of the submachine gun.

"Oh... and Pryze, if you come back, I'm shooting first. I'll question ya corpse!"

As soon as Dru heard Gunnz put his key in the door and open it, he began firing! Gunnz looked as if he was doing the 'electric boogie' as Dru pumped a minimum of six rounds in him. When Dru stood over him, Gunnz was bleeding from the mouth. He stripped Gunnz of his jewelry, watch, money and firearm. He turned to put one last slug between Gunnz eyes, but when he noticed the pool of blood about to ruin his black suede Timbs he changed his mind.

"Fuck it, if the bloods that dark, that li'l nigga's history!" Dru mumbled to himself, stepping off into the night.

CHAPTER 21
DESPERATE MEASURES

Skatz had no other choice but to sit by the phone. Around 12:45 Pryze called canceling his non-existent session. By 12:50 Shane called in confirming a 1AM session. Skatz knew that to mean Shane had handled his business and Pryze hadn't. Skatz figured Fatal probably gave Pryze the same message he'd gotten from Gunnz. It was 1:05 a.m. by the time Dru called.

Skatz answered before the first ring was completed. "Hello?"

"Skatz, I'm running late but that one o'clock session is definitely a go." Dru said, whipping the Benz in and out of traffic and admiring the Rolex watch he lifted off Gunnz's body. Skatz dropped the phone...

"Aw man!" Skatz said, letting the receiver lay where he'd dropped it.

Skatz said nothing until everyone arrived. Then he ran through the task of updating everyone on Gunnz's visit.

"He even knew about Peaches and didn't blow it up. So he couldn'ta been gaming us!" Skatz sounded stressed but Dru thought nothing of it.

"Look, fuck it! Son 'assed out' trying ta play the middle."

Shane didn't argue with Dru, he'd done exactly what Shane knew he'd do...get the job done!

Pryze broke down his story, explaining how Fatal had the drop on him from the jump. As far as Shane was concerned,

Pryze's story confirmed the fact that the two of them truly wanted to stay neutral. Had Fatal even thought of Pryze as the enemy, he wouldn't have hesitated at killing him.

Shane told his story, summing it up as, "He must've caught on at the last minute. All I can say is, we gotta hope Fatal thinks the Bloods killed Gunnz."

Dru rolled a blunt from a dime bag he took off Gunnz.

"I left a red bandana near the body. Can't never be too careful when there's no statute of limitations." Dru smiled, inhaling the smoke.

"Anyone want a toke of this *Dead Man Walking*?" he asked. He was the only one who laughed at the joke.

Shane sat in his living room along with Pryze and Dru. He had a feeling that the drama between Fats and him wasn't over. Pryze and Dru decided to stick around in case Fatal showed up to avenge his cousin's death. Pryze and Dru smoked all day while Shane laid in the cut getting his thoughts together.

Damn, he thought to himself. *I've got a family waiting on me and I'm laying up wit these niggas like we're 19 years old again. I'm not built for this shit no more. This shit ain't about franks! The hit on Fats was sloppy, Gunnz died for nothing, and I still feel paranoid.* Shane's cell phone rang, interrupting his thoughts. It was Skatz on the other line.

"Shane, you won't believe this shit! Turn on the news!" Shane grabbed the remote and turned to the news channel. The newscasters were in front of Gunnz's crib. He turned the volume up...

"Sources say at around midnight gunplay resulted in the shooting of Kelvin Griffiths. Mr. Griffiths is listed in critical condition at Mary Immaculate Hospital, under police protection. Law enforcement officials are unsure what prompted last night's attack, but detectives suspect gang violence..."

"Unbelievable! I saw that nigga in a pool of burgundy blood. He should be dead!" Dru pointed at the TV, drowning out the reporter.

"Dru, I can't hear the shit, shut up already," said Shane.

The reporter was speaking to the detective. "Do you have any leads?" she asked.

"From what we can see, the perp fired from inside the house. We're not ruling out professionals...."

"Thank you!" Dru said, once again interrupting. Shane gave him a stern look, silencing him.

The detective went on, "We're hoping the victim pulls through so we can question him. Although we have ruled out robbery, some of the victim's personal effects are missing. The fact that the perp was already inside shows premeditation."

Shane looked at Dru, pissed off that he hadn't followed orders.

Dru just shrugged it off. "Hey, it was cold outside!" Dru smirked, knowing his excuse sounded lame even to himself.

Shane turned the volume back up when the television flashed a picture of the Radisson Hotel. This time a different reporter was on the scene.

"In similar news, a shootout at the Radisson resulted in no arrest as two gunmen shot their way through the hotel escaping. Police suspect a drug deal gone bad..."

The news flashed to hotel security, who pointed at the spot Shane remembered Fats laying. The security guard spoke directly in the camera. "I saw the guy lying here. He wasn't moving, and I knew from TV not to contaminate a crime scene so I went to get help. When I came back the dude was gone!"

Shane turned the TV off and picked up his cell phone.

"Skatz, you still there?"

"Yeah, what's up?"

"Meet us at Digimon tonight at eight!" He hung up unable to fathom what he'd heard. *They're both alive?*

Maybe Gunnz wouldn't make it, but Shane knew Fats was healthy enough to flee... It wasn't over, not by a long shot!

Fats stood in Manny's living room pacing back and forth, occasionally glancing at the level three body armor that saved his life. He'd had the armor made *into* his green army flight jacket. Luckily he'd worn it ever since the hit on Shane went awry. What truly puzzled Fats was, who shot up Gunnz? To make matter worse, Fatal was nowhere to be found. Fats started barking orders.

"Manny! I need you ta round everyone up!"

"I'm working on it, won't you relax, letcha self heal?"

Fats' vest saved his life, but the force of the Magnum broke one of his ribs and fractured another.

"Fuck that! Get the FAM here!" Fats pointed toward the floor. "Fatal, Mark, Skillz, and us, we're settling this shit immediately!"

Manny saw Fats was losing control but said nothing. He reached Skillz and Mark but Fatal was nowhere to be found. Once Fats calmed down, Manny asked, "Do you think them Blood niggas did Gunnz dirty?"

"Hell no!" Fats pulled out a red bandana. "Shane left this, *after* he shot me. I'm sure whoever hit Gunnz left the same calling card. That's why Po-nine's talking that gang related shit. It don't take much ta get the pigs ta look right, so us niggas can go left."

The red flag Fats waved caught Manny's attention.

"That li'l set-up move of Shane's might interest Redrum and the GKB," said Manny, scheming up a way for the Family not to fight two wars.

"Fuck GKB! We're calling all of 'em out! Aye yo. Pretty,"

Fats yelled.

"What's up, Fats?" Pretty came from behind the bar jigged out in Mauri gators and a mink vest with a matching hat, proving pimping was a full time job.

"Change clothes, you're in this. Fuck that pimping shit, that's on hold fa now," Fats barked at the young don.

Pretty didn't feel up to arguing with him, so he went to change into the appropriate gear.

Mia called Shane's cell phone as he drove behind Pryze and Dru on the way to the studio to meet Skatz. She told him how Mark had kicked in her door, attacking her right in front of Isaiah.

"Boonk, Isaiah tried to help me and Mark knocked him down."

I don't have time for this, thought Shane.

"Is Isaiah OK, Mia?"

"Yeah, he's just shaken up, that's all." She sniffed, sounding as if she'd been crying.

"Mia, what do you want *me* to do?" Shane was tired and needed to get her off the phone.

"I've been saving up to relocate to Miami, but with all the bullshit going on, I'm trying to bounce now." He was glad that was all she wanted. He had no time to meddle in Mark's little jealous fits.

"How much?" he asked.

"Can you spare five grand? I'll try and pay it back."

"Done!" Shane cut her off. "I'll bring it tomorrow," he said, then hung up.

He felt bad not being able to console her, but he had more pressing matters to deal with. His cell phone rang a second time, this time it was Redrum.

What's up?" he answered.

"Fats sent me a message....said meet him on the square

midnight tomorrow. Said to tell us both ta bring our biggest gun and wrap up what we don't want broke up. You coming?" Rum asked.

"We'll be there. I'm ready ta end this shit no matter how it turns out." Shane hung up. Fats' call-out made him think of all the people and things he could lose if tomorrow didn't work out in his favor. He needed a pick-me-up, so he called Chyna.

"Hello?" she answered.

"Hey Babe," he said, feeling weak for his woman's touch.

"DuShane, come home, baby. Forget that bullshit out there. *Let's just* go!"

Shane didn't have the heart to tell Chyna the truth, so he did what he promised to never do again... he lied!

"I was thinking the same thing babe, matter of fact in two days won't you come and help me pack?"

Chyna agreed, delighted her and Shane were on the same page mentally. She'd expected some resistance from him at first, but now she laughed off her doubts. Shane asked to speak to Chauncey.

"He's sleep. And I'm not lying this time," Chyna joked, referring to the last few months of hell she'd given him.

"OK, but after I hang up, kiss him for me."

"Will do." Chyna smiled as she visualized their fresh new start at life.

"Yo Chyna, whatta you think about Atlanta?" Shane asked.

"As long as we're all together, it could be Alaska!" she answered.

"Love you, Babe."

"Love you more," Chyna answered and hung up.

When they reached Digimon Studios, Skatman was in the booth listening to old blends. Shane sat down, telling his men about Fats call-out. Everyone agreed they were sick of the cat and mouse game and that a showdown could end the bullshit once and for all. Mia had called back, informing Shane that Pretty called her saying Fats was hiding at Manny's. Shane thanked her even though Peaches had told him the same, a week earlier. What they did take notice of, was the fact that Pretty Boy telling them Fats whereabouts meant he wanted no parts of the impending war. Skatz handed Shane a piece of paper.

"Read that Shane, and tell me timing ain't a motherfucka!"

Shane read the paper. As his face turned solemn, he said, "I'm not superstitious Skatz, but even I've got to admit that's a sign."

"What?" asked Pryze and Dru in unison. They explained that the letter was from a major label who'd gotten wind of Skatman's music and wished to sit down and begin some form of negotiation, maybe a distribution deal.

"You nice like that, Skatz?" Pryze asked "Let us hear something."

Dru jumped in the conversation. "Word, son. We're stuck in here until tomorrow. So let's loosen the fuck up! Pryze, roll that weed. DuShane, haul that liquor over here. Jesus had the last supper and we gonna have the last session." The men all looked at Dru as if he put his foot in his mouth. Dru cleaned up his statement.

"OK that came out wrong." Putting his hands up in mock surrender, he smiled.

"What's your forte, Skatz?" Pryze asked.

"Storytelling! I spit the truth... without preaching I get my point across." Skatz loosened up as soon as they began talking music. Shane brought in the liquor. Pryze started rolling trees as Skatz punched up "For the Love of Money," the number three song Gunnz said was his favorite. Pryze caught the bass line immediately.

"That's that O'Jays shit, son!" He sang along. "For the

love of money, Whoo...."

"Who's honey on the hook?" Dru asked.

"Peaches," Shane answered.

"Shorty who helped set up Fats? She's got talent!" Dru said.

"Who did the beat?" Pryze asked, nodding his head.

"Shane! You didn't know?" Skatz smiled.

Like so many others, Pryze thought Shane just financed Digimon Studios. They never knew he had a true love for the art of producing tracks.

Skatz spoke up. "Aight ya'll this here's a listening session, so shut up and listen!" He joked, as Gunnz's favorite song played:

Baguettes in the bezel, Hoes in stilletos

I was packing heavy metal, pushed a Benz through the ghetto

But now I'm up top on the down low wit twenty

And it's all for the love of drug money...

It started out wit a cat name Cadillac Slim

Pushed a white Benz wit rims

Loved gems and Timbs

Had AM Gees on his E-class, knowing that he's ass

But I didn't revoke his ghetto pass, 'cause his metal blast.

But little did I know duke was frontin

Nigga talked about blasting something, but never hit nothing

He was sorta like that D.T. from In Too Deep

From Akron that missed when he shot the Mach One

See the nigga was a pimp wit nothing but a floss game

Tossed dames into his moss green, glossed Range

Talked wit a lisp, and stayed so crisp

In the Coogi so he hardly had ta say shit

And the hoes they would pull at least five a piece

At least, per night that's twenty grand a week.

So I ask myself time again in the pen

Skatman, why the fuck was you fucking wit him?

I had a ten year run, robbing payrolls, pushing yayo
In broad day yo, trying ta stay low...
I was a Queens cat...Adidas wit the shellified toe
Wit a hellified hoe, pushing a ...hell if I know?
Name Missy, pop shit, pop Cristal and pussy
Pop tops wit her pistol and her wrist glist too
She was my driver for the getaway, could hit or lay,
Spit a stray. She laid back and lit a tre off a HK
But when she got knocked up, I put the glocks up
Cuz working off pot luck'll have my ass locked up
But instead I'm up top on the down low wit twenty
And it's all for the love of drug money!

Skatz stopped the music. He never let anyone listen past the first verse, often reminding Shane that a good song should catch an A&R's attention during the first thirty seconds of playing time.

"Why'd you stop it? I was just getting into it," Dru asked, stating the same thing Pryze was thinking.

"Word Skatz, stop playing! How does it end?" he asked, puffing the trees before he passed the blunt to Dru.

Skatz began lecturing, "See that's what I'm talking about, the first thirty seconds should have music execs begging for the rest. And peep how I'm telling the story as if I'm regretting the choices I made, instead of glorifying it? That's a jewel fa the youth!" Skatz smiled, proud of his work.

"Homie, save that shit for the labels and play the shit!" Dru grinned at Skatz, knowing he'd play the rest of the song.

Shane sat in the corner, distancing himself from the others. He had the distinct feeling he'd be pressing his luck if he showed up at the Square to meet Fats. He sat sipping his drink, contemplating his thoughts.

If it was poker, you'd have cashed in your chips by now. Them Blood niggas could handle this shit cause lately I can't seem to do shit without prison coming to mind! Them crackers gave me twenty years! My lawyer got that cut in half, so if I get knocked again I'm dying in jail! I could see me now walking the yard talking 'bout I had this and that... *Not me!!* Pryze snapped Shane out of his thoughts.

"What you over there daydreaming, nigga? I said, did you do this beat too?"

"Oh...nah, Ron did that one," Shane answered.

"What's up with Ron anyway? I ain't seem him around lately." Pryze rolled another blunt, the first one Dru smoked on wasn't even finished. Pryze paused, waiting for Shane to answer his question.

"Ron went to visit Pops. He's been feeling under the weather lately." Shane's comment gnawed at his conscience. He had ten years over his brother Ron, yet Ron was the *responsible* one. Ron was the one who took the time to check on their parents while Shane ran the streets trying to dish out his own brand of street justice. At least thats what he told himself. He'd been beating himself down mentally ever since he'd killed the two teens Fats had sent after him. Shane decided he needed some time alone to think.

"Yo ya'll, I'm out." He gave his partners a pound as he exited the studio, thinking, *No matter how many angles I find, bottom line is something has to happen to Fats in order for me ta live in peace and not put my family in danger.*

CHAPTER 22
SHOWDOWN AT THE SQUARE

As Shane pulled up to Mia's place the first thing he noticed was the sloppy job the landlord did at fixing her front door. He could still see splinters of busted wood on the front steps as he rang the doorbell waiting on her to answer.

Mia lived near the 113th precinct. Shane shook his head as he reasoned that the precinct's presence wasn't enough to deter Mark's actions. When she answered the door, her eye appeared slightly bluish, apparently a remnant of Mark's rage. He stroked her hair away from her eye to get a better look. Upon seeing the bruise, he grimaced.

"You deserve better, Mia. How do you always end up choosing these losers?"

"I don't know, but I damn sure don't feel like talking about it." She invited him in, but he declined the offer.

"I'm in a rush, Little Mama. I just brought this by so you can handle your business." Shane handed her an envelope containing five grand.

"I'll pay it back as soon as I get situated, Boonk." Mia gripped the envelope, hugging him.

"You don't have to pay it back! Look at it as severance pay for raising Isaiah alone for eight years." He kissed Mia on the forehead and left.

"I think I'll be relocating soon myself," he yelled.

"You're welcome to come to Miami with me and Isaiah," she yelled back.

"I appreciate it, but I might relapse out there." He flashed her a smile and got into his truck, pulling off.

Five hours before midnight Shane sat with Redrum in his Lincoln Aviator on the square, going over their plan.

He pointed. "Me and my boys will be on the roof. We'll have sawed-offs and machine guns. Pryze, a Mach-11. Dru, a Tech-9. Our job will be to mow them down so ya'll can move in and *make sure* they're dead. Expect them to be wearing vests. It's kept them alive this long. If Fats dies, the war is over; he's our main target."

Redrum interrupted, "Skillz is a wild boy. He's gotta go too! He's *our* main target." Shane didn't argue, he just wanted this whole beef over with.

Redrum felt Shane out. "With Fats out the way, this area will be a poor man's dream. You trying to get some of this dough?"

Shane shook his head. "Nah Rum, my beef with Fats was never over cash, it was over peace of mind.

Rum nodded as if he understood. The truth was, he *didn't* understand.

It's always bout the paper, thought Rum.

Shane exited the truck. "See you tonight," he said, as he got into his own ride and never looked back.

Redrum knew Shane had no love for him and that the only reason they'd come together was based on their common goal of getting Fats out the way.

Who gives a fuck? thought Rum. *Long as 550 rides for the cause.*

Fats and the Family pulled up at 11:45, their first mistake. Redrum and the GKB were already in position, giving them the advantage. Fats' second mistake was riding into the square, which even surprised Shane. The Family was boxed in.

Fatal stood by the corner phone booth, the only member smart enough not to ride in. He hadn't been the same since Gunnz had been shot up. Gunnz was now in critical, but stable condition at the hospital. Fatal wanted to be there for Gunnz if he pulled through, which may have explained his indecision to spring into action at the present moment. Instead, he just lurked in the shadows smirking as if he was glad Fats finally had to get his hands dirty. Fatal's MP5 could have easily evened the odds for the Family, but he decided to do nothing.

Shane sat atop the roof with a sawed-off pump shotgun with Skatz who had a 150 shot calico rifle. Pryze and Dru were perched on the rooftop across from them. Their getaway was a hop, skip, and a jump away from the rooftop. Fats saw his team was in a fucked position, so he tried to bluff...

"I'm here ta offer you a way out, Rum," Fats shouted through the jeep's half-open window.

Rum and the GKB answered with gunfire, spraying the black Ford Excursion as it rocked back and forth from the impact of the slugs. Pretty Boy ran out first, firing wildly in Rum's direction. "Pow! Pow!"

Pretty Boy jumped behind a parked car Pryze laced with holes just to keep him at bay. Shane and Skatz waited on firing their weapons. They wanted Fats. Fats, Manny, and Skillz jumped out the truck, Skillz instantly killing Mumbles with his second shot and wounding Y.B. with his third. "KRAKOW!" The slug sounded as it hit Y.B.'s shoulder. Skillz stood his ground with no cover, nothing shielded him as he fired repeatedly. "PLAP! PLAP! PLAP!"

Skillz's weapon shattered the glass of a parked hooptie in front of Redrum. Dru took aim, hitting the ground two feet in front of Skillz, forcing him to duck behind an oversized green garbage dumpster behind the bodega. "PADOONK! PADOONK!" was all he heard, he could feel the slugs vibrating the Dumpster that shielded him from gunfire.

Manny broke in a run away from Fats since the majority of gunfire went his way. Manny saw they had Fats holed up as he made his way toward him to hold him down. Just then he saw Pretty Boy sneaking his way down the back street.

Manny snarled. "Bitch-ass nigga's leaving us!" Manny screamed. He popped two shots at Pretty, but he had already rounded the corner.

As Skillz reloaded, he heard the sound of a round being chambered. He spun around, looked up and squeezed but his gun dryfired. Pryze riddled his chest with bullets as Skillz realized he only had time to load one gun—the one stuck in his waistband! He fell face first, still gripping the empty auto in his hand.

Fats fired wildly yet accurately as he noticed Redrum hit the floor. As he stuck the next clip in his Desert Eagle, he popped Yellow, watching him go down.

Just might pull this off, thought Fats as he realized he and Manny were the only two left. Fats figured the GKB must've had a few men laying in the cut for Fatal.

Can't worry bout that now, thought Fats as he noticed Manny creeping toward him. Fats waved him over, providing cover fire for him. Shane nor Skatz could get a clear shot at Fats from the roof, due to the enclave he was squatting in. It was out of their hands. Manny fired a few shots.

"Manny you've gotta come better than that, son," Fats barked.

Manny bit his bottom lip, "I've got two bullets left; I dropped the S.K. in the truck."

Sirens sounded, signaling the police were closing in.

Since Skillz was dead, GKB sent all their gunfire at Fats

knowing this war wouldn't end as long as he was alive.

Fats turned to Manny who stood behind him and said, "We can shoot it out till the cops come or risk making a run for it...your choice?"

"Keep firing," Manny replied.

Fats let off a whole clip, when he heard, "POW!" He looked around puzzled.

"POW! POW!" the shots echoed in the enclave.

Fats felt dizzy, *wet* and dizzy! As his neck started burning, he reached up to rub the burn and was met with the stickiness of blood. Fats realized he'd been shot.

"But how?" he whispered hoarsely, as he fell on his back.

"Not how nigga... *who?*" Manny said, as he stood over Fats pointing a gun at his head. Manny laughed with a sneer on his face. "Don't look at me like that Fats. It's always the one that's closest to ya that'll do you in the end! Nigga, you a fool... The Cab Stand's pulling ten grand a day but you too busy *stunting* ta notice. I counted ya cash till my thumbs got sore. I tried ta get Shane to kill you by telling the detectives he was in on the Soffey heist, but I guess he changed so much he just accepted it. So I linked up wit Redrum, knowing once you hid in my crib you'd have ta tell me your connect. Yeah nigga, the connect was what made you the man. Now Rum'll run the Cab Stand and I'll supply. It's under new management, motherfucker!" Manny spit in Fats face, who already appeared dead, but he was taking no chances as he cocked back the revolved and squeezed.

Click! Manny had spent all shells. The gun was empty!

Rum pulled up. "Manny, get in! The pigs are getting closer." He snapped to attention jumping in Rum's jeep as they pulled off. Shane had heard it all. It sickened him that Manny would do Fats so dirty, but his main focus was his exit. He had a *family* to get home to!

By the time Chyna arrived with Chauncey, Shane had all his boxes packed and a U-Haul truck in his driveway. Him and Chyna would live at her house in Maryland while they hunted for a permanent home in Atlanta.

He refused to discuss anything that had happened to him in the last few days.

"That's all in the past," was all he would say about it.

Detectives Rogers and McCullem pulled up, getting out of their unmarked car. The Bull Mastiff, who rested on the front yard, stood up.

"Sit Bolo," Shane commanded, as he approached the detectives.

"How can I help you?" he asked. All the sarcasm had left him.

"Just came to see you off, West. This use ta be a decent neighborhood until recently. Why, not too long ago two teens got murdered just down the way. Well maybe not murdered given the fact the bodies were in possession of some pretty impressive hardware. Strangest thing, though, one of the bodies seemed mauled. You know, as if by an animal of sorts." Rogers glanced at Bolo.

"You've seen my dog on a leash at all times if I'm away from the house," Shane said defensively.

Rogers cut Shane off by throwing up both his palms. "Like I said West, we're not here *officially*, just passing through. Besides, I doubt you'd have any blood on your hands. You seem smarter than that. I don't think you're squeaky clean, but as long as you're leaving my jurisdiction, it's not my problem." Rogers turned to leave. Before opening the car door he paused... "Oh, by the way, Francis sends her regards."

"Who?" Shane asked, in no mood for games. The detective was now making him feel uneasy.

"Oh I forgot, you don't know Ms. Francis... You know

Mona!" He smiled, a sarcastic grin. "It's good to know people in high places, isn't it West?"

As the detectives pulled off Chyna asked Shane who they were. "A memory babe...just a memory."

Fats came to a few days after the incident on the square, handcuffed to a hospital bed with tubes and IVs hooked up to him. The nurses told him he was lucky to be alive. He didn't feel lucky. He had guards posted at his front door and as soon as he awoke, the DA's office charged him with two counts of murder, gun possession and an accessory to Skillz's murder, quoting the law that any homicide committed in the act of a felony is charged to the perp.

To make things worse, his one call was to no avail. Manny had snaked him, and Pretty Boy and Fatal all but disappeared off the face of the planet. The only one he could reach was Mark. Lucky for Fats, Mark still idolized the Family as something worth being a part of. Mark actually still considered himself part of the Family. It never occurred to him that the Family now consisted of him and Fats.

Once Fats reached Rikers Island, Mark came to see him. Fats signed his property over to him, which consisted of his Rolex watch and a six carat pinky ring. Fats had Mark sell the jewelry and cop from his connect so he could get himself a lawyer. Manny wiped him out. Fats blamed himself; he'd gotten so lax he let Manny handle *all* his affairs. Nothing was in Fats' name, so when he got knocked everyone on paper took whatever the documents claimed was theirs. Thanks to Khalid's money laundering techniques, Ray-Ray's cousin Selene was pushing Fats' Bentley to her job at Foot Locker. The DA's office offered Fats a flat forty at arraignment. He was put in Rikers Island's infamous NIC ward for high profile cases until a date could be set for trial.

EPILOGUE

Mark started seeing a little paper, thanks to Fats. He never could understand Manny's betrayal. Manny embraced Mark, and as far as he was concerned, he'd try his best to remain neutral. Deep down Mark knew Fats would one day ask him to put that work in. Mark spent his days finding and recruiting the new generation of thugs popping up and around Queens to form what he called the new "Black Rose Family." He spent his nights pulling up in front of Mia's old crib reminiscing on better days. He knew she no longer lived there, but stopping by gave him a feeling of nostalgia. *You never miss what you have until it's gone,* thought Mark as he pulled off into the night.

Manny tossed and turned all night. For some strange reason he felt uncomfortable. He strained his eyes, trying to adjust them to the darkness in his bedroom as he reached to turn on the lamp.

"Don't bother, I took the bulb out." Manny jumped up, startled by the familiar voice in the room. He reached under his pillow for the pearl-handled .25 he kept there. *It was gone.*

"Oh, I took that too."

Fatal flashed the gun at Manny, returning it to his pocket. "Fats did have his faults, Manny, but I can't help but feel you should've let his enemies deal him his hand." With that said, Fatal cut loose half a clip, slicing through Manny's midsection like butter. He never got out the scream.

Peaches relocated to Fayetteville, NC. She currently works at Magic City shaking her 'ass-ets' in hopes of catching that baller that will sweep her off her feet and make the everyday struggles of life disappear.

Mia started a modeling agency in Miami. She was nicknamed the *"female pimp"* by the industry. It was rumored her models would do 'anything' on or off camera for a fee, which may have had to do with the fact that the majority of her models consisted of Pretty Boy's old stable. The two of them were currently building on ideas for a website. Pretty Boy called his new hustle 'webpage-pimping.' Most of the models suspected Mia and Pretty Boy to be involved in a relationship, since they often sent Isaiah to visit Shane.

Even Pryze got hit by the entrepreneur bug. He opened a strip club in Virginia, but got raided for drugs being on the premises. He is out on bail pending trial.

Dru vanished as usual. He was still ready to help Shane out at the drop of a dime. "You know how ta reach me," Dru had told him.

Gunnz survived Dru's attack, but now walks with a permanent limp. He and Fatal own several weed spots in the Queens area and are very content with being ghetto fabulous. None of their spots have ever been robbed. Fatal bought Gunnz an ivory handled 14K gold cane to assist him with his limp... he's worn derbies ever since.

Skatz finally got a distribution deal and was up and coming in the rap game. Shane ran a division of Digimon in Atlanta, and Ron ran the New York office. Between FedEx, fax machines, e-mails, and frequent flyer miles, Shane was able to continue producing Skatz's music. However, he always declines a spot in his videos, choosing to keep it simple.

Shane and Chyna married that spring in a wedding ceremony under the waterfalls of Jamaica. Dana was Chyna's maid of honor. Chauncey was Shane's best man. They now own a string of condominiums in Atlanta. He and Chyna also own a Barber Shop, which is adjacent to

Chyna's Beauty & Nail Salon. Dana runs the beauty part of Chyna's shop. She stopped her gossiping and is now very professional and customers adore her. She has lost 20 pounds and is engaged to be married.

Sherry calls and visits Chyna often, giving her tips on improving the shop.

"Go down the hall to the left...wait till you're called!" the C.O. told Fats.

Fats had an attorney visit. His second visit in a week. As he shook his lawyer's outstretched hand, he told him, "I have some good news, Mr. Armstead."

"Last time you had good news, these crackers offered me forty years," Fats snapped.

"The ballistics test came back on your gun," the lawyer said, ignoring his rudeness. He was used to it in his line of work.

"I already told you, I was *defending* myself," he barked at his lawyer.

"Even better, Mr. Armstead, your gun did *not* kill those men." His lawyer smiled. It was a rare occasion that his job allowed him to bring this sort of news.

"What does that mean?" Fats asked, scared to get his hopes up.

"Well, depending on our story, which we will rehearse all next week by the way. I think our new evidence can turn that forty year offer into forty *months*."

It took his lawyer twenty minutes to break down the technicalities of their case. Fats hadn't fully grasped the concept behind his good fortune. He was too preoccupied with the possibility of revenge. On his way back to his housing unit, a sinister grin crept into the corners of his mouth, as he mumbled...

"*It ain't over yet motherfuckers!*"

The End...

FAMILY COMES FIRST

Questions for the Reader

1. From the moment Shane stepped out of Sing-Sing to the end of the book, did there ever come a point where you as a reader considered him a criminal?

2. Do you feel Shane took the action that was in his family's best interest? What would you have done different?

3. What do you feel was the moral of the story?

4. What message do you feel the author was trying to convey by emphasizing the plan's Shane had made prior to his release?

5. What do you feel was the author's reason for mentioning from the outside the family seemed more lucrative than it actually was?

6. Who was your favorite character and why?

7. Should Shane have gotten back with Chyna? If not who would, you have wanted to see him with.

8. Do you think there will be a sequel to *Family Comes First*? And why?

Email your answers to PenGameLLC@aol.com for a chance to win a free copy of Tracy's next book, *The Track*.

Sneak Preview of
THE TRACK
by Tracy Thomas

Coming Soon

CHAPTER 1
The Track

The beginning of the new millennium brought about a new breed of hustlers. Mayor Guiliani's *"quality of life"* campaign and crusade against New York's drug trade forced the masses of the city's street dwellers to seek an alternative means to making a dollar. Drug dealers began robbing each other, and crackheads began informing on low-level dealers in anticipation of the couple of dollars law enforcement officials threw their way, only to hand the money over for drugs to the next hustler sure to replace the last. Some headed out of town, hoping to lock down a small hood in the south. Burglaries rose, and drugs—the ghetto's stock market—experienced a slight depression. Even the hustlers appearing to be on top of their game had to resort to leasing their vehicles, a major regression in comparison to the days when a mid-level dealer could *walk* onto a car lot and exit *driving*.

However, the mid '80s were long gone. Law enforcement—through trial and error—now knew every trick in the book, making it harder for the average hustler to stay on his grind. Those fortunate enough to still have their luxury cars, jewelry, and bankrolls from their prime knew one thing never changed: the women!

Hustlers weren't tricking like they used to. A bad broad came a dime a dozen. But a successful street player was becoming a rarity with each day that passed. With so many young black men on lockdown, women outnumbered men in a 6:1 ratio. Chickenheads flocked like groupies to every diamond-studded, ghetto fabulous nigga cruising the streets. Lil Kim had given girls the go-ahead to give up the goods. *The freakier, the better!* Cats with enough sense to know their stock had just gone up made chicks compete for their time.

A breed of *new-millennium* pimps was born! Those ingenious enough to finagle an angle manipulated gold diggers into seeing their true selves. Dropping their soft-shoe, sugar-coated game and becoming straight-up hoes!

Pennsylvania Avenue was one of New York City's toughest strips, known as "The Track." Pennsylvania Avenue was located in Brooklyn's East New York on a dark industrial backstreet, and ran into Sunnydale Supermarket across from the Five of Diamonds Park. Another popular strip was Queens Plaza—better known as "The Plaza"—located in Queens near the 59th Street overpass, which was ironically the bus stop for the Q101 heading to Riker's Island.

This particular night, Platinum took his four hoes to Pennsylvania Avenue to work. Platinum's hoes named after the earth's precious metals and gems, thus complimenting the very name Platinum chose as his pimp handle. Pearl, Diamond, Ruby D, and White Gold were currently paired out on the stroll, humping up a bankroll for their "Daddy," while Platinum stood amongst a circle of young pimps talking shit. Old-timers took an immediate liking to Platinum, describing him as a colorful pimp. Unlike the new breed of young thugs who mostly gorilla pimped, Platinum had finesse. At a young ripe age of twenty-two, he was one of few who could still do a "toast." At the moment, he was in rare form, spitting his spiel. The younger and older pimps alike urged him on.

"Yo, Platinum, spit the Ten Pimp Commandments fa these niggas," said Green Eyes, who was pouring himself another glass of Cristal right in the middle of Pennsylvania Avenue. Green Eyes was Platinum's road dawg and a pimp who had a stable of two broads.

"The game is to be sold not told, Eyes. It's gonna cost you some of that high-priced piss," Platinum slurred, holding out his cup. Without hesitation, Green Eyes poured Platinum a cup of the high-priced champagne made popular by rappers everywhere.

Some of the newer pimps on Pennsylvania Avenue were surprised to see the veteran players openly getting intoxicated in the streets, not counting the flagrant use of marijuana amongst their peers up and down the strip. Unbeknownst to them, the squad only cared about firearms and runaways who were usually underage teens who had left the care and custody of one of the various state agencies forced to report their disappearance. Other than that, the pimps had a free pass to do as they wished, except for Tuesdays, the nights the squad did their weekly sweep.

The rowdy players lowered their tone as Platinum began spitting the Ten Pimp Commandments, his self-written manual to successful pimping. Green Eyes smiled as he watched his boy Platinum brush his shoulders off and clear his throat. Platinum began by raising his cup old-school style in the gesture of a toast.

"I crack that slang until she backs that thang up!
From the cradle to the grave, it's a Platinum thang...
what?!
I went from pimping hoes uptown ta pimping all around.
I'm a pimp pressologist, a game-a-cologist,
Wordsmith, chauvinist, bagging yo' bitch.
I be the extraordinary adversary extraordinaire,
extravagant nigga!
It's only right in the memory of Biggie Smalls
I drop these commandments ta hip y'all negrawll'z.
Rule No. One: *It ain't all games and fun;*
Ya reputation and ya name is one, so game 'em, son.
Fuck freaks and streets, this here's bread and meat.
And if they don't hoe...we don't eat!
Which brings me ta **Rule No. Two** *... the backhand slap!*
Perfect ya technique and collect that trap.
See, your brain is the boss, yo' dick is ya jone's.
If them chips is coming home, put tha dick fo' her,
holmes.
But don't...obey yo' thirst. The dough must come first.
So don't fuck around and fuck her first!
Then there's **Rule No. Three,** *the "P" ain't free!*
I don't care if it's a nipple; nigga, charge 'em triple.
Number Four, *self-esteem...you sell a bitch dreams at*
full speed ahead,
And all that square shit's dead!
I pump her head for the long con; it keeps her off
balance.
I tell a broad she's got no talent!
Five *is the stealing, lock, cop, and block it.*
Cuz what you call a pussy is a ho's stash pocket!
Six, *I teach a bitch ta work that dick. Pickpocket tricks*
and put the wallets back.
Seven, *listen to the jewels I'm spitting in ya ear. I'm*
pissing, no kissing! Man, listen...

Eight, I'm constantly stating...
When they pull up, ask them tricks, "pimping or dating?"
Now, some pimps will lie, but if I see she's tried,
She might save herself a self-inflicted black eye.
Number Nine, ain't none fine...a bitch is a bitch,
Just as long as she scratch that itch in yo' mitts.
Number Ten, go through one ta nine;
Wit my "bottom" bitch, bag her girlfriend then go through
'em again!"

As the young pimps chanted and hollered his name, some even applauding, Platinum jumped in his silver S-class Mercedes Benz to make his rounds, checking in on his girls. Platinum liked to keep an even number of hoes. It enabled his stable to pair up when working the streets. Platinum was strictly business when it came to the pimp game, running his hoes like a business.

As he approached the intersection of Cozine, he saw Ruby D leaning against a white Honda Accord, haggling with a trick over her prices. Platinum tapped his horn lightly as Ruby ran over, leaving the trick hanging.

"Hey, Daddy!" Ruby said as she approached, clicking her clear-heeled stilettos against the pavement.

"What's up, Ruby?" Platinum went about his normal routine of holding an open pack of Newports toward Ruby as she fished out a cigarette and smoothly inserted her and White Gold's bankroll into the pack. This was to ensure the police never saw the exchange of currency between Platinum and his hoes.

Platinum glanced over toward the Honda and noticed White Gold, his only white girl, take over the negotiations Ruby started.

"Where the hell is Pearl and Diamond?" Platinum asked, scanning the avenue's shadows and corners.

"They picked up a date five minutes ago," Ruby

answered.

Platinum noticed White Gold wave Ruby over. Ruby, signaling to her that she'd be right over, extinguished the cigarette and asked Platinum, "Anything else, Daddy?"

"How many condoms you got left?" Platinum asked.

Ruby held up ten fingers as Platinum nodded his head and pulled off.

The condom count would give him an idea of what each hoe's cash flow *should* look like, but like every other hustle, there were ways around the system. He didn't even count the stash; his mind was on finding Pearl and Diamond. He headed toward the rear of the Linden Complex. Anytime the girls caught a trick, they were informed to bring them to the Linden House's parking lot area.

Platinum pulled into the back of the complex, once again tapping his car horn. At first sight, a newcomer to the strip would only notice the dozens of men sitting slumped back in their vehicles. Once Platinum sounded his car horn, dozens of hoes picked their heads up from their trick's lap to see if it was *their* pimp honking. Platinum scanned the faces of different hoes, most getting back to business once they saw the disturbance was not from their pimp. Some quickly avoided eye contact for fear of getting *charged* for being "out of pocket," even though the charge wouldn't be legit in this case. Still, most hoes knew a thirsty nigga who was new to the game was known to try everything.

Platinum's eyes finally found Diamond, who held out her palm, signaling to Platinum to give her a minute. Platinum double parked and waited.

About five minutes later, Diamond jumped in the back seat of Platinum's Benz. As if she could read Platinum's mind, Diamond spoke. "Back up, Daddy. Pearl's in the alley fucking some broke-ass trick who ain't got no car. You know Pearl...if the money's right, the pussy's tight." Diamond laughed at her little jingle as she passed Platinum the money she'd made thus far.

Platinum reversed to the mouth of the alley, and sure enough, Pearl was standing, bent over with her skirt hiked up over her ass cheeks as the trick stood behind her pumping away. Platinum put the Benz in park and lit the half-smoked blunt he'd left in the ashtray.

"Can I get a pull off your blunt, Daddy?" Diamond asked, hoping to catch Platinum in one of his generous moods.

"Wait till we get home, Diamond. I don't want you out here getting lazy or off-point. You can smoke all the weed you want once we get in the house," Platinum told her.

The truth was Platinum had no intentions of smoking behind *any* ho. According to Platinum's bankroll, he figured she must've sucked at least a dozen dicks and it wasn't even 3AM. Pearl jumped in the passenger side of Platinum's Benz. Pearl was Platinum's bottom bitch, therefore allowing her the privilege of riding shotgun. Nobody said a word on the ride back to Pennsylvania, where Platinum parked in a small lot off the corner of Cozine and Pennsylvania to count his cash.

Thirty-two hundred and fifty, thought Platinum as he realized his hoes were eight hundred dollars short of their minimum. Platinum had *trained* his hoes to make close to at least a thousand a night each. At times, one ho would go over her minimum to allow for another to come up short, just as long as he made at least four thousand each night. The reward for the highest money-maker of the night was the chance to share Platinum's bed. This was a tactic he used to keep his hoes competing for his affection. Plenty of nights, when his hoes got real competitive, Platinum's bankroll was known to exceed five grand.

Pearl, an experienced ho and Platinum's first ho, turned him to the pimp game. Pearl met Platinum a year earlier during a brief hiatus from her "ho-stroll" days. Platinum, not knowing her past, made Pearl his girlfriend. After a few months of dating, Platinum found himself conned out of six thousand dollars in a drug deal gone bad. Pearl gave him his way out, exposing him to the pimp game. After the shock of learning Pearl's past profession, Platinum took to pimping with a passion. Never one to half-step, Platinum learned every rule of the game. By the end of the night, Platinum knew the ins and outs of pimping like the back of his hand. Or so he thought. He soon discovered *knowing* and *doing* were two different things all together.

By the end of the week, Pearl had brought Diamond home, which turned out to be an easy task considering the fact the two girls had a prior history together. By the end of his first month on The Track, Platinum was a force to be reckoned with. The other pimps kept their hoes on a short leash when Platinum came through. Platinum was savvy enough to catch even the most seasoned hoes "out of pocket." He'd snagged Ruby D in a similar fashion.

Platinum sat in his whip, reminiscing about the day he happened upon Ruby D.

Back then, Ruby D, under another alias, hoed for a pimp named King. Platinum pulled up in his Benz, newly purchased at the time and unfamiliar to Ruby. She'd done as King instructed her to when Platinum slowed to a halt, lowering his window.

"Pimping or dating?" Ruby asked.

The question was the standard jargon of hoes to elicit from a pimp the proper response. The rules of engagement stated that if a ho asked this question, a pimp was bound by the code to tell the truth. Otherwise, the *charge* was not legit, and a ho would be led to believe she was dealing with a trick and continue to proposition him. If the driver announced himself as a pimp, a bitch better make tracks in the opposite direction. Another word and she's out of pocket!

When Ruby asked Platinum if he was pimping or dating, he smoothly responded, "As good as you lookin' tonight, a nigga shouldn't have a problem spendin' some dough."

Ruby smiled, jumping in Platinum's Benz, believing she'd snagged herself a baller who'd decided to cut out the middle man and just pay for the pussy directly. That night, Ruby learned a lesson only experience could teach her: On The Track, *always* get a *straight* answer.

PenGame Publishing, LLC

Order Form

Family Comes First by Tracy Thomas   Qty. _____Price each: $15.00 **Total:**_____

                                                              Subtotal:_____

                                                                    +   **$4.05 (S/H)**

                                                              Total: _____

Ship To:

Name: _____
Address:_____
_____

City: _____

State: _____ **Zip:** _____
Email: (optional) _____

Correctional Institutions Only:

Family Comes First by Tracy Thomas   **Qty.** _____**Price each:** $12.00 **Total:**_____

                                                              Subtotal:_____

                                                                    +   **$4.05 (S/H)**

                                                              Total: _____

Ship To:

Inmate Name: _____
Inmate Number: _____
Correctional Institution: _____
Address:_____
_____

City: _____

State: _____ **Zip:** _____

Send Checks or Money Orders (make Payable to PenGame Publishing, LLC) to:

PenGame Publishing, LLC
PO Box 341361
Jamaica, NY 11434-3131

For questions, please call: (347) 632-2220